D1392782

About the author

Elmore Leonard was born in 1925 in New Orleans. He lived in Dallas, Oklahoma City and Memphis before his family settled in Detroit in 1935. He served in the U.S. Navy during the Second World War and afterwards studied English Literature at the University of Detroit, graduating in 1950. From 1949 to 1961 he worked as a copywriter in various advertising agencies but, apart from a few book reviews, he has been writing only novels and screenplays since 1967, including the screenplays for his novels *Stick*, *LaBrava* (winner of the 1983 Edgar Allen Poe Award for the best mystery novel) and *52 Pick-Up*; these and many other of his books are published in Penguin, including *Glitz*, *Swag*, *The Switch*, *The Hunted*, *Unknown Man No. 89*, *Mr Majestyk*, *Cat Chaser*, *Bandits*, *Split Images*, *Dutch Treat* and *City Primeval*. He concentrates mainly on westerns and thrillers, and many of his books have been filmed.

ELMORE LEONARD

52 PICK-UP

PENGUIN BOOKS

PENGUIN BOOKS

Published by the Penguin Group
27 Wrights Lane, London W8 5TZ, England
Viking Penguin Inc., 40 West 23rd Street, New York, New York 10010, USA
Penguin Books Australia Ltd, Ringwood, Victoria, Australia
Penguin Books Canada Ltd, 2801 John Street, Markham, Ontario, Canada L3R 1B4
Penguin Books (NZ) Ltd, 182–190 Wairau Road, Auckland 10, New Zealand

Penguin Books Ltd, Registered Offices: Harmondsworth, Middlesex, England

First published in Great Britain by Martin Secker & Warburg Ltd 1974
Published in Penguin Books 1986
Reprinted 1986, 1987, 1988

Printed and bound in Great Britain by Cox & Wyman Ltd, Reading

For J.S.

1

He could not get used to going to the girl's apartment. He would be tense driving past the gate and following the road that wound through the complex of townhouse condominiums. Even when it was dark he was a little tense. But once he reached the garage and pressed the remote control switch and the double door opened he was there and it was done.

It was cold in the garage, standing in the darkness between his car and Cini's, feeling for the key on the ring that held all the keys he had to carry. He didn't like keys and wished there was another way to do it. He wished he didn't have so many doors that had to be kept locked.

It was warm in the kitchen, with a warm glow coming from the light over the stainless steel range. Shiny and clean, nothing on the sink or the countertop. She was neat, orderly, and for some reason that had surprised him.

The rest of the apartment was dark, though dull evening light was framed in the sliding glass door across the living room. To the right was the front entrance and a suspended stairway that made one turn up to the hallway and two bedrooms. Beyond the stairway the door to the den was closed.

He called out, 'Cini?'

Usually music was playing and in the silence the place seemed empty. But she was here because her car was in the garage. Probably in the shower. He listened another moment before going back into the kitchen to the wall phone.

The sound of the plant came on with the voice answering and he said, 'This is Mr. Mitchell, see if you can find Vic for me, will you?'

The ice bucket wasn't on the counter. Usually there were the ice bucket and two glasses, ready. Maybe at other times when he came in they weren't on the counter, but tonight he was aware of it.

'Vic, it's Mr. Mitchell. I'm not going to be back today. . . . No, I'm tired. Son of a bitch has four vodka martinis, shish kebab, coffee and three stingers. We go back to his office and I have to listen to all this shit about delivery dates.'

He was patient for almost a minute, leaning against the counter now, at times nodding, looking at the window over the sink where a stained-glass owl hung from the shade string.

'Vic, I'll tell you what. You call on the customers and eat the lunch every day, I'll run the shop. . . . Victor . . . All right, you got a problem, but we know weeks ahead when we have to deliver, right? We take into account the chance of screw-ups, breakdowns and acts of God. But, Victor, we deliver. We deliver, we pay our bills and we always take our two percent ten days. That's what we always do, as long as I've been in business. If you've got a machine problem then fix the son of a bitch, because I'll tell you something, I'm not going to go out every day and eat lunch, Vic, and run the shop too. You see that?'

He listened again, giving his plant superintendent equal time. 'All right, I'll talk to you first thing tomorrow. . . . Right . . . All right, Vic. Listen, if anybody wants me I'm there, I'll call them back, right. . . . Okay, so long.'

He hung up, took time to light a cigarette and dialed his home. Waiting, he was thinking he could have handled that a little better with Vic, not sounded so edgy.

'Barbara, how you doing? . . . No, I'm back at the plant. Finally. Spent the afternoon at the Tech Center. . . . No, you better go ahead, I'll probably be late. Vic's got a problem I have to look into. . . . I know it. That's what I told him. But getting somebody else doesn't turn out a job that's due tomorrow. Listen, if you want me for anything and my night line doesn't answer, I'm back in the shop somewhere. Leave a message, I'll call you. . . . Okay, see you later.'

He wasn't finished with the cigarette, but didn't need it now and stubbed it out as he hung up.

In the living room he turned on a lamp. He liked the furniture, all the orange-and-white stuff and abstract paintings and plants that were like trees. He had paid a decorator to pick them out and they were his. He was finally starting to get used to the place; though he still had the feeling, most of the time, he was in a resort hotel suite or someone else's house. At the foot of the suspended stairway he looked up and called the girl's name again.

'Cini?'

He waited. 'Hey, lady, I'm home!'

It sounded strange. He said it and could hear himself, but it sounded strange, not something he would say. He stood there, listening.

But the sound he heard, finally, did not come from upstairs. It came from the den, the faint, whirring sound of a motor, and he looked toward the closed door.

He identified the sound as he opened the door and there it was, the movie projector going, lamp on, illuminating a hot white square across the room; the screen, set up, waiting. There was the sound and the shaft of light. Nothing else, until the figure moved out of the darkness to stand in front of the screen: a man he knew immediately was a black man, though he wore a woman's nylon stocking over his face that washed out his features. At the same time he knew that the revolver in the man's hand was a .38 Colt Special.

Even with the stocking over his face the man's words were clear. He said quietly, 'Take a seat, motherfucker. It's home movie time.'

Later, he remembered saying, 'What do you want?' and 'Where is she?' and then half turning as he heard the sound behind him. Later, he tried to concentrate on what he saw in the moment before the living room lamp went out: two men, seeing them as a heavyset guy and a skinny guy with long hair, but not seeing their features or even their clothes, only remembering an impression, the contrast of a thin guy with bony shoulders coming toward him and the thick-bodied guy hunched over the lamp. That was all he saw of them. The black guy poked him with the revolver, moving him to a chair, and Mitchell said, 'You mind telling me what's going on?'

The skinny guy, in the room now at the projector, said, 'No talking during the show, man. Just watch, and listen.'

The black guy pushed him into the chair and moved around behind him. Mitchell sat staring at the screen. He leaned back and felt the barrel of the revolver press against his head. In a moment he saw the countdown of numbers as the film started through the projector.

'You've seen some of this before,' the skinny guy said. 'Stuff your girl friend shot. I want you to know what we know, so it'll be clear in your head. You dig?'

Mitchell saw himself on the screen in full color, green bathing trunks and suntan lotion shining on his arm. He was reclined in a lounge chair reading *The Wall Street Journal*. The projector hummed in the dark room. After a moment he saw himself lower the newspaper and look up and shake his head and then smile patiently. He remembered the moment. He remembered almost telling her for Christ sake, *no*. But he had not said anything because no one but the two of them would ever see the film.

As he watched himself the skinny guy's voice-over said, 'Lucayan Beach. Grand Bahama, March seventeen through twenty-one, while your wife thought you were at a convention in Miami. You rascal. The broad's shooting you. Now here's you shooting the broad.'

Cini came glistening out of the surf in the tan bikini he remembered very well and from this distance, for a moment, she looked naked. Now she was closer, smiling, smoothing back her wet blond hair.

The voice-over said, 'A nice body, but a little weak in the lungs. What do you think?'

He remembered Cini going over to the hairy bald-headed guy and talking to him and handing him the camera.

'Now you and the broad together. There he is, Mr. Clean. Member of the Urban Renewal Committee, Bloomfield Village Council, Deprived Children's Foundation and the Northwest Guidance Center. You don't mind my saying, for a successful businessman and generally active in all that community bullshit, I think you got fucking rocks in your head, man, to let yourself get put on film. I mean, as you can see it's plain fucking dumb.

'Shots of the pool now ... and all the schmucks laying around in their resort outfits. Hot shit, huh? Seventy-five bucks a day, couple hundred bucks for the jazzy outfits. ... Here comes sport now, rum collins for the broad and a Heineken. Loaded and he still drinks beer. That's your background showing, man. Eleven years on the line at Dodge Main. Couple of shots and a beer every day after the shift. Right?'

Eleven and a half years, Mitchell was thinking, seeing himself in the green bathing trunks that were too big for him because he had lost fifteen pounds in one month after meeting Cini. Eleven

10

years and seven months exactly. Two-eighty an hour when he quit.

He saw the beach again, deserted now in the early evening. Their last day. He had stayed in the room to take a nap and she had gone for a walk.

'And as the sun sinks slowly in the west ... we leave the beautiful Bahamas, isles of intrigue and plenty of extra-curricular screwing, and get back to real life.'

He saw his car on a street, moving, the bronze Grand Prix.

'We spliced this in with the other,' the voice-over said, 'so we wouldn't waste your valuable time changing film. You recognize it, sport? That's you. Now watch where you go.'

Mitchell knew where the car was going. He remembered the day and the time and the street and the Caravan Motel.

There it was.

A zoom lens on the camera got him coming out of the motel office and driving over to unit number 17. There was a good shot of him looking out toward the street before he opened the door and they went inside.

Fifteen bucks. Not a bad place. It had been their third time. They had taken a shower together and drunk a bottle of champagne in bed, before, during and after, with a lot of kissing and squirming around, kissing the way he hadn't kissed in twenty years. She had said to him, 'I think I'm falling in love with you. If I'm not already.' But he did not say anything about love to her that time.

Over footage of them coming out to the car the narrator said, 'I like this one, the expression. Mr. Casual. We cut to ... sub-urbia.'

Now Mitchell was looking at his home in Bloomfield Hills and saw himself in a tennis warm-up suit jogging down the driveway past the big red-brick/colonial to the street.

'Keeping fit,' the voice-over said. 'You start chasing twenty-one-year-old tail you got to stay in shape. Mile-and-a-half jog every morning before going to ... the plant.

'Here we are. Ranco Manufacturing near Mt. Clemens. Gross sales last year almost three mil. Forty-something employees working two shifts. You bank at Manufacturers, you pay your bills on time and you have a very clean D and B. I like that. I also like the hundred and fifty grand you make a year on the patent you hold. What is it, some kind of a hood latch? Doesn't cost two bits to stamp out, but all the cars got to have one and, man, you own it.'

Mitchell had never seen his plant before on a movie screen. It didn't look bad: the front ledge-rock and Roman brick, and the aluminum sign that said RANCO.

'One of your trucks going out on a delivery,' the voice-over said. 'Or is it making a haul to the bank? We like your style, sport, so we're gonna make a deal with you.'

The film stopped, holding on the plant that was now slightly out of focus.

'The deal is, you get to buy this complete home movie for only a hundred and five grand. Not a hundred and fifty, no, we're not greedy and we know you got to pay capital gains on your patent royalties. So we'll let you pay it and give us approximately what's left. That's all, one year's royalty check. You won't even miss it and you'll have this fun movie for your very own. Nice color footage of what must be the most expensive piece of ass you ever had in your life.'

There was a silence before Mitchell spoke.

'Is she part of this?'

The narrator paused. 'Well, I wouldn't say she's a hundred percent pure. We had a talk and the chick is not dumb. She decided to move out, figuring fun and games were over.'

Mitchell sat in the chair, not moving, realizing he was calm and in control and this surprised him.

'What happens if I don't pay?'

'We get stills made of you and the broad -- on the beach, the motel -- and pass them around. A set to your wife. Set to your customers at G.M. Maybe a newspaper. I don't know, we'd think of ways to mess you up. Maybe it's no big deal, but you don't seem like the kind of guy would want to get smeared around. On the Keep Michigan Beautiful Committee, you go to church every Sunday, all that shit.'

Mitchell thought about it. 'You think I just go to a bank and draw a hundred and five thousand dollars?'

'No, it could take you a little time. But we want ten grand tomorrow. Like a down payment. Show us you're acting in good faith. You dig?'

'Give it to you where, here?'

'I'll call you at work, let you know.' The voice paused. 'Any more questions?'

'I'll have to think about it.'

'You got all night, sport. We'll pack up and leave you alone.'

'When do I get the film?'

'After the last payment. When'd you think?'

He sat in the dark room for perhaps a half hour after they had left. Finally he went into the kitchen and poured Jack Daniels over ice, took a drink of it and thought of something. He opened the door to the garage and saw that Cini's car was no longer there. Then he called his lawyer.

2

From the bedroom window Barbara Mitchell watched her husband for several minutes. Sometimes in the summer, while she was still in bed, she would hear him in the pool doing his twenty-five lengths. This morning it was cold and there was no sound.

He was directly below her on the patio, sport coat open, hands in his pants pockets. He never wore gloves, and only occasionally a raincoat during the cold months. She wasn't sure what he was looking at or how long he had been there. When he moved finally it was to walk along the edge of the swimming pool, looking down, as if inspecting the pale plastic cover that was stained and streaked with dead leaves and the dirt of winter and spring.

When she came outside, wearing a housecoat over her nightgown, he was still at the pool.

'Thinking about going for a swim?'

A trace of a smile appeared as he turned. 'Pretty soon. Get her cleaned out, be ready for Memorial Day.'

Barbara's hands were deep in the pockets of the housecoat, her shoulders hunched against the chill.

'Did you sleep at all?'

'Little bit, on my couch. Couple of the turning machines were giving us the trouble. They got them adjusted and set, then I had to wait while they started the run again and checked the pieces, cylinder rod couplers. Some reason the outside diameters were coming out trimmed a hair undersize and we had to scrap thirty percent of the run. That costs money.'

She knew he was not explaining but was talking to be talking, filling a void. She knew his sounds. Something was on his mind and it could be cylinder rod couplers or it could be something else.

'I'm going to change and get back. Sit on the job till it's out. Supposed to be in Pontiac this afternoon.'

'You make the deliveries now, too?'

'Sometimes it looks like it's coming to that.'

'Well, how about breakfast first?'

'Couple of soft-boiled eggs would be good. Four minutes.'

'I know,' Barbara said.

*

She was in the bedroom waiting for him. She heard the shower turn off. He would be drying himself now. In a few minutes he would open the bathroom door to clear the steam from the mirror and would shave with the towel wrapped around his waist that was flat through the stomach, hard-muscled, but bulged slightly above his hips and around into his back. You could never get that area, he said. You could do two hundred situps and twists a day and never quite get to those little bulging handles of fat. Love handles, Barbara said. Or she would say it was because he wore his pants so low, down on his hips. Something left over from younger days. And he would say he would never wear his pants way up high, the way fat old men did. Where did they get those pants? The goddamn zipper must be two feet long.

When he came out, with the towel around his middle, and went over to the dresser, Barbara said, 'I'll wait until you come down before I put your eggs on.'

He said, 'Fine,' and got a pair of jockey shorts out of the dresser. He never wore an undershirt top or a T-shirt.

Watching him, Barbara's expression was calm, her dark hair combed, her skin clear and clean-looking without make-up. She was forty-two; a very attractive forty-two. She had confidence in herself and in her husband, but she was worried about him and wasn't sure why.

She took off her housecoat, then timed it, waiting until he turned before she stepped into her panties, raising the short nightgown and pulling it up over her head.

'I probably got about two hours sleep,' Mitchell said. 'I need a bigger couch.'

'Usually it's the wife who makes the excuse.'

He looked at her, her body, the lines showing her tan and the white breasts. 'What?'

'The wife says she has a headache as the husband reaches for her.'

'I'm not making excuses. I'm not only tired, I got to get back to work.'

She reached behind her to hook the bra. 'I've seen you dead on your feet, but you could always move other parts of you.'

'Barbara – do people argue about making love?'

'I don't know what other people do.'

'Don't you think it's better when it happens naturally? You both want to do it?'

'Let me know when you feel natural again,' she said and put the housecoat back on and went downstairs.

*

Now she was at the breakfast table with *The Detroit Free Press*, her coffee finished. He came into the kitchen, wearing a clean shirt but the same sport coat, one that had been his favorite at least eight years. He took the sports section out of the paper and began to scan it as she served his eggs, English muffin and coffee. When this was done Barbara sat down again.

'Sally called last night.'

'She did? What's the matter?'

'Nothing. She just wanted to talk.'

'Still likes Cleveland? And the battery salesman?'

'She's happy, you can tell. But she misses us.'

'Is she pregnant yet?' His eyes roamed over the sports page as he began to eat, passing up a report on the Tigers' spring training camp that yesterday he would have read.

'No, she's not pregnant. They're going to wait a while.' Barbara paused, watching him. 'Did you see the mail?'

He looked up, momentarily interested, or pretending to be. 'No. Anything good?'

'A letter from Mike.'

'Another one? No, I didn't see it.'

'In the front hall.' She waited again as he returned to his breakfast, eating slowly, not finishing the eggs and pushing the plate away. 'Don't you think it's sort of amazing? He's written on the average of once every two weeks since he's been at school.'

'When he needs money.'

'I think he's a good writer. He tells you what's going on. How many do that?'

'I don't know. I guess not many.' Mitchell looked up at the big railroad clock on the kitchen wall.

'I got to go,' he said, but took time to finish his coffee before getting up. He looked at the clock again, then leaned over to kiss his wife on the cheek.

'Mitch?'

'What?'

'If it's such a pain in the ass, why don't you sell the business? Is it worth it, being tense all the time?'

'I'm not tense.'

'I don't know what you call it then. You're preoccupied, something. You don't talk anymore. All you think about is business or one of your committee things. You're so busy you don't even come home for dinner anymore.'

'Come on, maybe a couple nights a week I stay at the office or have to go to a meeting or something.'

'Mitch, it's almost every night, except the weekends.'

'Okay, I've been busy lately. What am I supposed to do. I've got machines breaking down for no reason. We're behind on orders. I got to keep customers happy, take them out to lunch. I got union contract negotiations coming up. I got to keep all these balls up in the air at once.'

'Poor me,' Barbara said.

'What'd you say that for?'

She shook her head. 'I'm sorry, it was dumb. I guess what I'm trying to say is you're different lately. Somehow. I can't put my finger on it.'

'Listen, I got to go.' He kissed her again, this time lightly on the mouth, and patted her shoulder. 'I'll try to get home early and we'll go out to dinner. Okay? Go to Charlie's Crab, get a good piece of fish.'

He was out of the drive, turning into the street, when Barbara reached the front door and got it open. She stood there, holding the letter from their son.

3

O'Boyle kept staring at him. Jim O'Boyle, his lawyer and friend, sitting across the desk now in the wood-paneled office.

'I never knew you fooled around,' O'Boyle said. 'You really surprise me, Mitch, I never thought of you that way.'

'I *don't* fool around.' Mitchell leaned in, emphasizing his words, being open and honest. 'I never fooled around in my life.'

'Then what do you call it?'

'I mean before. I never did anything like this before in my life.' O'Boyle kept watching him and Mitchell added, in a lower tone, 'I didn't consider this fooling around. I mean I didn't honestly feel that's what I was doing.'

'What did you consider it then? The girl's what, a year older than your daughter.'

'I didn't consider it anything. I didn't put a label on it.' He wasn't sure what to say next and the sound of the buzzer on his telephone saved him. He picked it up. 'Yeah? . . . All right, tell him I'll be out in a couple minutes.'

Mitchell hung up. 'Victor wants me.' He took a reel of tape from his desk drawer and held it in front of him with both hands, as though it might be fragile or of special value.

'I came back here after I talked to you on the phone last night, while it was fresh in my mind. Jim, I put it all down on the tape recorder, everything I could remember that happened. What the guy said, what he sounded like, what the film showed, everything I could remember that might mean something.'

'But you never saw any of them before. You're sure of that.'

'Jim, I don't know. I didn't see them last night, just a glimpse like half a second, how do I know? The machine's over there. Listen to it, Jim, I'll come back soon as I can.' Moving around the desk he said, 'I got a plant supervisor pulling his hair out because the fucking machines keep breaking down or the bearings freeze up. I got more downtime than production and now I got these clowns want to sell me a movie for a hundred and five thousand bucks. You ever have one like that before?'

'Go fix your machines,' O'Boyle told him.

And Mitchell said, 'Yeah.'

In the outer office his secretary, Janet, who was efficient and always in control, gave him a funny look, a quick, warning xpression.

The man standing by her desk said, 'Are you Mitchell?'

He's a cop, Mitchell thought. That was the instant impression the man gave him. But there was also something familiar about him. He had seen him before, somewhere.

Janet said, 'I've tried to tell this gentleman you can't see anyone. He walked right in, said he'd wait.'

'I'm sorry,' Mitchell said, 'I've got a full day,' and walked past the man toward the hall.

'My name's Ed Jazik, business agent Local one-ninety-nine.' He was a step behind Mitchell, extending a card as he followed behind him down the hall, past the glass partitions of the accounting and engineering offices.

That was it, Mitchell had seen him in the parking lot the week before, talking to some of the employees. He felt himself relax and took the card, putting it in his pocket without looking at it.

'We've never met before, have we?'

'No, I been assigned to handle negotiations this year,' Jazik said.

'Well, that's not for a couple of weeks.'

'I thought we might talk about it before. See where we each stand.'

'That's what the contract negotiation's for,' Mitchell said.

'I just want you to know,' Jazik said, 'I'm not taking any token cheap shit you might happen to offer. We don't come to a quick agreement you got a walkout on your hands.'

They came to the end of the hall, to a fire door with a sign that said NO ADMITTANCE. AUTHORIZED PERSONNEL ONLY. Mitchell stopped and looked at the man now.

'I thought everybody was happy.'

'From where you sit,' Jazik said, 'in your wood-paneled office. You don't happen to be operating a fucking machine all day long.'

Mitchell was tired and didn't want to lose his temper. He said, 'What're you pushing me for? You don't have a grievance. Let's wait, okay? Contract time we'll talk all you want.'

'Maybe some people don't want to wait,' Jazik said. 'They want to let you know conditions got to be a lot better.'

'Here's the thing,' Mitchell said. 'We get in an argument now I'm liable to forget who you are and knock you on your ass. So for the time being, why don't we stay friends?'

He pushed through the heavy door, into the high-level vibrating sound of the plant, and let the door swing closed in the business agent's face.

*

O'Boyle said, 'I thought you quit smoking?'

Mitchell leaned over the desk to get a light from him. 'I started again. You listen to the whole tape?'

'Twice.'

'Well?'

'I think you're being blackmailed.'

'How much do I owe you so far?'

'Mitch, you're in fairly serious trouble.'

'Fairly serious. What's really serious?'

'Tell me how you met the girl and started seeing her. Everything.'

'I met her in a bar—'

'Wait a minute, I want to get it down.' O'Boyle moved the tape recorder closer to Mitchell and turned it on. 'Okay.'

'I met her in a bar, a little over three months ago.'

'What bar?'

'I forgot the name. One of the topless go-go places down on Woodward.'

'What were you looking for, some action?'

'Jim, you want me to tell it? I was out with Ross. Once a week I take him to lunch, and I try not to make it a Friday, because he starts his weekend with the first martini. But it was

Friday. I pay the bill, we're walking out, it's only two o'clock, I'm thinking, thank you, God, I did it. And he says, "I don't feel like going back. Let's stop someplace and have a tightener." '

'So you stopped at the go-go bar.'

'We stopped at four of them. Nice sunny afternoon we're doing the topless tour. The last place, she's sitting at the bar. Ross sees her, pats her on the ass thinking she's one of the go-goers and tries to move in.'

'What kind of shape were you in?'

'Not bad. I just had beer.'

'So you sat down with her?'

'Ross did, I sat next to him. He begins with the usual bullshit about his forty-two-foot boat and his place in Canada. Pretty soon he's dropping the news that he's president of Wright-Way Motor Homes and how would she like to go up north in one this weekend. You know, that ski lodge he's got an interest in. She says, "Wow, ride up north in a house trailer." Ross says no, a *motor home*, with a built-in bar, the whole thing custom-designed and equipped, including a chauffeur. And she says, very innocently, "Gee, I don't know, sport. I don't know if I'd be able to handle it, a custom-designed motor home." You know, putting him on a little. He says, "I got a ski lodge up there, near Gaylord. I own it." She says, "That sounds great. What do you ski on this time of the year, the grass?" '

O'Boyle, watching the tape recorder, looked up. 'She used the word *sport*. That's what the guy called you a couple of times, didn't he?'

Mitchell paused, nodding. 'You're right.'

'Go on. Wait a minute,' O'Boyle said then. 'If she doesn't work in the place and I assume she's not a hustler, what was she doing there?'

'A friend worked there. Cini used to pick her up sometimes, drive her home.'

'Where did Cini work?'

'I'll get to that,' Mitchell said. 'I didn't start talking to her until her friend joined us. Actually I came back from the can and the other girl's there and Ross's already switched over, giving her the business. So I sat down next to Cini.'

'You know the friend's name?'

'I forgot. Donna. No, Doreen something or other. She's col-

20

ored. The best-looking colored girl I ever saw. That's why Ross jumped on her. Really good-looking.' Mitchell paused.

'Go on,' O'Boyle said.

'I don't remember how Cini and I started talking. I mean, what about. But it was nice. She didn't give me the innocent big eyes she gave Ross. We just started talking – I think about meeting people, you know? How people meet and start dating and then sometimes they get married? She told me she was married when she was eighteen and divorced two years later. So now she was taking a secretarial course at Wayne, night school, and working as a model during the day.'

'What kind of model? Ads? Commercials?'

'Let me get to it. We started talking and, Jim, I'll be a son of a gun, I asked her to go out to dinner.'

O'Boyle looked at him, saying nothing.

'I mean we started talking and I *liked* her. She was *real*. No bullshit put-on or, you know, cute acting.'

'She was real.'

'She was very honest and sincere, down to earth. She used a few words once in a while like "shit," but it was natural. She was easy to talk to and we started laughing at things each other said.'

'So you took her out to dinner.'

'Yes. Listen, you try and think of a place to go you're not going to run into somebody. It's almost impossible.'

'I've never been faced with the problem,' O'Boyle said.

'Yeah, well good for you. We ended up in someplace downtown, I'm looking around the whole time we're there expecting somebody to walk in. Place you never even heard of, all of a sudden you start picturing all your friends and neighbors walking in.'

'Guilty conscience.'

'That's what I pay you for, huh?'

'You score that night?'

'Jim, we were having a nice time, that's all. I didn't even think about it.'

'Well, when did you start thinking about it?'

'I guess when I saw her without any clothes on.'

'That could do it.'

'I told you she was a model? Well, when I first met her she

21

worked in one of those places you go in, take pictures of a nude girl, fifteen bucks for a half hour.'

O'Boyle stared; he didn't say anything.

'Thirty bucks you can body-paint them.'

'How much for a plain old-fashioned lay?'

'She didn't do that. Maybe some of the others did, I don't know.'

'She just took her clothes off for any guy who came in.'

'Jim, she didn't see anything wrong with it. She said a body's a body, everybody's got one, so what's the big deal? I told you she was . . . natural, honest.'

'A real person.'

'She was different. Jim, I'm not good at describing people. But I'm telling you I liked the girl. In fact, you want to know the truth, I fell in love with her. Can you hear me saying that? I fell in *love*. I felt like I was twenty years old. We had a good time together, we enjoyed each other and we didn't even do anything. I mean exciting. We didn't go out and spend a lot of dough. I'd come to the apartment and most of the time all we did was talk. Have some wine, listen to music and talk. You understand what I'm saying?'

'You're going through your menopause and you thought you were in love.'

'I *was* in love. Christ, I know the feeling. When I wasn't with her I'd think about her all the time. I'd get a pain inside.'

'Where, in your crotch?'

'In my *gut*. Jim, I'm telling you it's a real honest-to-God feeling that's got nothing to do with sex. We went to bed, of course, naturally. But that wasn't the big thing. We liked being with each other. Listen, we'd sit there and ask each other questions like what's your favorite color? What's your favorite vegetable? What's your favorite movie?'

'*Brief Encounter.*'

'I don't get it.'

'What about Barbara?'

'What about her?'

'I mean if you were so in love, why didn't you leave Barbara and marry the girl?'

'Come on, Jim.'

'I'm serious. You say you think about her all the time, you're deeply in love. Why didn't you get a divorce and marry her?'

'Jim, last night when I went there, the reason? I was gonna tell her I wasn't coming back anymore.'

'Why?'

'Try faking it for three months,' Mitchell said. 'Whether you're faking one or the other it isn't worth the state you get yourself in.'

'Conscience,' O'Boyle said.

'You said that before.' Mitchell was silent for a moment, thoughtful. 'I'll tell you a funny thing though. I've been married twenty-two years. All of a sudden I fall in love with a young, really nice, good-looking girl. But you want to know something, Jim? Barbara's better in bed.'

*

O'Boyle was still in the office when the call came. Mitchell recognized the voice. Nodding toward the extension phone on the table by the couch he said, 'Yeah, I know who it is.' O'Boyle went over and very carefully picked up the phone.

'Have you thought it over?' the voice asked.

'I'm still thinking,' Mitchell said. 'A hundred and five thousand, that's a lot to think about, isn't it?'

'Not for you, sport. A little side money.'

'I guess I'm tight with it then. I work hard for what I make. I say to myself why give it to some asshole comes along trying to con you?'

There was a silence and O'Boyle made a face, closing his eyes. Finally the voice said, 'This is no con. You don't come across you're going to find yourself up to your chin in shit, buddy, and I mean it.'

'But it's my decision,' Mitchell said. 'If I want to be in up to my chin or not is up to me, right?' Again there was a silence.

'You can have it any way you want,' the voice said.

'All right, then give me a couple more days to think about it.' Mitchell looked over at his lawyer. 'You've probably been working on this for a while. What's a couple more days? I mean you lay it on me all of a sudden, I have to have a little time to make up my mind.'

'We'll give you till tomorrow. First payment, ten grand, to show your good faith.'

'Where do I send it?'

'I'll call you tomorrow, let you know.'

'What time tomorrow?'

But the voice was no longer there.

Mitchell hung up. 'Now what?'

'You're sure,' O'Boyle asked, 'you've never heard his voice before?'

'Not before last night.'

'Could he be somebody who used to work here?'

'I don't know, I guess so. The guy knows more about me than my accountant. So what do we do?'

'Eventually,' O'Boyle said, 'we'll probably have to go to the police.'

'You're kidding.'

'You want to give them a hundred thousand dollars?'

'I want to give them two feet of pipe across the head.'

'Let me work on it,' O'Boyle said. 'I'll talk to a guy I know in the prosecutor's office and find out the procedure.'

'Not like drawing up a contract, is it?'

'I'll admit it's been a while since I've done any criminal work.'

'Just suppose,' Mitchell said, 'what if I pay them and forget about it?'

'You know better than that. If you pay they won't let you forget about it. You'll pay forever.'

'But if I don't, then people find out.' Mitchell saw his wife on the patio in her housecoat. She always looked good. In the cold morning light she looked good.

'Let's wait and see what happens.'

'I guess I ought to tell Barbara.'

O'Boyle, getting fifty dollars an hour for his advice, thought about it a moment. 'Mitch, I wouldn't say anything that you don't have to. Not yet, anyway. These guys could chicken out for some reason, get scared, change their mind. The whole thing could blow over like it never happened.'

'The clouds break and the blue sky appears.'

'Mitch, no one ever got in trouble keeping his mouth shut.'

That was all the advice he could buy for one day. Some encouragement, but not much. Maybe there was something he could do about it himself. He wasn't going to sit here thinking about it.

4

It had been a sporting goods store at one time – Mitchell remembered it because he had stolen a baseball glove from the place when he was in the seventh grade and his dad was working at the Ford Highland Park plant. It was on Woodward six miles from downtown in a block of dirty sixty-year-old storefronts. The showcase windows of the sporting goods store were painted black now and whitewash lettering four feet high said NUDE MODELS.

The girls sat around the lobby in aluminum porch furniture with green-and-yellow-plaid cushions. They weren't bad-looking, they weren't especially good-looking. They were girls in their early twenties who could have been waitresses or counter-girls at a dry cleaner's. On the walls were nude photos of girls, but not of any of the girls who were in the room now. A customer walked over to a secondhand office desk, paid the man in the swivel chair fifteen dollars, rented a Polaroid for five more if he wanted to or if there were any cameras working or any film available, and then would pick a girl and go down the hall to one of the eight-by-ten cubicles, or studios, as the girls called them.

The first time Mitchell came here he rented a camera and picked Cini right away, though without giving any indication that he knew her. He remembered being very self-conscious walking into the place and paying the fifteen dollars. Cini grinned but didn't say his name until they were in the room and she was taking off her sweater and jeans. She didn't wear anything under them. It was the first time he had seen her naked. She smiled again and asked if he was really going to take pictures. He said he thought that's what you were supposed to do. She said most of the guys just sat in the chair and stared at her boobs and crotch. Sometimes they'd ask her to lie down on the cot and put her legs apart, but very few of them ever brought a camera or rented one. Mitchell asked her if the guys ever tried anything. She said yes, sometimes; but most of the guys were creepy; they were nervous and mostly just wanted to look. There was a sign on the wall that said, LOOK OR TAKE PICTURES

BUT NO TOUCHING. Really? Mitchell asked her. None of the girls put out? Probably, Cini said. She never discussed it with them. It was an easy way to make a hundred and fifty a week, part time, and not have to worry about getting arrested. It was more than she needed to pay for school and to live on. She said she was glad she wasn't into drugs anymore and didn't have to work every day. Pretty soon, that first time, she started to play around, striking exaggerated nude-model poses. He took a half dozen pictures that came out sharp and clear in the brightly lighted room, but didn't take the pictures with him when he left. That evening they went to the Caravan Motel for the first time. Three weeks later he leased the apartment and she quit the modeling job.

Now, the second time Mitchell had come here, he was again self-conscious walking in and seeing the three girls and the guy behind the desk look up at him, knowing they were judging him: horny, middle-aged guy who had to pay to see a naked girl; dirty old man trying to act casual.

The guy behind the desk was heavy, soft-looking, with sculptured sideburns and thin hair combed carefully to the side in an attempt to cover his baldness; a thirty-year-old thirty-pounds-overweight guy in a tight mod sport shirt. He smelled of after-shave lotion and stared at Mitchell, not moving, as he approached the desk.

Mitchell said, 'There was a girl named Cini, Cynthia, used to work here. Is she still around?'

The fat man, whose name was Leo Frank and was the owner of the place, stared at Mitchell another moment before he said, 'We got a Peggy, we got a Terry, we got a Mary Lou, but no Cinis.'

'Nice-looking girl about five-four,' Mitchell said. 'Blond hair. She was going to school at the time.'

'They're all going to school,' Leo Frank said. 'These are probably the most educated young ladies you ever met in your life. Pick any one you want.'

'Her name's Cynthia Fisher,' Mitchell said.

The fat man looked off with a thoughtful expression. Finally he said, 'Yeah, she worked here a while. Quit sometime ago. Couple months at least.'

'You haven't seen her since then?'

'Can't help you. They come and they go. They don't leave any forwarding address.' Leo Frank nodded toward the three girls, lowering his voice. 'That Terry there, one in the middle, you want to look at some nice goodies.'

Mitchell glanced over at the girls, not wanting to stare at them. 'How long she worked here?'

'About a week is all. Her and Mary Lou just started.'

'What about the other one there?' Mitchell said.

'Peggy? Yeah, Peggy's been here maybe a couple of months.'

'I'll take her.'

'Nice goodies,' Leo Frank said. 'Peggy might have a little extra going, if you know what I mean.'

Mitchell paid the fifteen dollars and walked over to the girl, not looking at the other two. All three of them were watching him now. He said, 'Peggy?' The girl took her time getting up. Mitchell waited. She walked past him toward the hallway. Mitchell followed, feeling his age and the two girls watching him.

Leo Frank swiveled around in his chair, putting his back to the two girls across the room. He picked up the telephone and dialed a number. When a voice answered, Leo Frank said, 'He's here. . . . Who the fuck do you think I mean? The guy. He's here.'

*

The girl stared directly at Mitchell as she unbuttoned her shirt and took it off. For several moments she stood there, bare to the waist, before she said, 'You don't happen to be a cop, do you?'

Mitchell said, 'I thought it was legal.'

'It is,' the girl said. 'I was just wondering.'

'Do I look like a cop?' He was thinking that probably he did. On the force twenty years. The vice squad.

She said, 'You can't tell anymore,' unzipping her slacks now and stepping out of them. She wore bikini panties. 'Some of them, vice and narcos, they got long hair, mustaches, even beards. There ought to be a law they have to wear their uniforms at all times.'

'I'm not a cop,' Mitchell said. 'I just like to look at bare-naked ladies.'

'That's all you do, just look?'

'That's what the sign says.'

'Would you be interested in something else?' She hooked her

27

thumbs in the panties, like a cowboy, giving him a hip-cocked pose. 'Well, would you? I'm not going to come out and say it, that's called soliciting. But I imagine you get the general idea.'

'Do all the girls work here, are they all … pros?'

'Shit, you're not a cop,' the girl said, 'you're a newspaper reporter. How'd you get into this? How much you make? Does your mother know you ball? Cop, you know where you stand. Newspaper reporter, he's got a dirty mind, wants you to say dirty things he can't write in the paper anyway. No, I'm sorry, I'm not answering any questions at all today about anything.'

'I'm not a cop,' Mitchell said. 'I'm not a newspaper reporter. I just want to ask you if you know somebody. Girl used to work here, her name's Cini, Cynthia. Do you know her? It's a personal matter. I'd like to get in touch with her but I don't know where she lives anymore. She moved.'

The girl hesitated. 'You know where she used to live?'

'Apartment by Palmer Park. On Merrill.'

The girl said, still cautious, 'She moved from there months ago.'

'I know she did.' Mitchell waited.

'She was going to school,' the girl said. 'I think Wayne.'

'Not anymore,' Mitchell said. 'I called. She hasn't been to class in over a week.'

'Well, you know more about her than I do,' the girl said. 'I never saw her much. I didn't even know she quit school.'

Mitchell was silent, thoughtful for a moment, before he said, 'Well, thanks anyway,' and started for the door.

The girl said, surprised, 'Hey, don't you want to see my thing?'

Leo Frank waited until Mitchell was outside before he swivelled his back to the girls for the second time and picked up the phone. When the voice came on he said, 'He just left. … No, he was asking about Cini. … What do you think I told him for Christ sake? … Yeah, he went in a room, but the broad didn't know shit. … Right, I'll see you. Let me know.'

*

Alan Raimy put down the phone and came out of the cramped, cluttered, one-desk office into the lobby of the Imperial Art Theater; 'Adult features – continuous 10 A.M. to 10 P.M.' He took time to check the house again, counting one, two … six,

28

nine, twelve, sixteen, a couple guys over in the corner, maybe a couple more down low in the dark, somewhere in the rows of nearly empty seats. He could hear the projector throwing black-and-white images on the screen that were fuzzy, out of focus. The steam room scene. The stud is sitting there. The chick comes in. Oh, she says, isn't this the ladies' bath? The stud stands up. Her eyes lower and widen and there's the close-up of her reaction. Holy shit, mom. The twenty or so guys in the audience who have paid five each would see the stud and the chick on the massage table in about four minutes, then the group thing in the whirlpool bath shortly after. Same old shit. Slower than usual and enough out of focus to be annoying. Alan Raimy decided if the picture didn't start to draw in a couple of days he'd sail it and bring in *Going Down on the Farm*, they said it was grossing like crazy in Chicago and L.A.

Alan Raimy didn't own the theater, he was the manager. The owner lived in Deerfield Beach, Florida, and stayed down there from November through May; so Alan booked the features and took enough off the top to make the extra work more than pay for itself. A hundred guys come in today, only pass out tickets to half of them. It was easy to rake it off a dumb shit who lived in Deerfield Beach seven months of the year. The nice part, Alan got to see all the movies at the screenings. Alan dug movies. He was going to make one himself sometime: a good hard-core porno, but done well, with style; not just a dirty movie, a dirty *film*.

He went out through the lobby to the street and began walking south along Woodward Avenue, hands in his hiphuggers, bony shoulders hunched against the damp cold, dark hair curling over the collar of his safari jacket: young guy going nowhere in particular, in no hurry, looking at the storefronts and the cars going by – until he saw Mitchell on the corner.

When the light changed Mitchell started across Woodward. He was on the other side by the time Alan reached the corner.

The pedestrian warning light flashed WAIT. Alan fixed his gaze on it and was in the middle of the six-lane avenue when the light turned from red to green for the northbound traffic. He kept walking. A horn blasted close to him, to his right. Alan didn't look over until the driver yelled, 'You idiot, you want to get killed?'

29

The front three cars were waiting for him to pass. Alan walked over to the middle car, where the guy who had yelled at him was looking out the side window, ugly-looking middle-aged guy wearing a white hardhat.

Alan said to the guy, pleasantly, 'Hey, sport. Fuck off,' and kept walking. The guy wasn't going to get out, not with all the traffic behind him. Alan threaded his way through the waiting cars and got to the sidewalk in time to see Mitchell going into the Kit Kat Bar.

＊

It was the place where he had met her and first talked to her, after Ross had realized he wasn't getting anywhere and had switched over to her friend. Donna. No, Doreen.

There were three men at the bar and another half dozen, including two women, sitting alone, at the tables closer to the oval stage where the skinny girl with small breasts was moving to a slow rock number, her eyes closed, showing them she really felt it; or else she was asleep and doing it by rote. The only other girl Mitchell could see was standing at the end of the bar in a blouse and sequined panties with her can sticking out.

He ordered a Bud from the bartender. When the bartender came back and poured it and said that would be a dollar and a quarter, Mitchell said, 'Doreen still work here?'

'Which one's Doreen?' the bartender said. He had been tending the bar since 1932 and looked as though he had seen most of the Doreens there were in the world.

'Colored girl,' Mitchell said. 'You got more than one here?'

'Just a minute.' The bartender walked down to the end of the bar where the girl in the blouse and sequined panties was standing. She looked his way as the bartender came back.

'Doreen's off today,' the bartender said. 'It's her day off.'

Mitchell nodded. He looked at his watch. It was twenty to four. He took a sip of beer and was glad it tasted good and went down easily. Maybe he'd have another one before he went home. He looked around at the skinny girl with the small breasts doing her number, eyes still closed. After a moment he turned to his beer again, finished it and left.

Alan Raimy, at the end of the bar near the door, signaled the bartender.

'You want another Fresca?' the bartender said.

Alan shook his head. 'Eddie, that guy just walked out, what was he looking for, some tail?'

'I don't know what he was looking for. He asked was Doreen working today.'

Alan grinned. 'No shit. Goes for the black stuff. You never know, do you?' The bartender didn't answer, and Alan said, 'You seen Bobby? He been in?'

'Unh-unh,' the bartender said picking up the empty Fresca can, 'I ain't seen him all day.'

The Gray Line sightseeing bus was approaching the foot of Woodward Avenue when Bobby Shy started up the aisle in his light-gray business suit and sunglasses, past the thirty-six heads he had counted from his seat in the rear. They were mostly couples, out-of-town conventioneers and their wives, middle-aged or older, almost all of them wearing glasses and name tags.

'That beautiful structure on the left is the City-County Building,' the driver was saying into the mike clipped to his lapel. 'And the statue in front is the world-famous "Spirit of Detroit." Sitting there that man is sixteen feet high and weighs over sixteen thousand pounds. Ahead of us now you see the Detroit River.'

As the bus turned left onto Jefferson, heads raised and gazes shifted to look at the river and the dismal gray skyline beyond.

'Across the way, beautiful downtown Windsor, Ontario,' the driver said. 'You can get over to Canada by tunnel or bridge. There used to be a ferry, but I believe he was arrested sometime back. The amazing thing is that, at this particular point, Canada is *south* of the United States.'

At the front of the bus now Bobby Shy ducked his head to look out. Straightening again he reached inside the jacket of his light-gray business suit, came out with a .38 Colt Special and placed the barrel gently against the driver's ear.

'Give me the mike, man,' Bobby Shy said.

The driver's head turned, eyes raised, and the bus swerved abruptly into the next lane. The sound of a horn came from behind them. Bobby Shy looked back past the faces staring at him, then at the driver again. He said, 'Be cool, man, everything will be lovely. Turn left at the light. Three blocks up take a right, then left again. You dig? Just nod your head.'

Bobby Shy unclipped the handmike from the driver's lapel and turned to the faces again, the rows of eyeglasses and white round nametags.

He said, 'Ladies and gentlemen, you all see how it is? I'm sure you all want everything to be lovely same as I do. Because if you don't, if anybody tries to be brave, I'm going to blow this motherfucker's head off.' He paused and nodded toward the back of the bus.

'As we continue this sightseeing tour of the dynamic Motor City, my assistant is going to pass up the aisle for your contributions.'

Doreen was wearing sunglasses and a blond wig with a nice little flip-up where it reached her slim shoulders. She got out of her seat and started up the aisle with an A & P supermarket grocery bag, the top of it folded back tightly so it would stay open.

As the bus turned the corner, Bobby Shy said, 'Feel free to give my assistant your wallets, bill-folds, money belts, watches, jewelry. I mean don't hold back, 'cause we robbing the stage-coach, friends, taking everything you got.'

Doreen offered the open bag from one side of the aisle to the other, not missing anybody, saying, 'Thank you, love . . . thank you . . . God bless you, ma'am, I sure admire those earrings. They real diamonds? . . . Sir, we'll take your watch too, if you don't mind. Thank you, love. God bless you.'

When the bus turned north, onto a main street in the black ghetto area, Bobby Shy said, 'On the left coming up, past the hockshop and the poolhall, is the world-famous K.O.'s Bar-b-que y'all heard so much about. Past two A.M. you can get a drink in there with your ribs. Any kind you want, comes in a Co'Cola can.' Looking down the aisle, Bobby Shy paused.

'Man, put your wallet in there, will you please? Thank you.'

He ducked his head to look through the windshield again. 'For you gentlemen, up over that bar on the corner? That's a whorehouse. Nice clean establishment. Those places you see boarded up? Historic remains of the riot we had a few years ago. Got me a fine hi-fi set and a 'lectric toothbrush . . . color TV for my mama.' To the driver he said, 'Right at the next corner. Go to the end of the street.'

Doreen was near the front of the bus now, finishing up.

'How we doing?'

'Looks good,' Doreen said. 'Some junk and travelers' checks, but looks good.'

At the end of the street the bus came to a stop in front of a black-and-white-striped dead-end barricade.

Bobby Shy grinned at the rows of tense, blank faces watching him. He said, 'Detroit's a great big wonderful town, ain't it, gang? Enjoy yourselves. And thank you.'

The driver and the sightseers watched Bobby Shy and Doreen make their way down the grassy embankment to the Chrysler Freeway, gauge the traffic, run across to the median, wait for the oncoming cars to pass and then run across to the other side and up the embankment. A car was waiting for them in the service drive. The car started off, in plain sight, moving through an area that had been razed for redevelopment, then reached a tree-lined block of old apartment buildings and was out of sight.

*

The John waited in the doorway. He didn't move until Doreen had turned on a lamp. He walked in then, slightly drunk, looking around the apartment living room and nodding.

'You got a nice place here,' the John said. 'Very sexy. You must do all right.'

When he looked at Doreen again her flip-up wig was perched on a fat candle in the center of the coffee table and she was at the record player, turning it on. Her hairstyle was natural, moderately full.

'You want a drink or something first?' Doreen asked.

'You got any ... pot?'

'I think so, I'll look. Sit down, take your coat off if you want.' Aretha Franklin came on softly as she spoke.

The John watched her remove a book from a shelf, open it and take out a white number 10 envelope. He sat down on the couch, making himself comfortable.

'Hey, you didn't tell me your name.'

She knelt at the coffee table to roll the joint. 'I told you, you forgot. Doreen.'

'You never told me how much, either.'

'Kick your shoes off, love. Then we can talk business.' She lighted the joint and handed it to him and watched him draw in.

33

As he did his eyes opened, fixed on something, and he coughed, exhaling the smoke.

'Man,' Doreen said, 'you supposed to hold it *in*.' She noticed the direction of his gaze and looked around.

Bobby Shy was standing in the doorway that led to a bedroom, standing there in his undershorts, an unlighted cigarette in his mouth.

'What time is it?' Bobby Shy said.

Doreen glanced at her watch. 'Quarter to eleven. I thought you were sleeping.'

He came over to the coffee table and picked up the lighter. The John didn't move. He stared at Bobby Shy, at the flat gut and sloping shoulders and the veins that stood out in his arms like cords. Lighting the cigarette Bobby Shy said, 'How long you going to be?'

Doreen shrugged. 'All night if he's up to it. No pun intended.'

'I got to go out for a while.' Going back to the bedroom he said, 'Come here a minute.'

The John watched Doreen get up and follow the black man to the doorway. When the black man looked at him, the John shifted his gaze quickly and studied an orange day-glo painting of Spanish galleons at sunset.

Bobby Shy said to Doreen, 'He look like anything?'

'You want to hustle a shoe clerk,' Doreen said. 'He been saving his money and his little dick a month for this.'

'I'll see you later,' Bobby Shy said. Going into the bedroom, closing the door, he heard Doreen say, 'He's just a friend of mine, baby. He don't mind.'

*

Bobby Shy got to the Kit Kat Bar about eleven-thirty. He liked the beat of the number and felt very fine right now with twenty dollars worth of top-shelf coke working in his head. There was a good crowd for a weeknight; he had to look around before he saw Alan and Leo sitting at a table toward the back of the place.

Alan looked up at him. Leo was anxious and asked him right off, 'Where you been all day?'

'Sightseein',' Bobby Shy said. He took a seat, glancing over at the white skinny chick on the oval stage and pausing to watch her a few moments: a new one, not too bad; maybe he'd look into some of that.

'We been trying to get ahold of you,' Leo said.

Bobby Shy nodded. 'I got the message. I'm here, ain't I?'

'You want something to drink?' Leo had had six vodkas and Seven-Up in the past few hours; Alan, one Fresca.

Alan kept his eyes on Bobby Shy. 'How you doing?'

'I'm fine,' Bobby said. 'Mellow.'

'I can see it,' Alan said now. 'Coming in about five thousand feet.'

'Not coming in, man. Staying up a while.'

'You better land,' Alan said. 'The guy's been around. Looking for Cini.'

'So what'd you expect?'

'He's holding back,' Leo said. 'Stalling.'

'What you want me to do, run him over?'

'I talked to him on the phone,' Alan said quietly. 'He wants more time. He's figuring ways to get out of it.'

'I would too,' Bobby Shy said. 'Look all around me for ways.'

Alan was patient. He liked the idea of not ever raising his voice. 'No, there's more to it,' he said. 'We got to look at the guy a little closer. He's not scared yet. He's nervous, but he's not scared. He doesn't sit home biting his fingernails, he asks for more time and then comes around looking for Cini. Maybe he doesn't believe it. Maybe he thinks it's a joke. You see what I mean? I mean I think we're going to have to dig the hole a little deeper for the guy and put him in, so when he looks up he doesn't see any way to get out. You follow me?'

'You want to dig a hole,' Bobby Shy said. He looked over at the new go-go dancer again.

'In case we need it,' Alan said. 'Just in case.' He grinned then. 'I'll tell you, I got an idea, man, a way to do it that's un-fucking-believable. I mean it, I tell you and you're not going to fucking believe it at first.'

Slowly Bobby Shy looked away from the go-go dancer. 'Well lay it on me. See if I like it.'

Alan was in control again. 'There's time,' he said. 'First we see if the man makes his down payment.'

5

Barbara said, 'You want a drink, don't you?'

'I guess so.'

She looked at him a moment, about to say something. Mitchell waited and it passed. He watched her take a fifth of Jack Daniels and two lowball glasses from the cupboard and place them on the counter that separated the kitchen from the breakfast room. Mitchell stood on the side away from the kitchen, leaning on the counter. He watched Barbara fill the glasses with ice from the freezer side of the refrigerator. He could smell something cooking in the oven. Pot roast. With browned potatoes and carrots.

'I thought we were going to eat out.'

'I didn't think you really wanted to.' Barbara poured two inches of whiskey into the glasses and added a splash of water from the sink faucet. 'You looked tired this morning,' she said, her eyes raising with a calm, nice expression.

'I guess I am. Last few days I haven't slept much.'

'You should go to bed early tonight.'

'I'm planning to. If Victor or somebody doesn't call.'

'Haven't they fixed . . . whatever it is yet?'

'Still some machine problems. And now I've got a smart-ass union guy on my back trying to show me how tough he is.' He saw her watching him and he said, 'I'm not making excuses. It's a simple fact.'

'I didn't say anything.'

'I know you didn't.'

There was a silence as they sipped their drinks. Mitchell lighted a cigarette and handed it to Barbara, then lighted one for himself.

'You didn't read Mike's letter this morning,' his wife said. 'Now I don't know what I did with it.'

'That's right, I forgot. Anything new I ought to know about?'

'He still hasn't said how he's doing in class. It's mostly about parties. He's repairing his motorcycle in the apartment and there's no place to sit down. He has another rice and mushroom recipe he wants to fix for us when he gets home.'

'Doesn't know whether to be a cook or a mechanic.'

'Marion called. We're going there for dinner Saturday night.'

'Fine. Who's going?'

'I didn't ask. I'm sure we'll know everybody.'

'Yeah, I guess we usually do.'

'The disposal's acting up again. It works and then it doesn't.'

'Why don't you call somebody?'

'You said you were going to fix it.'

'That's right, I did.'

'About a month ago,' Barbara said. 'The first time it got stuck or whatever it does.'

'Yeah, I keep forgetting.' Mitchell looked over at the sink. 'This weekend, I'll open it up, take a look.'

'That would be nice,' Barbara said.

'Probably the blades're out of line.' He watched his wife sip her drink and place the glass on the counter again.

'I've been seeing a girl,' he said.

Barbara's gaze remained on the lowball glass, still holding it. He couldn't see her eyes. He knew she was waiting for him to continue and he didn't know what to say.

'I met her about three months ago.'

He waited again as she took a sip of her drink, her eyes still lowered.

'Go on.'

'I don't know how to tell it.'

'Try,' Barbara said. She looked at him directly now. She seemed calm. 'Do I know her?'

'No. We met in a bar. I've been seeing her maybe two, three times a week.'

'You go to bed with her that often?'

'No, it's not like that.'

'Then what are you seeing her for?'

'I'm trying to say, we started seeing each other, it wasn't just sex.'

'Is she good in bed?'

'What're you asking something like that for?'

'Why, does it offend you? Your sense of morals?'

'I met the girl, we liked each other. It just happened. I don't know why. I wasn't looking for anything.'

'How old is she?'

'Twenty-two.'

'A year older than Sally.'

'I know. But she doesn't seem that young.'

'Sally's married.'

'She was, too. She's divorced.'

'What's her name?'

'Cini.'

'That's cute.'

'Cynthia. Her real name's Cynthia.'

'She's young,' Barbara said. 'She's different. You met her in a bar but she's really a nice girl. She's in love with you and she's ready to get married again. Anything else?'

'That's not the way it is.' He was trying to appear calm and raised his glass slowly to finish the drink.

Barbara waited, staring at him. 'If that's not the way it is, then why are you telling me about it? If you've got something going on the side, why in hell would you want to tell *me*?'

'You want another one?' He was already pouring whiskey into his glass.

'I might as well,' his wife said. The glass was something to touch and turn and look at thoughtfully. She couldn't stare at the wallpaper or the cupboards for very long. She couldn't look at Mitchell for more than a few moments at a time. She couldn't press down on him with her gaze and purposely make him uncomfortable. The son of a bitch.

She said, 'All right, two supposedly intelligent people who have been living together for twenty-two years are now having a little talk. If you're not planning to marry the girl – can I assume that?'

'No, I'm not planning to marry her.'

'Then what are you telling me about it for? Why wouldn't you use a little sense and keep it to yourself? Are you bragging about it or what?'

'I don't know. I guess it's been bothering me.' He looked at his wife and made himself hold her gaze. 'Barbara, I don't do things like this. I can't get used to sneaking around. I feel like I'm somebody else.'

'It's been bothering you,' Barbara said. 'Poor baby.'

'Do you want to hear about it or not?'

'I don't know. Maybe I don't.'

'All right, let's forget about it.'

'*Forget* about it!'

'I mean talk about it some other time. Maybe I shouldn't have brought it up.'

Barbara shook her head, almost in wonderment. 'You're too much. *Maybe* you shouldn't have brought it up.'

'Look, it isn't a simple thing to explain.'

'I guess not, if it could blow a perfectly good marriage that's lasted twenty-two years.' She paused. 'Or hasn't it been so good? God, all of a sudden I'm not sure I know you. Much less her. Is she pretty or flashy or what? She have big knockers?'

'Barbara – she's not what you picture. She's kind of plain-looking.'

'Well, tell me what the big attraction is. She know a lot of kinky sex tricks?'

Mitchell shook his head. 'We got along, that's all. We laughed, we had a good time together.'

'*We* get along,' Barbara said. '*We* laugh. At least we used to.'

'I know it. It doesn't make sense. It's just something I felt.'

Barbara frowned. 'Wait a minute. Why the past tense? Aren't you going to see her again?'

'I don't know. Right now I don't even know where she is.'

'You mean she left you? But you're still interested?'

'It's a little more complicated than that.'

'What is?'

'If I told you the whole story – I don't know, I guess my timing's bad. It'd sound like I was sucking around you for sympathy.'

'Boy, it would have to be an awfully sad story to get any sympathy from me.'

'Well, it's not something that happens every day.'

'But you won't tell me about it.'

'Not yet.'

'So all I know is you've been fooling around.'

Mitchell let it pass and took a sip of his drink. Barbara stared at her glass. She said, 'I never thought it would happen to us. I never even considered it. Ever.'

'I didn't either,' Mitchell said. 'I think about it now – it would've ended, you never would have known the difference.'

'I think I have known,' Barbara said, 'for at least a month. But God, I wish you hadn't told me.'

*

From ten until twelve that morning Barbara Mitchell played doubles with her regular Wednesday group at the Square Lake Racquet Club. It was twenty-five minutes past twelve when she reached home and turned into the drive. Barbara didn't get out. She sat in the Mercedes and lighted a cigarette. She was alone. She could hear the engine idling and, faintly, Roberta Flack's voice on the radio. It was warm in the car, reasonably comfortable. She wore a scarf and a suede coat over her tennis whites, no pantyhose; her legs were still tan from two weeks in Mexico in February. She could go in the house and change into slacks and go to Marion's for lunch and talk to the girls and laugh and pretend nothing had happened. Or she could back out the drive and get to a freeway and go north or south or any direction, it didn't matter, and keep going and feel the speed of the car – see how fast it would go – and see fields and trees and road reflectors rushing past and . . . what?

Or she could drive over to Ranco Manufacturing and go into Mitch's office and kick the great lover in the balls. The bastard. The rotten son of a bitch. Twenty-two years. And he had to tell her about it.

She wondered if he'd ever had a girl friend before. No, he would have somehow given it away. Or, with his conscience killing him, he would have told her. She doubted that he had ever lied to her. Harry Straightarrow. The good guy.

But God, he was dumb. Falling for some little ass-shaker, cute little mindless fluff who probably didn't wear a bra and said 'groovy' and 'cool' and smoked pot.

She could see Mitch trying it, holding the twisted cigarette delicately in his big tool-grinder fist, trying to hold in the smoke curling out of his nose. The dope. The wrong dope got the dope. Bob Hope had said that in a movie. She remembered the line but didn't know why. She didn't remember the name of the picture, only that they had seen it together before they were married: Mitch working days at Dodge Main and taking engineering courses at night – while she was working on her masters in English lit, which she never completed – and every Saturday or

Sunday they'd go to a show or a ball game, Tigers or the Lions, depending on the season.

Twenty-two years used up, gone. Photographs in a bottom drawer. She remembered sitting on the floor with Mitch – a year ago, right after Sally was married – looking through the pile of snapshots they were going to sort out someday and put in albums, chronologically, with dates, a pictorial family record. But there were no dates on most of the photographs. Sally and Mike, little kids on the beach. Sally and Mike standing by the car. Barbara younger, with a tight hairstyle and a long skirt. By the car. Mitch, heavier, with a crewcut. By the car. Why did they always take pictures standing by a car? It was a good thing, Mitch said. It was a way to identify the year. The cars changed and the people changed. A time they could look at but not remember as a particular day. There were pictures taken at a party at least eighteen or twenty years ago. Look at how young everyone looked. Good friends who were still friends, most of them. Everyone laughing. Every weekend. Bring your own. A case of beer or a bottle of Imperial, two-forty-nine. No money, but they talked and laughed and seldom seemed to worry about anything. She remembered saying to him – perhaps a month ago – 'Why don't we have fun anymore?' And he said, 'We have fun. We go to Florida and Mexico, we've gone to Europe, we play tennis, we go out to dinner every week, we go to shows.' And she remembered saying, 'You haven't answered the question.' That time, looking at the photographs, she said, 'Can you hardly wait till Sally has a baby?' And she remembered him saying, 'I guess so, except then I'd be married to a grandmother, wouldn't I?' Being funny, but telling her something at the same time.

Go upstairs and throw his clothes out the window. His drip-dry shirts and jockey shorts and ratty sport coat and the blue sweatsuit he jogged in every morning. Let him come home and find all his things in a pile on the front lawn, the bastard, and have to shovel them into his showboat bronze Grand Prix.

Grow up, she said to herself, and go to lunch.

Barbara got out of the car and crossed the lawn to the front steps. She was reaching for the handle when she noticed the door slightly open, the copper weatherseal touching the jamb but not closed all the way. This morning she had gone out the back to the garage. Had she opened the front at all? Yes, to get *The Free Press*. Then had slammed it closed. She could have left it unlocked easily enough – they had lost the key to the front door and usually didn't make a point of locking it until they were in for the night. But, she knew, she had not left the door open this morning.

In the foyer she took off her coat and draped it over a chair. It was when she paused then, listening, that she knew someone was in the house. There was no sound that she heard; she sensed it. Someone was here, now.

*

Alan Raimy was sitting in a big chair by the fireplace, his legs crossed, an attaché case on the floor at his feet.

He watched Barbara come into the living room: nice tan legs in the short tennis dress, yes, very nice. A good-looking well-preserved broad. Nice hips; she moved nice.

He said, 'Slim, I'll tell you what I'm going to do.'

Barbara turned abruptly to see him fifteen feet away from her in the easy chair: a bony, pale-looking young man with long hair, wearing a dark business suit, sitting in Mitchell's chair. She noticed his boots and the attaché case.

'I'm going to give you a personalized monthly accounting service,' Alan said. 'Take care of all your bills and expenditures for a low three and a half percent charge, guaranteed to be accurate or we eat the difference.'

'Who are you?'

'In fact, that's our motto. Silver Lining Accounting Service – we satisfy or we eat it.'

'How did you get in here?'

'I walked in, Slim. I knocked, nobody answered. The door was open so I walked in.'

Barbara kept her voice cold, dry. 'Well, would you mind getting up now and walking out?'

'For example,' Alan said, 'I figure you got about an eight-, nine-hundred-dollar mortgage payment. You got all the credit cards ever invented and you spend in excess of four thou on monthly bills, right?' Barbara stared at him and Alan shrugged. 'All right, let's say four for right now.'

'I'm going to ask you once more—'

Alan held up a hand. 'Another couple hundred for restaurants. You sign because it's easier, am I right?'

'Or I can call the police,' Barbara said.

'What for?'

'What *for*? You walk in my house, you refuse to leave—'

'I didn't refuse to leave. You haven't given me a chance.'

'All right, you've got it. Now get out.'

Alan took his time rising, picking up his attaché case. 'Forty-two hundred times three and a half, that's roughly, in round figures ... five fours are twenty, three fours are twelve ... about a hundred and forty bucks a month, you never have to balance another bank statement. How does that sound?'

'What's the name of your company?'

'Silver Lining Accounting. I told you.'

'What's your office phone number?'

Alan started across the room. 'That's all right, I'll get back to you. Never inconvenience the customer, put them to any trouble.'

'Give me the number,' Barbara said. 'Or your card.'

Alan patted his side pocket. 'I ran out of cards.' He smiled at her then. 'Don't worry, Slim, we'll be in touch.'

He walked through the foyer and out the front door.

Barbara reached the door, opening it again part-way, to see him crossing the lawn to the street. He waited at the edge of the pavement. After only a few moments a white Thunderbird appeared and rolled to a stop. The bony, pale young man got in with his attaché case and the car continued up the street.

Barbara turned again to the living room. From the arched entranceway she looked around. Nothing seemed to be out of place. She ran upstairs to the master bedroom, went directly to her dresser and took out the case that held her good jewelry. Nothing was missing. She looked around. The room didn't seem to have been disturbed.

She knew she should call the police. But she'd have to wait here for them and answer questions and what, specifically, could she tell them? It hardly seemed worth the trouble – in the light of eternity, or just in the light of current events. The bastard. She began to change, taking off her tennis dress. She'd have something to talk about at lunch and wouldn't sit there like a clod, thinking.

*

'I see the car pull in,' Leo Frank said, 'and I think, Christ, what's he going to do?'

'I was upstairs,' Alan said. 'You can't ever get caught upstairs. They don't believe shit they catch you upstairs. But she stayed in the car a while like she was sneaking a smoke. So when she comes in I'm sitting in the living room in my blue suit.'

Leo drove carefully, watching the speedometer, as the Thunderbird followed Long Lake Road east, through a rolling wooded residential area of large homes set far back from the road. Leo didn't know the area and it made him nervous to be here. He was anxious to hit Woodward and turn south, toward the hazy skyline of the city.

'I gave her Silver Lining Accounting Service,' Alan said. ' "We satisfy or we eat it." '

'Silver Tongue Service,' Leo said. 'You chow-hound.'

'She's not bad,' Alan said. 'It wouldn't be bad duty at all.'

'I'm surprised you didn't proposition her.'

'Who says I didn't?' Alan sat with the attaché case on his lap, his palms flat on the leather surface, his bony fingers drumming slowly, in silence.

'Well,' Leo said, 'you going to tell me what's in there, or what?'

'You won't believe it.'

'Tell me. Let's see if I do.'

Alan's thumbs snapped the brass fasteners open. 'You ready? Ta-*daaa*.'

'Come on, for Christ sake.'

Alan opened the case. 'I got a sport coat.'

'Yeah.' Leo glanced over. The coat was folded neatly to fit in the case and seemed to fill the inside.

'I got a shirt. Underneath.'

'Yeah.'

'I got a tie. Just in case.'

'Sharp-looking tie?'

'He doesn't own one. And I got – you ready for this? The fucking good luck jackpot award of all times.' Alan raised the coat, folded, out of the case and Leo glanced over again.

'Jesus Christ,' Leo said.

'A genuine no-shit thirty-eight Smith and fucking Wesson, man,' Alan said. 'How's that grab you? The piece, the paper that goes with it and a box of thirty-eights.'

'Jesus Christ,' Leo said again. 'You're hoping for something like that going in, unh-unh, never in a million years.'

'Clean living,' Alan said, closing the attaché case. 'It pays off every time.'

6

Mitchell waited.

Ross's hand was now up under the waitress's brief skirt, resting on her can. They were at Ross's table, the good table in the corner where he believed no one could ever see what he was doing.

'Do you still love me?'

The girl smiled, holding the order pad in front of her with both hands. ' 'Course I do.'

'Then when the hell are we going to consummate it?'

She smiled again. 'Two of the same?'

'How about this weekend?' Ross said. 'We'll go up north. You're a good girl, I'll take you up skiing next winter.'

The girl wrote something on the pad. 'I'll have to ask my mother.'

'Your mother skis?'

'Vodka martini and a Bud,' the girl said, and took off through the Motor City Mediterranean décor, through the roomful of businessmen having the businessmen's lunch at the tables with maroon lamps and maroon checkered cloths.

'Irene's twenty,' Ross said, 'but she's got the mind of a fifteen-year-old. I'm sorry, what were you saying? About the plant problem.'

'No,' Mitchell said patiently, 'I told you we'd handle that.'

'Right. I tell you we're putting in some improvements at the lodge? I mean big ones,' Ross went on. 'Blasting out a couple of hills, making the runs longer, putting in a couple more chair lifts. You don't ski, do you?'

'No, I never tried it.' Mitchell wanted to say something, but he waited too long and Ross was off again.

'I look for a dynamiter, you know, for the job. I have to go all the way to Colorado to get a guy who knows what he's doing.'

'There was something I wanted to ask you,' Mitchell said.

'What?'

'Remember the day we went to all the go-go bars? About three months ago.'

'Vaguely.'

'We met a girl the last place, sitting at the bar.'

'We did?'

'You were interested in the colored broad that worked there. Doreen. Very nice-looking.'

Ross began to nod, lighting a cigarette. 'Right. Big eyes. Cute little nose.'

'The other girl, the one you were talking to first,' Mitchell said and paused a moment, 'I've been seeing her the past three months.'

Ross looked at him, not grinning, not coming right out with it, but with a relaxed, comfortable expression, a look of quiet satisfaction as he settled back in his chair.

'You ... son ... of ... a ... gun. So you're normal after all. Healthy, red-blooded American boy—' He leaned against the table again. 'How is she?'

'Ross, Barbara knows about it.'

'Oh, Jesus. How'd she find out?'

Mitchell looked up as the waitress approached with their drinks.

Ross said to her, very seriously, 'Irene, you know you're driving me right out of my goddamn mind. When're you going to run away with me?'

'How about Monday?' the waitress said. 'It's my day off.'

Ross nodded. 'Monday, five o'clock. I'll pick you up right here.' She moved off and Ross looked at Mitchell again, showing concern.

'How in hell she find out?'

'I told her.'

'You told her? For Christ sake, why?'

'It's a long story,' Mitchell said. 'I just want to ask you, all the fooling around you've done—'

'Mitch, I don't *fool*. I fall in love. Like anybody else.'

'All right then, with all the experience you've had. What I want to ask you, when you were still married to Pat, did she ever find out?'

Ross thought about it, sipping his drink. 'I suppose so. Once or twice.'

'Well, what happened? What'd she do?'

'She didn't do anything.'

'You explained it somehow? I mean what happened?'

'Nothing. It never came up.'

'Come on.'

'Really,' Ross said. 'Why would she want to bring it up, cause a sticky situation? And I certainly wouldn't. Mitch, you must be out of your mind. Why'd you tell her?'

'I don't know. I just did.'

'Mitch, they don't want to know about things like that. They want everything to be nice. Don't rock the boat. Don't fuck up what appears to everyone to be a perfect marriage.' Ross pried an olive up from the bottom of his martini and put it in his mouth. Chewing, he said, 'It sounds to me like your conscience grabbed you by the balls.'

'Maybe that's it,' Mitchell said. 'The point is, she knows.'

'Well, how did she take it, when you told her?'

'She was pretty calm about it. Didn't say much.'

'Is that right?' Ross seemed surprised.

'She said a couple of times, "What'd you tell me for?" '

'See what I mean? What else?'

'I don't know. She said she never thought it would happen.'

'She didn't sound pissed off at all?'

'Yeah, she was mad, said a few things. But that staring at you, you know, giving you the look, that's worse.'

'So how'd it end?'

'I don't know. That's what I'm asking you. What happens now?'

'She kick you out?'

'No, I slept in Mike's room.'

Ross was thoughtful again. He sipped his martini and lighted a cigarette.

'I think you ought to move out, Mitch. Really. You want my advice, I think you ought to clear out and let her think about it a while. You see what I mean? She's there by herself, the house isn't the same. It's too quiet. She gets lonely. She thinks, maybe I was too hard on him. So he fooled around with some broad for a while. It happens. But it isn't the end of the world.'

'Well, I don't know if it's that simple,' Mitchell said. 'She's not sure it's over. I mean I wasn't asking to be forgiven, I was just telling her how it is.'

Ross's eyebrows raised. 'Is that right? It's still up in the air?'

'I don't know what she's going to do. So you can say it's still up in the air.'

'What about the girl?'

'That'll end. If it hasn't already.'

Ross nodded, leaning in closer. 'You know, I wouldn't want to have Barbara mad at me, Mitch. She's very nice, probably the smartest woman I know. But, if you don't mind my saying, as nice as she is, she's a very tough lady.'

'Ross, I been living with her twenty-two years.'

'You know what I mean, I'm not being insulting, Mitch. I love Barbara.'

Mitchell nodded. 'I know.'

'What I'm suggesting, I think you ought to move out and lay low for a while. Let her cool off.'

'You think so?'

'That's what I'd do, Mitch. If I were married to Barbara I'd stay out of her way and play it very cool for a while, couple of weeks at least.'

'Maybe you're right,' Mitchell said. 'Instead of hanging around and getting into arguments, try and let the thing die.'

'That'd be my advice,' Ross said. He picked up the martini, leaning back in his captain's chair. 'And as you say, I've had a little experience with women. God help me.'

*

His secretary, Janet, said, 'Mr. O'Boyle called. Just a few minutes ago.' She followed Mitchell into his office. 'I told him you were still at lunch,' and added, 'you're back early.'

Mitchell looked at her. 'My wife call?'

'No. Your mail's on the desk. Nothing important. Except maybe the envelope on top. I didn't open it.'

Standing behind his desk, Mitchell picked up the envelope. His name and company address appeared in a faint black typewriter face. The words PERSONAL AND CONFIDENTIAL, in capital letters, were typed in red. There was no sender's name or return address. Janet waited, but he didn't open it or comment.

'Also, Vic would like to see you as soon as possible.'

'Tell him to come in,' Mitchell said. 'And get me O'Boyle.'

He sat at his desk now, looking at the envelope, feeling something small and hard inside. He knew it was a key and he knew who had sent it. Mitchell tore open one end of the envelope and let the key slide out onto his blotter pad: a short dull-metal shape with the number 258 etched into the flat part of its surface. His telephone buzzed.

'Jim . . . Pretty good . . . Yeah, well listen, before you go into that, Jim, I told Barbara.' He paused again. 'I didn't mention the blackmail, but I told her about the girl and it's done. So they can show her the film or shove it up their ass, I don't care, it's done.'

He listened for a few moments. 'I've got a few other things on my mind too, Jim. I've got a goddamn plant to run.'

Mitchell looked up, listening to O'Boyle again as his superintendent appeared in the open doorway.

'Jim,' Mitchell said, 'how're they going to confiscate the film? You think the guys carry it around with them? I don't even know who they are. How do I identify them?' Mitchell paused again, listening, and then said, 'Let me get back to you, Jim. Vic's here, we have to discuss something, all right? . . . Right . . . No, I won't. I'll see you later.'

Hanging up, Mitchell looked at his superintendent. 'Now what?'

'All the trouble we been having,' Vic said. 'I don't know why I didn't see it. You know what's going on?'

'What do you mean do I know what's going on? The goddamn machines are breaking down.'

Vic shook his head. 'Not by themselves, Mr. Mitchell. I don't know why I didn't see it before this. I guess because I trust people or I expect too much, I don't know.'

'So it's a slowdown,' Mitchell said.

'It's got to be.'

'Who's behind it? You know?'

'Guy was my second-shift leader, John Koliba,' Vic said. 'Maybe three or four other guys. You remember the breakdowns started on the second shift. Week ago Koliba comes up to me, says he wants to work days, he's in some bowling league. I say okay, but I don't need a leader on the first shift, I'll have to put you on a Warner-Swasey. He said that's okay. Right away we start getting breakdowns on the first shift. I say John, you been operating a fucking turning machine ten, twelve years, what's the matter with you? He says I don't know what's wrong, the goddamn thing freezes up on me. Acting dumb. But he knows I know. Maybe that fucking Polack is dumb a lot of ways, you're not going to get any arguments, but he isn't that dumb.'

'So fire him,' Mitchell said.

'I can't prove he's behind it,' Vic said. 'I *know* it, but I can't prove it. I fire him you got a grievance on your hands.'

With negotiations coming up, Mitchell was silent. You dumb shit. He could see the guy from Local 199 – the business agent, what was his name? Ed Jazik – following him down the hall, trying to push him or scare him, practically telling him he was going to have trouble – something to think about with contract bargaining time only two weeks away – practically writing the threat on the wall for him, SLOWDOWN!

But he had been too busy thinking about something else.

'Shit,' Mitchell said. After a moment, getting up, he said, 'Well, I guess it's time to kick ass.'

*

Within a 25,000-square-foot area Ranco Manufacturing milled, bored, shaped and ground machine tool and machine accessories for the automotive industry. They turned out powered actuator clamps, cylinder rod couplers and adapters, switch actuator assemblies, transfer bar guide rolls, rest pads and bushing plate stops, locating and positioning blocks, tool block clamps, screw adjusting units, grippers, neoprene cushion conveyor rolls, vacuum lifters and handling systems, air exhaust silencers and ball swivel assemblies. Mitchell had designed about a third of the products: improvements of industrial applications in use.

It was a Detroit backyard operation. A specialty house. High-volume production out of a cinder-block building that looked like a hangar. Banks of fluorescent lights and power lines, a pair of five-ton overhead cranes, high above bins and racks of metal materials, raw stock or half-finished and heat-treated parts that would be fed into the rows of Bridgeport milling machines, grinders and big Warner-Swasey bar-turning units – and come out in an assembly of parts and products that most people, even in Detroit, had never heard of before.

Someone at a party or in a foursome would get around to asking Mitchell, what do you do or who are you with, and he'd say Ranco Manufacturing, and they'd nod and say, oh yes. He was in machine tools and he knew the business and if they wanted details he'd provide them. Otherwise . . .

He didn't often talk shop. But now he was in the shop, in the glassed off testing room, Quality Control, looking out at the machinery and the racks of material, listening to the never-ending noise of the place that he was used to, and here the only thing he talked was shop.

Vic had a dozen or so rotary-motion clamp housings on the test table: small, dull-metal hollow cylinders threaded on the outside.

'Like these,' Vic said. 'Start to spot-check and every one of them's off tolerance, cut undersize. Scrap. Got to set up and run half the job over again. This is the way most of it shows up, which the son of a bitch was supposed to've been checking. Then we got seven instances of tool breakage I know we can trace to him. I see oxidation on his machine, honest to Christ, *rust*, on the turret spindle. I realize he's mixing too much water in the coolant. Christ yes, it's gonna freeze up, or tear the fixture apart.'

Mitchell turned from the window, hands in his pockets. 'Where's he working?'

Vic looked out past him, his gaze moving. 'He must be on his break.'

'I think we better do it in my office,' Mitchell said. 'We don't need an audience.'

'That wouldn't be so good. No.'

'Okay, tell him to come see me.'

•

Janet said, 'Mr. Mitchell will be back in a minute. Go right in.' John Koliba looked like he didn't know what was going on. He'd never been in Mr. Mitchell's office before. He came in wiping his hands on his gray work pants, looking around the office at the dark paneling and the hunting dog prints, the green-and-white-striped draperies, green carpeting, the TV set on a darkwood cabinet, big seven-foot desk and black-and-white Naugahyde chairs. She hadn't said to sit down so he stood there until Mr. Mitchell came in from the conference room next door. He was carrying some papers, studying them, and didn't look up until he dropped the papers on his desk.

'Have a seat.'

'Vic said you wanted to see me.'

'John, sit down, will you please?' Mitchell waited until Koliba was looking up at him with a serious, intent expression, sitting forward with his elbows on the chair arms, heavy shoulders hunched, his hands folded over the beer belly stretching his T-shirt into a tight mound.

'How's it going, John?'

Koliba shrugged. 'Pretty good. I got no complaints.'

'I have,' Mitchell said. 'I got a problem.'

'Yeah? What is it?'

'I'm going to ask you a simple, direct question, John. You ready?'

'Sure, go ahead.'

'Are you pulling a slowdown on me?'

'A *slow*down – there ain't any slowdown I know of. We had some *break*downs, we been having some problems, but you think it's on purpose, no sir. Or if it is I had nothing to do with it.'

Mitchell took his time. He said quietly, 'All right, John, now we both know where we're at. *You* know I'm aware what you been doing. And *I* know you're going to sit there and give me a bunch of shit.'

Koliba straightened, pushing his shoulders back. 'I'm telling you I never fooled with the machines. You don't believe what I'm saying, then you're calling me a liar. Is that right?'

'That's right, John,' Mitchell said. 'You're a fucking liar. You want a drink?'

'Listen now, nobody calls me a liar.'

'I just did, John. You want a drink or not?'

'You start accusing me, calling me a liar – let's see you prove I done anything.'

52

Mitchell walked over to the darkwood cabinet, took out two glasses and a fifth of Jack Daniels that he held up, showing it to Koliba.

'I don't like somebody calling me a liar. I don't care *who* it is.'

Mitchell poured whiskey into the two glasses, walked over and handed one to Koliba, who took it, but kept watching Mitchell. He watched him walk slowly around his desk. He watched him sit down and lean back in the chair and then take a drink.

After a moment Koliba raised his glass and swallowed about an ounce of the whiskey.

'John,' Mitchell said, 'I don't need a slowdown.' He picked up a ledger sheet and extended it toward Koliba. 'You want to look at this week's P and L statement? That's profit and loss. Here ... current sales analysis chart. Computer printout shows labor costs the past two weeks are up to eighteen percent of our gross sales volume. To make a profit we have to hold that figure at twelve. John, we go up six points we got a one percent loss. We're selling, but we're losing money. Here ... sales department report. Competitor comes up with a lower price and we lose an account we've had for three years. But we can't cut our price because we're as low as we can get. This one ... notification from the insurance company, workmen's compensation rates are going up again. The government's increasing F.I.C.A. rates. And I got to make all this look good on a balance sheet. John ... I'll tell you, I don't need a fucking slowdown.'

Mitchell paused, watching Koliba.

'You been here two and a half years, John. You were at Ford Rouge, how long?'

'Six years,' Koliba said. 'Then over Timken three years.'

Mitchell nodded. 'You know I was on the line at Dodge twelve years.'

'No, I didn't know that.'

'Twelve years. I've had some luck, John, but I've also worked my ass off. And the harder I work the luckier I get. I don't expect any gifts or favors. Nothing is free. But I also don't expect any shit from anybody. No, I take that back. I *do* expect it. What I mean is, when it comes it doesn't come as a surprise. I watch where I'm walking and I don't step in it if I can help it. Why should anybody take any shit if they can help it? John, you agree with that?'

'Certainly. I don't take any shit I can help it.'

'Right,' Mitchell said. 'Who needs it.'

'Guy tries to give me some shit,' Koliba said, 'I let him know about it.'

'Why put up with something you don't have to,' Mitchell said. 'Like this plant. I see it's losing money I shut it down, sell the equipment. Maybe take a bath. But, John, I'd rather lose it quick and forget it than piss it away while the goddamn business goes down the drain. You see what I mean? I own the joint, so I can do anything I want with it, can't I?'

'Sure,' Koliba said. 'I guess so.'

'I can lock the door tomorrow I want to, right?'

'Yeah. Hell, you own the place.'

'Hey, John,' Mitchell said. 'That's exactly what I'm going to do if one more machine breaks down. Close the place.'

'Listen, I said before, I don't know anything about any slow-down.'

'John, I believe you, because I see I can talk to you. You were a shift leader, and you got to have a feeling of responsibility to be a shift leader.'

'Sure, I always want to see the job's done right.'

'You see my position,' Mitchell said. 'I can't go out in the shop and make a speech to everybody. I got to rely on key people like yourself, people who see a future here and advancement . . . more money.'

Koliba waited, thinking about it. 'Well, I guess maybe we could watch it a little closer,' he said. 'You know, stay more on the ball so to speak.'

'That's the way I see it, John,' Mitchell said. 'I've learned it's always better to stay on the ball than it is to fall off and bust your ass.'

*

Mitchell swiveled his chair around to put his feet on the corner of the desk. The envelope marked PERSONAL AND CON-FIDENTIAL, the single sheet of typed instructions and the locker key, lay on the blotter close to his leg. He stared out the window at the pale gray afternoon sky, taking a rest now, a breather. He felt good. He felt his confidence coming back and, with it, the beginning of an urge to get up and do something. That was the essence of the good feeling: to be able to remain calm and relax while he was keyed up and confident. Never panic. Never run. Face whatever had to be faced. Be practical, reasonable, up to a point. And if reason doesn't work, get up and kick it in the teeth. Whatever the problem is. He smoked a cigarette, taking his time, looking at the dull afternoon sky that didn't bother him at all now.

When he finished the cigarette he took a sheet of letterhead and a 10 × 12 manila envelope from a desk drawer and buzzed his secretary on the intercom.

Janet waited while he wrote something, slowly, deliberately, on the sheet of paper, folded it once and slid it into the manila envelope that was fat and rounded, bulging with something inside.

'Give this to Dick or somebody,' Mitchell said. 'And this key. Tell him to run it out to Metro and put it in locker two-fifty-eight. Number's on the key. Hey, and tell him to be sure and put the key in with it.'

'If the key's inside,' Janet said, 'how's anyone going to open the locker?'

'I just do what I'm told,' Mitchell said.

She gave him a funny look. 'What?'

'It's not our problem, Janet, so we're not going to worry about it.'

His secretary took the envelope and went out, not saying any more.

*

Bobby Shy shot snooker on the mezzanine floor of Detroit Metropolitan Airport until the place closed. He went into the men's, paid a dime for a stall and sniffed a two-and-two, scooping the coke out of the Baggy with a silver Little Orphan Annie spoon. Man, almost immediately it was a better, brighter world. He bought the current issue of a magazine dedicated to 'Sophisticated Men About Town' and studied the breasts and beaver shots for about a half hour, read an article that tested his sex I.Q., but didn't bother to total his answers to see how he scored. At ten past one in the morning he went to locker number 258 across from the Delta counter that was empty now, used the duplicate key Alan had given him, opened the locker and took out the plain manila envelope.

There was no one near him; no one in sight as far down as the Eastern counter; no one who could possibly reach him before he made it down the central arcade to the men's room and went inside.

'Mail's here,' Bobby Shy said. He flipped the envelope with a backhand motion, watched it hit the tile and slide beneath the door of the third stall. He turned around and walked out.

Leo Frank, sitting on the toilet, picked up the envelope. It felt good and thick. The switchblade was already open in his hand, ready to cut the envelope and everything in it to shreds if anyone came banging in and tried to open his stall or ordered him to come out. Cut it quick and flush it down the toilet. They were good toilets with a high-speed force flush; you could keep flushing them without waiting for the tank to fill up.

Leo looked at his watch. Ten minutes later he stood up, shoved the envelope into his waist beneath his snappy double-knit, eight-button, checkered blazer and walked out.

The white Thunderbird was where it was supposed to be, on the Arrival ramp across from the American sign.

Alan moved over as Leo got in behind the wheel and tossed him the envelope.

'Shake hands with ten grand,' Leo said. 'Twenties and fifties fill up the space, don't they?'

Alan's fingers felt the envelope as the Thunderbird curved down the ramp and straightened out on William Rogell Drive.

Leo said, 'Open it, man. What're you waiting for?'

Alan didn't say anything. His fingers worked along the edges of the envelope and moved up to the clasp. His fingers said something was not right. They said somebody was trying to pull some shit and they didn't like the feel of it at all.

The Thunderbird turned right beyond the underpass and merged with the headlights going east toward Detroit.

Alan snapped open the glove box. In the framed square of light, hunched over, he pulled a folded copy of *The Wall Street Journal* out of the envelope. With the paper, resting on it, was the sheet of letterhead. Alan unfolded the sheet and read the three-word Magic Marker message in capital letters. BAG YOUR ASS.

He said, very quietly, shaking his head, 'Leo, honest to Christ, I don't know what this fucking world is coming to. You honestly, sincerely tell the guy how it is and the mother doesn't believe you.'

7

At ten after nine Mitchell called his wife. He was still at the plant and had not seen her or spoken to her in four days.

'I wanted to make sure you were home,' he said, 'or if you're going to be home this evening. I want to stop by and get some clothes.'

She said, 'Are you moving out?'

'Well, I thought under the circumstances. It might be easier. Give you some time to think.'

Barbara's voice said, 'What am I supposed to think about?'

'All right, give us both time to get our thoughts together. Are you going to be home?'

'I'll be here.'

'I was wondering—' He paused. 'You didn't get anything in the mail? Some pictures?'

'Pictures? Of what?'

'Never mind. I'll be leaving in a few minutes,' Mitchell said. 'I'll see you about ten.'

'I can hardly wait,' Barbara said, and hung up.

Shit. For the past few days he had felt pretty good, but now he was tired again and wondered if he should go home. Maybe wait a while. And then said to himself, You started it. Let her have her turn.

Going out through the plant, past the rows of machines, he saw John Koliba in the Quality Control room. Mitchell paused, went over and stuck his head in the door.

'Second shift agreeing with you?'

'Yes, I don't mind working nights,' Koliba said.

'It's where we need you, John. Keep the goddamn place from falling apart. Any problems?'

'Not a thing.' Koliba held up a small metal part that fit in the palm of his hand. 'We been running switch actuator housings since three-thirty. Every one's up to spec.'

Mitchell didn't smile, but he felt better again. He said, 'That's the eye, John,' and continued on through the plant and out the rear door.

There were two spots above the door on the wall of the plant and light poles at the far end of the yard where a cyclone fence enclosed the plant property: bleak lights that laid a soft reflection over the rows of cars in the parking area. Mitchell unlocked the Grand Prix and opened the door. He was sliding in behind the wheel before he realized the interior light did not go on – though the goddamn buzzing noise sounded as he turned the key and kept buzzing until he slammed the door closed.

Beginning to back out he turned to look past his shoulder. The face with the stocking over it was staring at him from less than three feet away. When the .38 Special appeared the stocking face leaned in somewhat closer and the barrel of the revolver touched his right shoulder.

Bobby Shy said, 'Keep your head on, man. Everything will be cool. Go west to Seventy-five. We going downtown.'

On Metropolitan Parkway Mitchell reached up to adjust the rearview mirror. Bobby Shy said, 'That's fine. Look all you want, you know I'm still here with my eyes stuck to the back of your head. Hey man, and no smoking. Don't reach inside your clothes for nothing, not even to scratch yourself. You listening to me?' But Mitchell didn't answer or speak until they had turned onto Interstate 75 and were moving south in the light freeway traffic.

'My wife didn't get any pictures yet.'

'We didn't send any,' Bobby Shy said. 'It was an idea, you know? I told them shit, guys fool around all the time. Names you read about. Man could be President of the United States, fucking somebody, nobody gives a shit. So the man's getting something on the side, everybody say he probably need it, don't get enough at home. No, it was an idea is all. So we scratch it and make you another offer.'

'Why don't you do yourselves a favor,' Mitchell said. 'Get into some other business. I don't think you guys could sell water to somebody on fire.'

Bobby Shy laughed. 'Try us one more time. I think you going to dig this trip.'

'Tell me what you've got,' Mitchell said.

'You got to see it.'

'Another movie?'

'Only better. More excitement in it.'

'I should've brought some friends,' Mitchell said. 'Or some guys from the plant. We don't like the movie we make you eat it.'

Bobby Shy laughed again. 'Hey, I know you not going to like it. That's why you don't want to have anybody with you. I mean you wouldn't want to have anybody in the whole fucking world to see this flick but you, man, and that is absolutely word of honor, no bullshit.'

They turned east onto Jefferson and after a few minutes, passing the Uniroyal plant and the Belle Isle Bridge and the Naval Armory, Bobby Shy hunched forward to study the street, a continuous row of dark storefronts.

'All right, pull in, anywhere this block.'

'It's no parking along here,' Mitchell said.

'Man, stop the fucking car, will you, please. Go in that gas station, it's closed.'

Get a ticket now, Mitchell thought. That would be something. What're you doing around here? Well, you see this guy with the gun's taking me to see a movie. Oh, you're going to see a movie. Yeah. Well, where is this movie?

'Cross the street,' Bobby Shy said.

They crossed Jefferson toward a theater marquee, Mitchell thinking of the policeman and then of his lawyer, Jim O'Boyle. I saw another movie, Jim. This time in a theater. A closed theater. In a closed theater, uh? It sure looked closed, with its bare marquee and dark foyer that was like the boarded entrance to a mine tunnel. A car passed on Jefferson, a faint sound behind him that faded to silence.

'Go on in,' Bobby Shy said.

Mitchell tried one of the doors – the handles showing between the protective sheets of plywood – then the other door and stepped inside, into a deeper darkness.

'This way,' a voice said. Not a voice he had heard before, or a face to go with the voice, only a small flashlight beam at knee height, pointing to the floor. 'You come through here.' The light began to recede.

Mitchell followed it into the theater, past an empty candy counter to the right-side aisle. The voice told him to hold it there, facing in toward the seats.

Then the black man with the stocking must have taken the flashlight, because as the beam made a spot down the aisle in front of him, it was the black man's voice, close behind him, that said, 'Where you like to sit, man? Take a seat.'

Mitchell wondered if one place was better to sit than another. If it made any difference. If he was going to sit here or if he was going to do something. He walked about a third of the way down the aisle and into a row, taking the second seat. Behind him, maybe two rows, he heard a seat go down, hitting hard.

'I'm right here, baby, case you 'fraid of the dark.'

A voice from above them, a familiar voice, coming from the projection room, said, 'Can you hear me all right?'

'He hear you,' the black man said.

Mitchell looked around. The black man was seated, head and shoulders without features. High on the back wall two squares of light showed the projection room.

'Turn the fuck around,' the black man said. 'You making me nervous.'

For several minutes there was dead silence in the theater. Mitchell sat in darkness that had no form and reached to nothing, wondering what he was doing here, wondering if he could get up and walk out. He said to himself, They won't shoot you. They get nothing by killing you. But he was here now and he knew they would keep him here if he tried to leave. Probably. Unless he hit the guy first. The black guy. If he could get to him and belt him.

But Mitchell didn't move. In the moment he might have, if he was ever going to try it, a bright square of light appeared on the screen and he could see the rows of empty seats now in front of him and the pale, high walls of the theater.

'Titles would go here,' the familiar lazy-sounding voice said. 'And credits. Slick pictures presents ... *Tit in the Wringer.* Or, how Harry Mitchell agreed to pay one hundred and five thousand dollars a year and found happiness. Note, I said a hundred and five a *year.* Not just the first year, not just the second. No, every year of your life. But wait ... here's the star of our picture, little Cynthia Fisher, not having any idea what the fuck is going on.'

The girl's face, in color, nearly filled the screen, her expression puzzled, changing, frowning, nearly obscuring the look of fear in her eyes.

Her lips moved and the narrator said, his voice slightly higher and almost in sync with the screen, ' "What is this? Come on, what're you guys doing? I told you, I don't want to *be* in a movie." '

The camera began to pull back, out of the close shot of the girl's face. 'Some people,' the narrator said, in his natural, lazy tone again, 'you got to tie down to convince them they can act. I told Cini she's a natural. But, as you can see, she's very modest.'

Mitchell was looking at her full figure now. She was sitting in a straight chair against a vertical pipe; a cement wall in the close background; a basement room brightly lighted. He could see that her hands were tied behind her. A rope circled her waist tightly and seemed to go around both the chair and the pipe. She was wearing a print blouse that he recognized and faded blue jeans.

'Next,' the narrator said, 'to keep your interest or whatever up, a little skin.'

The girl's eyes raised expectantly as the camera began to move in again. She was looking off to the side of the camera and her lips said, in silence, 'What're you going to do?'

The camera held on her face. The picture on the screen moved unsteadily and the camera dropped to her blouse. Two hands came in from the side – hands and forearms in a dark shirt – clutched the front of the girl's blouse and ripped it open to her waist, then pulled it back tightly over her shoulders. One hand lingered, lifted a bare breast and let it fall.

'Not a lot there,' the narrator said, 'but then this is a low-budget flick, done on pure spec. Next scene . . .'

Mitchell was looking at a square of what seemed to be half-inch plywood, the size of a newspaper folded once. Hands, the same hands as before, lifted the square from where it was leaning against the cement wall and turned it around.

'No marks on either side, right? Right.'

The hands raised the sheet of wood. Again there was a close shot of the girl's breasts before the tan grained surface of the wood appeared, filling the screen. The camera pulled back, unsteadily, and Mitchell was looking at the girl again from perhaps ten feet: the sheet of plywood resting upright on her lap, covering her from waist to shoulders, the upper end propped beneath her chin.

'Now what have we here?' the lazy tone said.

For a moment Mitchell wasn't sure what he was seeing.

'A reverse angle,' the narrator said. 'We're now looking past Cini from behind, over her shoulder, to see what she sees. And what is it?'

The camera began to zoom slowly toward a table fifteen feet away.

'Right. A gun.'

The revolver was mounted in a vise that was clamped to the edge of the table.

'You recognize it?'

Mitchell recognized it.

'Let's see it from the side. There. A thirty-eight S and W. You ought to recognize it, sport. It's yours. The box of thirty-eights on the table? Yours. The piece of paper? That's your permit.'

As Mitchell watched, an arm extended a sport coat into the frame and dropped it on the table.

'And the coat. I believe you wore that to our first home movie session. Ratty-looking goods, if you don't mind my saying. What I like about it is your name inside. Now then—

'Hello, what is that tied to the trigger?'

The camera moved in to feature the revolver.

'Why it looks like a wire. Funny, it extends back someplace, so that if you pull on the wire it fires the piece. That's pretty clever, isn't it? You can shoot the gun without messing up any prints that're on it. We'll let you think about that a moment. Meanwhile, here's our little star again.'

The girl's face, above the plywood sheet, showed an expression of fright and bewilderment.

'Looks like she's sticking her head out of a box, doesn't it? Honey, relax. You're gonna do the scene. Don't worry about it.'

Mitchell could see it coming. He pays or they kill her. And this is the way they would do it.

So what do you tell them?

He was watching her face. The face he knew and could picture clearly when he wasn't with her; but now he almost didn't recognize her. The awful expression. He could see tears glistening on her cheeks. He didn't understand the plywood, what it was for. He sat in the darkness looking at the screen and didn't know what he was going to do.

'This setup took some doing,' the narrator said. 'To get the full effect. Back and a little off to the side. So you can see the gun as well as our star. Okay, suspense time is over.'

The view was level with the revolver and the wire that extended out of the foreground. Mitchell didn't move. Past the barrel of the revolver Cini seemed to be looking directly at him.

'Ready,' the narrator said, 'aim . . . fire.'

The wire jerked taut again and again and continued as the lazy voice said, 'Bang, bang . . . bang, bang, bang,' as the five splintered gouges appeared in the plywood sheet and as the girl's eyes and mouth stretched open and her head hit against the pipe and fell forward with the last lazy-sounding *bang*.

In a silence, hearing only the faint sound of the projector, Mitchell sat staring at the screen. He said to himself Unh-unh, come on. He said, People get killed in movies all the time, but they don't get *killed*. He had experienced the same reaction before in a movie, making something jump inside, believability stabbing him in the belly, and it had never ever been real any of those times. It couldn't be real because people didn't really honest-to-God shoot people in moving pictures.

The narrator said, 'Hey, you still there?' He paused. 'The thing about Cini that makes her a star, she not only lives her part she dies it. And if you don't believe me, watch.'

The camera followed the plywood sheet as it was pulled aside and turned over.

'Note, the bullet holes go all the way through.'

The camera returned to Cini. Mitchell looked and closed his eyes.

'Take my word, man, that's real blood, not catsup. Now watch this.'

The hand pulled the girl's head up by her hair and laid it against the pipe. Her eyes, wide open, stared out from the screen and continued to stare into the hot light as the hand appeared again and seemed to press against her mouth. After a few moments the hand twisted to show a mirror held in the palm.

'Note, the mirror's clear. No breath to fog it up. Actually we didn't need the mirror,' the narrator said. 'Look at the eyes. Keep watching. They never blink, do they? That's because they don't see anything.' There was the sound of the narrator clearing his throat.

'Now, what we want you to see, sport, is that you got your tit tightly in the wringer and there ain't any way at all to pull it out. No, because we have this package hidden away: the broad's body, your coat with the broad's blood on it, the thirty-eight with your prints on it, the permit, a few snaps of you and the broad on the beach, all in this package where nobody can find it. Not unless we tell them. Like we call the cops and we say, hey, you want to know where there's a dead broad and all? We tell them, hang up. Pretty soon there's about eighteen fucking police cars outside your house and the neighbors are looking out. What the fuck's going on? They read about it in the paper, Christ, imagine, he seemed like such a nice guy. Yeah? Some fucking nice guy. Takes the broad's clothes off and shoots her five times in the left tit. Probably raped her after. Fucking pervert. Should be electrocuted. What does he get? Life in S.M.P. Jackson. He's over there making our fucking license plates we got to put on our car for Christ sake.' The narrator paused.

'Or, as I said. You pay us the hundred and five a year the rest of your life or until we say stop, we got enough. Listen to me, sport. No more fucking around. Ten grand tomorrow, ten grand a week from tomorrow, ten grand a week later. Thirty thou in good faith, giving you time to get it together. Then you plan ahead and come up with the balance in cash monthly payments. You got it? Tomorrow night you go out to Metro yourself, personally, with ten big ones. At exactly eleven-thirty you put it in locker two-fifty-eight and put the key in with it. If you hang around, or if you don't show, or if you pull any kind of shit at all, the cops get a phone call.

'Now sit there a while and relax, watch another movie. When it's over, come up and get the reel and the projector if you want. They're rented from Film Outlet, over on Larned. In your name.'

Sitting alone in the darkness, Mitchell watched a cartoon cat chase three cartoon mice all over the house. He watched the cat get clobbered, flattened, blown up, set on fire and electrocuted and the dumb goddamn cat hardly ever got close to them. When it was over Mitchell walked across the street to his car. He wasn't sure for a while where he was going.

8

He made himself wait until the next morning before going home. He made himself spend the night at the apartment he had leased for Cini, and for most of the night he sat near the floor-to-ceiling living-room window, in darkness, looking out at the dim shape of trees across the lawn. Sit down and think it out. That was the idea. Think about what to do and think about a girl he had – what? – gone with, fooled around with, had an affair with, laughed with, made love to, loved, maybe loved, for three months and who now was dead. He knew she was dead, but he couldn't accept it in his mind. Because when he thought of her he thought of her alive. But he told himself she was dead. She was dead because of him. He didn't drink that night in the apartment. He didn't want to feel sorry for himself or make excuses. He wanted to think it out as it was. But all he could think of was that she was dead and there was nothing he could do to change it.

When it was light he thought of calling Jim O'Boyle – because he had to begin doing something *now* and because he had called him before, from this room, six days ago. But he didn't reach for the phone this time; he hesitated and thought about it. He would hear O'Boyle saying they would have to go to the police. Maybe not right away but eventually. A girl was dead. Murdered. It wasn't simple blackmail anymore. But if he went to the police the newspapers would find out about it. Story and picture on page one – could he face that? He told himself, Yes, the girl was dead because of him. He wasn't going to run and hide; he'd have to face it.

But wait a minute. She wasn't dead because of Barbara. She wasn't dead because of his daughter or his son. He had to think about them also. How it would affect them. He had a business to run and responsibilities and, Christ, pretty soon a union contract to negotiate. He had more to consider than himself, his own feelings. Conscience said go to the police. Reason said wait, what are the consequences? What are your alternatives? The roof was coming down on him and he could yell for help or try to put it back himself.

How?

He didn't know how. Sitting in the girl's apartment, in the early-morning light, he didn't have the slightest idea what he was going to do. Though he was sure now he wasn't going to call O'Boyle or go to the police. At least not right away.

Take it a step at a time. Walk, don't run. Never panic in an emergency. Find out who they are first. If he could do that, if it was possible—

He was beginning to get the good feeling of confidence again, the feeling of being keyed up but able to remain calm. There it is, he said to himself. Simple. Find out who they are. And then kick ass.

*

Barbara was in a housecoat. She opened the front door and stood looking at him for several moments before stepping aside.

'It's your house too,' she said. 'You don't have to ring the bell.'

'I didn't want to walk in the back. You don't know who it is, you might be frightened.'

'I think I know your sound,' Barbara said.

'You're doing something, go ahead. I just want to pick up a few things.'

He walked past her to the main stairway and started up. Barbara watched him. She hesitated, making up her mind, then followed him upstairs. He was at the dresser when she entered the bedroom, going through the top drawer, pushing aside his socks and handkerchiefs.

'I thought you were coming last night,' she said. 'I waited until Johnny Carson was over.'

'I went to a movie,' Mitchell said.

'You went to a movie. That was nice. With your girl friend?'

Mitchell turned from the dresser. He looked at her and seemed about to speak, but said nothing and walked over to his closet.

Barbara watched him. 'You know what I almost did? I almost threw all your clothes out the goddamn window. I get urges too, buddy, but I restrain myself. Usually.'

'I'm sorry,' Mitchell said, turning from the closet.

'For what? I don't know, Mitch. You can talk quietly and sound very sincere — but that doesn't change the fact you're a bastard. I'm the one who's hurt, for God's sake, not you.'

'Barbara, who's been in the house in the last few days? I mean besides you.'

'Who's been in the house?' The abrupt change in the conversation stopped her. 'What do you mean, who's been in the house?'

'Has anyone come in that you don't know?' Mitchell asked quietly. 'Or that you do know. A plumber or a painter, somebody like that.'

'The only thing needs fixing,' Barbara said, 'is the disposal. You said you were going to take care of it.'

'All right, then have you noticed anything out of place? Like someone might have walked in or broken in while you were out.'

She shook her head slowly. 'The milkman comes in . . .'

'Or door-to-door salesmen.'

'No—'

She shook her head again. 'No, there *was* somebody. A man from an accounting service. In fact he was *in* here when I got home from tennis.'

'When?'

'A few days ago. Sitting in the living room. Can you believe it? Sitting there waiting for me.'

'What company's he with?'

'No company. I looked it up, Silver Something Accounting Service, he said, but there's no such company.'

'What did he look like?'

Barbara thought about it. 'Kind of hippie looking, and the way he talked, very cheeky. He was wearing a dark suit and carried an attaché case.'

'He had a car?'

'A car picked him up. A white one. I didn't notice the make or year.'

'Did he talk . . . slowly?'

Barbara nodded thoughtfully. 'Like it was an effort.'

'You're sure you've never seen him before?'

'Fairly sure. Mitch, what is it? Did he take anything?'

'A few things,' Mitchell said, answering her but seeing the movie screen, his gun in the vise aimed at the girl and the old sport coat on the table. He saw the soundless gun fired and saw the gouges appear in the plywood as the girl's head snapped back and heard the lazy sound of the skinny guy, who had been in this house, this room, saying bang, bang . . . bang, bang, bang. Five times. Five shots. Making sure, when one would have been enough to murder her.

Barbara, with a tense, concerned look now, was asking him, 'What? Mitch, what did he take?'

His wife looked good. She looked clean. He liked the navy-blue housecoat and her hair and, this morning, the trace of dark circles beneath her eyes. He knew that if he held her he would feel the familiar feel of her body and she would smell good. She had seen the man and maybe she could identify him. She could be a part of this. Right now, not knowing anything about it, she could become involved – another woman involved because of him – and he didn't want her to be, if he could help it.

He said, 'The guy took my gun—'

'You're sure?'

'It's not here. He took the gun, my old sport coat and maybe a few other things.' She would look after he was gone and find this out herself.

'But why?'

'Some people who steal need guns. The sport coat I don't know, maybe he just liked it.'

She was staring at him, listening to his sound, analyzing it. She said quietly, 'Mitch, that's not the reason he took it.'

'I don't know why. I'm only saying it's gone.'

'I think you do know,' Barbara said.

Mitchell hesitated, but in the same moment said to himself, *No.* 'I've got to get to the plant,' he said, and started out of the room.

Barbara's voice followed him to the hall. 'Mitch, tell me what's going on. *Please.*'

But he reached the stairway and went down without answering.

*

O'Boyle said, 'Mitch, this is Joe Paonessa. From the prosecutor's office.' He saw the flicker of surprise on Mitchell's face, gave them enough time to exchange nods and a glad-to-meet-you, and then offered a brief explanation. 'Joe was able to come at the last minute, Mitch. He's been kind enough to give us some of his time, talk to you personally and give his views on your situation.'

The man from the prosecutor's office was younger than Mitchell. He was bald and wore a little mustache. He had dark sleepy-looking eyes and a mild expression. But, Mitchell noticed, the expression didn't change. The man didn't smile. He raised himself barely a few inches from his seat as they shook hands. O'Boyle was drinking a scotch and soda. The man from the prosecutor's office had a cup of coffee at his place. He was already eating his salad, spearing at it, fork in one hand and a slice of French bread, thickly coated with chunks of cold butter, in the other. Mitchell ordered a Bud.

'I've never been here before,' Paonessa said. 'I don't get out to the high-rent district very often.'

'I've never been here either,' Mitchell said.

'It's pretty popular for lunch,' O'Boyle said. 'In fact I think it's busier now than at night.'

That was the end of the small talk.

'Most situations like yours,' Paonessa said, 'never get to us. We don't find out about them because the individual is too ashamed to tell anybody. Usually it's a Murphy game. The individual gets caught with some whore and he pays to keep from getting his balls cut off. Naturally he's not going to go to the police and tell them he was with some whore and take a chance his wife finding out.'

'I wasn't with some whore,' Mitchell said.

'In your case,' Paonessa said, 'it's the amount of money involved. It's not a simple Murphy situation. You're loaded and they know it. Pay them or they fuck you. Maybe they can do it,

I don't know. At least they can tell your wife you've been seeing this whore and that might be enough to screw up your life to some extent, I don't know that either, or how much you can afford to pay to keep people off your back. Jim says you're a respected businessman, never fooled around before. All right, I'll take his word for that. Though I know a lot of respectable businessmen who do fool around.' Finishing the salad, he began to mop the bowl with his bread.

'Naturally you don't want to pay them. Okay, but they're not going to let you off, are they? Assume that. They got some dirt on you. You're caught sticking your thing where it doesn't belong. You want to keep your secret a secret. So let's say they feel pretty sure you're going to come across. In fact, they have to feel that way. They have to believe they've made a deal you'll go through with, or else we never get close enough to them, the police don't, to find out who they are. They tell you meet us such and such a place with the money. Or they say leave the money such and such a place. The police either have to tail you or put a bug on you, get voices or whatever information they can from the bug, or stake out the place and pick the guys up when they come for the money. In other words the only way to apprehend them is if you pay or look like you're paying, offer the bait to bring them out in the open. We going to order or what?' He opened the big red menu that was bound by a red tassel around the fold.

'Or I don't pay them,' Mitchell said.

'That's up to you,' Paonessa said. His eyes roamed over the inside of the menu.

O'Boyle looked at Mitchell before turning to the man from the prosecutor's office. 'Joe, Mitch is asking, if he doesn't pay them, and he's considered it, there isn't much they can do to him, is there? He's already told his wife about the girl.'

Paonessa's eyes raised, his mild expression unchanged. 'Yeah? You told her? What did she say?'

'I don't think that's got anything to do with the people blackmailing me,' Mitchell said. 'I've told my wife – all right, but I'd still like to see them caught.'

Paonessa's eyes were on the menu again. 'Then you have to pay them, or attempt to.'

'That's the only way, uh?'

'Unless you can identify them,' Paonessa said. 'File a complaint, we see what we can do. I don't know, Jim, I think I'm going to have the New York strip sirloin. How's it here, any good?'

Before O'Boyle could answer, Mitchell said, 'If they were to contact me again. I mean, let's say they get something else.'

Paonessa's eyes held on the menu. O'Boyle said, 'What do you mean, Mitch?'

'Like what if they threatened the girl's life unless I paid?'

'That's called extortion,' Paonessa said. 'Now you're into something else.'

O'Boyle continued to stare at Mitchell. 'Have you heard from them again?'

'I'm talking about if I did. Then what?'

Paonessa shrugged. 'It's the same situation. Extortion, or kidnapping – they set up a meeting or a drop and the police handle it from there.'

Mitchell waited, took a sip of beer. 'What if the girl's already dead?'

'What if?' Paonessa said. 'They still make arrangements with you to get the money. They're not killing the girl for nothing, are they?'

'But what if they could work it so I pay? Somehow they do it. But nobody ever sees them and they get away with it.'

Paonessa looked up again with his dead expression. 'I'll tell you something. I've got cases, real ones, to prosecute for the next two years, on my desk, on my files, all over the goddamn office. I don't need any what-if ones at the moment. For all I know somebody's pulling a joke on you. And that's a good possibility, with all the fucking nuts there are around these days. So unless you tell me all this is real and you can prove it, and you're willing to cooperate with the police – what are we talking about?'

'But if it is real—' Mitchell began.

'If what's real? Blackmail or extortion? What are we talking about?'

'Either,' Mitchell said. 'Or both.'

It was a free meal, if it ever came, but Joe Paonessa was not getting paid anything more to sit here. He said, 'Look, you have to provide evidence. You have to show us, the police, a crime was committed. Otherwise it's just a story, and I know some better ones if you want to hear some real true-life crime stories, okay?'

Mitchell said, 'Joe—' He almost said, 'Fuck you,' but he didn't. He said, 'Joe, I'm looking at possibilities, that's all. I want to know, if things come up, what my alternatives are, if I've got any. What I don't need is any bored-sounding bullshit. I appreciate your coming and thank you very much.' Mitchell pushed his chair back and stood up.

'Jim, thank you. You get this one and I'll get the next.'

They watched him walk through the restaurant toward the front of the place. Paonessa said, 'Christ, what's the matter with him?'

O'Boyle didn't answer. After a few moments he said, 'Yes, the New York strip sirloin, it's pretty good here.'

*

Barbara was perspiring when she came off the court and it felt good; the soreness in her legs and right arm felt good. She had played singles for an hour with one of the assistant pros – who had not taken his sweater off – and lost two sets, 6–2 and 6–3. She had not gone out expecting to win; but she wished the long-haired good-looking son of a bitch would have taken his sweater off, at least after the first set. Today she would have beaten any girl she knew. She probably would have beaten Mitch. He was an unorthodox player who slapped at the ball instead of stroking it, but God, he hit it hard and he was all over the court. They had a doubles match coming up this weekend – arranged two weeks before – with Ross and a young girl with tight slender thighs they had played before and beaten. She wondered who would cancel the match, if Mitch would remember or if she would have to do it . . . or if Mitch would ask his girl friend to be his partner. No, the girl wouldn't play tennis. Barbara knew nothing about the girl, except that she was certain the girl did not own a tennis racket and had never played in her life. She said to herself, sitting down in a canvas chair and lighting a cigarette, You're a snob, aren't you? She sat looking down the length of the indoor courts that were five feet below the level of the lobby and saw Ross coming off number 4 with the head pro.

She stubbed out the cigarette, with time enough to reach the women's locker room before he saw her. But she waited, wondering if he knew. Coming up the steps to the lobby, seeing her then, his expression answered her question.

'Barb—' The sad, sympathetic look, coming over to her with his hand extended. He was the only person she knew who called her Barb.

Ross got two cans of Tab from the machine, steered her over to a couch — where they'd be more comfortable and out of the traffic — and they went through the preliminaries. I'm so sorry. Thank you. God, when Mitch told me I couldn't believe it. I'm really extremely sorry. Well, I guess it happens. Do you think he's serious? I mean how serious is it? I was going to ask you the same question.

'I've got an idea,' Ross said. 'Why don't we have dinner tonight?'

'Thank you, but I don't think so.'

'Now wait. Have you talked to anyone about it?'

'No, not yet.'

'I mean do you have someone you can talk to?'

She said, 'A shoulder to cry on?'

Ross gave her a sad smile. 'Maybe you do cry sometimes, Barb, but I'll bet not very often. You keep it inside, and that's not good.'

'I cry,' she said. 'I can probably cry as well as anyone you know.'

'Barb — I'm sorry. Really. I'd like very much to help you any way I can. I'm not a professional counselor, I'm a friend, and I know both of you very well. I've talked to Mitch and now, if you'll let me, I'd like to talk to you, or I'll keep my mouth shut and listen if you'd rather. Or we can talk about anything you want, take your mind off of it. Barb—' He paused. 'I think a quiet dinner would do you good. In fact, it might do us both good.'

She did not need Ross: his pseudosympathy or help or whatever he had in mind. God, she knew Ross well enough. But he had obviously talked to Mitch and maybe he did know a little more than she what was on her husband's mind. It was a possibility. He might even know the girl.

Barbara waited, making up her mind, before nodding slowly,

looking at him. 'All right, Ross,' she said. 'Let's do it. See what happens.'

9

Leo Frank was tired of sitting and tired of reading the article about the 130-year-old jig who lived down in Florida somewhere. It sounded like a bunch of shit, what the guy was supposed to have remembered, and was written with a lot of dialect that was hard to pronounce and didn't make much sense. So he got up from his desk and went outside for some air. He stood on the sidewalk with his hands in his pockets, his back to the painted glass that said NUDE MODELS. It was cool, about forty degrees out, damp and over-cast with a shitty-looking sky – spring in Detroit – cars streaming up and down Woodward Avenue making hissing sounds on the wet pavement. He had one customer inside. Three in the last two hours. There was nothing to do. The guy was supposed to drop the money tonight and they'd go out to Metro. But until then there wasn't a goddamn thing to do.

When he looked over and saw Mitchell across the street – the *guy*, actually the *guy* standing there – he felt something jump inside his stomach and he knew he had to move, right now. He thought of running. But he made himself turn and go back inside. The three girls looked up at the sound of the door and glanced at Leo as he walked past them.

'I'm going out for a while,' he said. 'One of you can handle it, okay? Box's in the right-hand desk drawer.'

The three girls went back to their cigarette smoking, magazine reading and nail filing as he walked down the hall.

Leo Frank opened the back door that led to the alley where he parked his car. Looking over his shoulder, down the hall, he let the door close again and ducked quickly into the last cubicle, the one that served as his private office and interview room and was practically wallpapered with photographs of nude girls.

When he got Alan on the phone – after seven rings, the slow-moving son of a bitch – he said, 'He's coming here again. Honest to Christ, crossing the street.'

Alan asked him where he was and Leo told him, in his office.

That was good. Alan Raimy, in his own confined office at the Imperial Art Theater, could picture Leo surrounded by the nude shots, sweating. He could almost hear him sweating, mixing the odor of his body with the smell of the cheap cologne he practically poured all over himself.

Alan said, 'Leo, stay where you are, all right? Jesus, wait a minute. What'd you tell the girls? ... That's fine, Leo. See, you're thinking. There's nothing to get excited about. ... No, stay right where you are. Leo, listen to me. Sit there, have a joint, play with yourself or something, but don't move. I'll be over, I'll come in the back door. Just keep in mind he doesn't know who you are. Keep telling yourself that, Leo. He doesn't ... know ... who ... you ... are.' Alan hung up. He said to himself, Jesus Christ.

*

Mitchell remembered their names, the same three girls sitting in the same left-to-right order on the porch chairs: Peggy, Terry and Mary Lou. They looked up, stared at him and Peggy said, 'You ever find her? What was her name? Cini?'

He shook his head. 'I'm looking for the manager. The guy that was at the desk before.'

'Leo stepped out. Said he'd be out for a while.'

'How long ago was that?'

'Just a few minutes.'

'His name's Leo?'

'Leo Frank,' the girl said.

'Well ...' Mitchell looked around the room, his gaze finally going to the desk and the empty chair next to it. 'I might as well sit down then, huh?'

Nobody seemed to care. Peggy said, 'Help yourself.'

After a few moments he reached over and picked up the magazine that was open on the desk and began reading about a 130-year-old colored man who lived in Florida and sat all day on a bus-stop bench in front of his one-room house. He was reading about how the man had lived in the West and claimed to have known Jesse James and Billy the Kid, when Doreen came into the room from the hallway. She was followed by a young guy who passed her quickly without saying anything, glanced at Mitchell and went out the door. Mitchell watched Doreen drop into a chair, shaking her head.

'Those shoe clerks get spookier every day,' Doreen said. 'You know what he wanted me to do?'

Peggy said, 'Go pee-pee on him.'

'On his *face*,' Doreen said.

'I know, I've had him,' Peggy said. 'How'd he like it?'

'I told him he want a kick, go stick his head in the toilet and flush it.'

'He probably does that at home,' Peggy said. 'Weird ones don't bother me anymore. After a while, what's weird?'

Mitchell looked down at the face of the 130-year-old man. He was sure. Still he waited a moment before looking up at the black girl again.

He said, 'Doreen?'

Her expression brightened as she met his gaze. 'Yeah, love. You want to take my picture?'

*

In the room she said, 'You know my name, you must've been here before.'

'Couple of times,' Mitchell said. 'And I saw you over at the go-go place. You don't work there anymore?'

'Kit Kat? Yeah, I work here and there, and around.' She untied her blouse, knotted beneath her breasts, and let it fall open. 'I've seen you too, but I'm having trouble placing the face exactly.'

'Times I came here, I stopped over at the bar first.'

'Get up your nerve?'

'No, I don't see anything wrong coming here. As long as it's legal.'

'I admire your liberal attitude,' Doreen said. Her hands were in the waist of her tight white slacks. 'Now, are you just a tit man or do you want the whole show?'

Mitchell raised the Polaroid he'd taken from the front desk, aimed it at her and snapped a picture. 'We can start and see what happens. Work up to it.'

Doreen grinned. 'Work *you* up. Whatever you want to do, love, long as it ain't against my religion.'

'It was at the bar,' Mitchell said then. 'I remember, I met you there a few months ago.'

'You met me?'

'I was introduced to you. There was a girl used to work here, I think her name was Cini. She introduced us.'

Doreen hesitated, though her expression remained calm and told him nothing. She said, 'Yeah, Cini used to work here some time ago. Very nice person. You used to see her?'

'A few times, that's all.'

'I think maybe she quit to go back to school.'

'Probably,' Mitchell said. He pulled the print out of the camera and peeled off the negative. 'I understand a lot of the girls doing this are working their way through college.'

'That's as good a story as any,' Doreen said. 'How'd it turn out?'

Mitchell studied the print. 'Not bad. A little dark.'

'That's me, baby.'

'I mean the light. It's a little underexposed.'

'Then I say, "Wait till I take my pants off, you want some more exposure."'

Mitchell gave her a big friendly grin. 'That's pretty good.'

'Or the dude says, "Hey, honey, what size is your aperture?"'

'There must be something you do with focus,' Mitchell said.

Doreen nodded. 'Dude's taking a picture of two of us? Paid double for the treat. I say, "Hey, are you trying to foc-*us* or what?"'

'Lots of laughs in your work, uh?' Mitchell snapped another picture of her and grinned. 'Gotcha.'

'You really do take pictures, don't you?'

'Doesn't everybody?' He sounded honest, sincere.

Doreen's calm brown eyes lingered on Mitchell. 'You ever go up to Cini's place?'

'You asked me if I used to see her. That's where it was.'

'Where exactly?'

'Apartment over on Merrill. You've got one in the same building,' Mitchell said. 'Once in a while Cini used to drive you home.'

Doreen raised her nice soft eyes. 'You did know her, didn't you?'

'Pretty well, I guess.'

77

'How much she used to charge you?'

Mitchell was pulling the print out of the camera. He looked up abruptly to meet Doreen's calm gaze watching him. He said, 'She didn't charge me anything.' And looked down again to peel open the photograph and study it.

'Not even the first time?'

'Not any time,' Mitchell said.

'Well, I guess that's her business,' Doreen said. 'Or I guess I should say that was *not* her business.' Doreen grinned then. 'Unless you're bragging, telling me a story.'

'What difference does it make,' Mitchell said, 'if you believe it or not?'

'Well, love, I was entertaining the thought, maybe we ought to leave this store to the shoe clerks and head for my place. The only thing is, the management over there don't hand out any freebies, not to anybody.' She waited and said, 'Well?'

He could see Cini in this room. He could see her in the apartment and he could see her on the beach in the Bahamas, the natural, nice-looking girl who smiled easily and made him feel good.

He said to Doreen, 'How much?'

'A hundred dollars. With that you get tea, a smoke and a chance to try for seconds.'

Mitchell nodded. 'All right, let's do it.'

Doreen worked her eyes again. 'Hey, I like you. Whether it's my charm or you're just in heat I still like you. But there's one thing, love, you're going to have to pay for this little session first, twenty with the camera or else the boss'll cut off my business.' When Mitchell opened his wallet and handed her a fifty-dollar bill, Doreen smiled and said, 'You come ready, don't you?'

*

He was ready to go with her to her apartment or anywhere, to try to find out everything he could about a girl named Cynthia Fisher and how she lived and the people she knew. But there was a delay.

Doreen opened the cash box in the desk drawer. There wasn't enough change inside for Mitchell's fifty.

Doreen said, 'Goddamnit, where's Leo, in the office?'

Peggy looked up from her magazine. 'I think he went out.'

Doreen turned to Mitchell. 'I'll go look. You can come along if you want, love, or wait here.'

Mitchell followed her down the hall past the studios. He was still holding the Polaroid, but did not realize it or think about it at the time. He wanted to look at this man again whose name was Leo and ask him something about Cini. He wasn't sure what he would ask; but that was the reason he followed Doreen down the hall to the last door and was standing behind her when she opened it and he saw Leo behind the desk, the heavyset man straightening and seeing him at the same time. Doreen was saying, 'Leo, give me thirty dollars for this, will you please?' But Leo was not looking at Doreen. His expression was fixed, frozen for a short moment, and Mitchell would remember the look on his face.

'It's good to see you again,' Leo said, forming a smile. 'Seems like you're becoming a regular.'

Doreen said, 'Leo, take this and give me thirty back, okay? The man's waiting.'

Mitchell knew in that moment what he was going to do. He said, 'Doreen?'

She said 'What?'

He said again, 'Doreen?'

This time she half turned, looking around at him, and he said, 'One more.'

Mitchell raised the Polaroid and pressed his eye to the viewfinder. He heard Leo say, 'Not here, no!' But it was too late. He clicked the shutter, paused a moment and lowered the camera to wait for the development process to take place.

Leo said, 'Hey, I mean it. I'm going to have to ask you for that camera. You rent it to take pictures of the models, but now the time's up, you don't get to use it after that.'

'My time isn't up,' Mitchell said.

'Well, what I mean,' Leo said, 'it's all right to take pictures in the studios, but this is private property. You can't take any pictures you want. You know what I mean? You rent the camera to take pictures of *models*.'

'She's a model,' Mitchell said. He saw Doreen's expression. She had no idea what was going on.

'Yeah, she's a model,' Leo said, 'but you aren't in a studio. That's the rule. You have to be in a studio. You can understand that. I mean how would you like somebody to come in here and take your picture if you don't want it taken?'

As Mitchell raised the camera, pulled out the print and peeled it away from the negative, Leo Frank was saying, 'I can demand you give me that picture.' Mitchell looked at it a moment and slipped it into the inside pocket of his coat.

'Now come on, man, I'm serious.' Leo Frank got up and came around his desk toward Mitchell, his hand extended. 'Give me the picture.'

Mitchell said to him, 'If you want it, you'll have to take it. The question is, How bad do you want it?'

Mitchell waited, giving him time. When Leo didn't move or say anything Mitchell turned and walked out.

*

Leo was still at his desk when Alan entered the back way and came into the office.

'He took my picture,' Leo said.

'What're you talking about? Who took your picture?'

'The guy, he came in here with Doreen a couple minutes ago, he tells her to turn around and takes a Polaroid shot.'

Alan was sitting down. 'You mean he took a picture of Doreen.' Sitting forward in the office chair now, his hands on the edge of the desk.

'No, he made it sound like that, telling her to turn around. But I'm in the picture, I know I am.'

'He show you the print?'

'No, he said, "You want it, try and get it," and walked out.'

Alan stared at Leo before sitting slowly back in the chair. 'All right, let's say he's got your picture. So what? He's seen you here a few times before, he knows what you look like. So what? Leo, think, all right? What good's the picture going to do him?'

'He's onto something,' Leo said. 'I know it.'

Alan gave him a weary look, a slow shake of the head. 'Leo, he's onto shit. He doesn't know you. There is no possible way he can tie you into it. Unless you tell him yourself.'

'*Tell* him. Christ, you think I'd tell him?'

'I don't know,' Alan said, 'but you look like you're ready to have a fucking heart attack.' He hunched forward again. 'Leo, the guy takes your picture. You could've given him a picture, personally autographed, he can carry it around in his wallet. But Leo, listen to me, how's it going to help him?'

Leo didn't say anything and Alan stroked him again with a quiet, easy tone. 'You got absolutely nothing to worry about. Go home take some pills and go to bed. Start counting up to a hundred grand, Leo, slowly.' He grinned at the fat man behind the desk. 'Hey, Leo, you'll be asleep before you get to your cut.'

*

Alan got hold of Bobby Shy, just in time. Bobby was going out to Royal Oak to see his dealer and pick up some stuff. So Alan went along for the ride and told him about Mitchell taking the picture.

'What can the man do with it?' Bobby Shy asked him.

'Nothing. I'm talking about Leo,' Alan said. Shit, he was more worried now about the way Bobby was driving in the fast-moving stream of night traffic on North Woodward. Bobby was up, gunning it away from lights, keeping up with the rods and muscle cars heading out to the drive-ins or for some street racing, past the flashy neon motel signs and used-car lots.

'What's wrong with Leo?'

'Leo is starting to whimper. He sees the guy again I think he's going to bust out crying.'

'Talk to him,' Bobby said. 'Hold his little fat hand.'

'Listen, I'll rock him to sleep every night if I have to,' Alan said. 'But if that doesn't work, then, buddy, we got a problem.'

'Not a problem can't be fixed though, is it?'

'I'm not saying anything like that,' Alan said. 'Not yet. But from now on we got to keep a closer eye on him. Especially when he starts drinking.'

'He can put it away,' Bobby said. 'I seen him.'

'He can also fall off the stool and bust wide open,' Alan said. 'That's what we don't want to happen.'

10

Ross usually made his move during the after-dinner drinks. Over a Stinger or a Harvey Wallbanger he would lean in close and say, quietly, 'Sweetheart, why don't we finish these and go to a motel?' Or, depending on the girl, 'Sweetheart, you wouldn't want to go somewhere and screw, would you?' Responses to the direct approach ranged from, 'Wow, you don't waste time, do you?' to 'No, but I wouldn't mind fooling around.' Once in a while he even got a straight 'Sure.' Very seldom a flat 'No.' Ross was successful because he was a good salesman and never afraid to ask for the order.

Tonight, though, was a little different. Barbara was a friend. The wife of a friend. And she didn't want an after-dinner drink. Just coffee. Black.

What he had going for him was the place. They had eaten dinner in the bar section of the restaurant. It was getting crowded and noisy and the wavy-haired middle-aged entertainer at the piano bar was singing things like 'Some Enchanted Evening.'

Ross said, 'I think this place is going downhill. It's getting to be like a neighborhood bar. The local hangout.'

'An expensive neighborhood bar,' Barbara said. 'Someone was telling me that hookers come in here now, pros. How do they compete with all the amateurs?'

Ross said, 'That's in the afternoon the bored housewives stop by. Today the ladies either drink or play tennis.'

'I would like to believe,' Barbara said, 'that somewhere, right now, a woman is sitting with a sewing basket on her lap, darning socks.'

Ross said, 'Would you?'

Barbara shrugged. 'It doesn't matter.' Her gaze moved past faces and raised glasses to the piano bar. 'The thirty-five–to–sixty set. Out having a swinging time. How many do you think are married? Or how many have been married twice? Three times?'

'Those things happen,' Ross said.

Barbara looked at him. 'I'm sorry. I didn't mean it the way it sounded.'

He saw the opening and said, 'Barb, we haven't really talked yet. But I don't think this is the place.' He sounded sincere.

She said, 'That's all right. It's about time I was getting home.'

'No, no – I mean I think we should go somewhere else. Have a quiet talk. It's only a little after ten.' He leaned closer now, beginning to move in. 'Is there someplace you'd especially like to go? Have one drink? Maybe a couple? Relax, and have a good talk?'

She shook her head. 'No, I don't care. Wherever you want to go.'

'Good,' Ross said.

He paid the check, got their coats and walked past the dining rooms and down the hallway that was lined on both sides with original paintings for sale to the lobby of the hotel-motel that was called an inn, the *in* Inn. Barbara hesitated.

'Ross—'

He took her arm. 'Don't say anything yet. All right?' And guided her through the lobby around planters and down another hallway to suite number 112, his hand in his coat pocket holding the key.

In the sitting room, on the coffee table – the first thing Barbara saw as she went in – was a bottle of champagne in a silver ice bucket, a bottle of good cognac and glasses. Closing the door behind them, Ross said, 'I had this for a customer who was here a few days. He left this afternoon, it's paid for, I thought why not use it? – nice quiet spot.'

Barbara said, 'And the champagne. Is that left over?'

Ross laughed. 'No, that's for us. Seriously though, folks—' Ross paused. 'Barb, really, I thought this would be more comfortable. But if you feel ... funny about it, we can always leave.'

'It's fine,' Barbara said.

'I promise you, I don't have any sneaky motives. Say the word, we'll turn around and walk out.'

'Don't overdo it,' Barbara said. 'Right now I believe you.' She sat down on the couch by the coffee table.

'I'll admit I've always been attracted to you,' Ross said, opening the champagne. 'I will even admit to having entertained fantasies about you.'

'Sexual fantasies?'

'What other kind is there? But you know I didn't bring you here to get you in bed.'

'Without my consent.'

Ross grinned. 'Well, maybe the possibility flashed through my mind. Any way I can give comfort, I'd be pleased to oblige. No, really.' Serious again. 'There's nothing better in a situation like this than to talk it out with someone, see what you think and how you honestly feel.'

She watched him pour champagne, then open the cognac bottle.

'Touch of this? Make us a couple of French seventy-fives.'

Barbara shook her head. 'No thanks.'

Ross poured about an ounce of cognac into his champagne and sat down on the couch, leaving a little space between them.

'Now then – have you told Sally and Mike?'

'No, I haven't really even talked to Mitch yet. I have no idea what his plans are.'

'Does it matter?'

'Does it matter? Of course it matters.'

'I mean, what if he wants a divorce?'

'Then we'll get a divorce,' Barbara said. 'Do you think I'd hold him against his will?'

'You wouldn't try to talk him out of it?'

'I'm not going to chase him,' Barbara said. 'He knows how I feel and what we've had for a long time. God, he's more sentimental than I am. The bottom drawer of his dresser, it's full of pictures of the kids when they were little. Birthdays, Christmas, a lot of them taken in Florida. We still have some of the old furniture, in the basement, my folks gave us to start out with when we got married. It's falling apart. He won't get rid of it; he won't even give it to the Goodwill.'

'Sort of a bleeding heart,' Ross said.

'Don't make him sound dumb,' Barbara said. 'He's not dumb. I'm saying if he wants to throw away twenty-two years to play house with some young broad, he's doing it with his eyes wide open.'

Ross raised his arm to lay it on the backrest of the couch. The tip of his fingers touched Barbara's shoulders.

'I'm not saying he's dumb. But I do think he's out of his mind.'

'Why, because he told me?'

'No, to get involved with somebody else. Do you know if he ever fooled around before?'

'I don't know when he would've had time. Now I think all of a sudden it's his age. Wanting to be twenty-five again.'

'The trouble is, once they start . . .'

Barbara turned her head to look at him. 'Is that the way it happened with you?'

'No,' Ross said, 'I always fooled around. Looking, I guess.' His fingers moved idly on her shoulder. 'What I'm saying – why I think he's out of his mind – I don't think I would've ever fooled around if I'd been married to you.'

'You weren't happy? Either time?'

'Not really. I always had the feeling something was missing. I guess because I thought I loved my wives at the time, but never particularly liked them.' He watched her sip the champagne. 'How is it?'

'Very nice. Good and cold.'

'Taste this.'

She took a sip of his champagne-cognac because she knew he would insist.

'I like it, but it's a little heavy.' She realized he was closer now as he took the glass from her hand.

'I'm not too concerned with Mitch,' Ross said, 'or how he got involved. I'm thinking more about you. I look at you, I think, what a waste.'

'I haven't exactly been scrapped.'

'No, what I'm saying, I think you're better-looking now, more attractive, than at any time since we've known each other.'

'Trying to grow old gracefully. Like everyone else.'

'You're not old.' His fingers touched her cheek. 'Not a line. Smooth, clear skin . . . a great figure. God,' Ross's eyes raised to her face. 'How long has it been since you've made love?'

'Do you want to know the exact day, and hour?'

'Barb, if we can relax and enjoy each other, what's wrong with that? Does it hurt anyone?'

'Maybe some other time, Ross. All right?'

'Barb, I'm not trying to rush you. I'm terribly attracted to you, I want to go to bed with you, and I'm not afraid to admit it.' He paused and said, even more quietly, 'Barb, I'll make love to you like you've never had it before.'

Barbara studied him for a moment before she said, 'How do you know?'

'I promise.'

'Really, why do you think you'd be better than Mitch?'

'After twenty-two years, Barb, I promise you, a little change, just the fact that it's new and different, can't help but be better.'

'What do you have in mind?'

'Come on, don't be clinical. Relax and let it happen.'

'I could, couldn't I? No one would know the difference.'

'I certainly won't tell,' Ross said. He placed his glass on the table. He brought Barbara to him gently, his hands on her shoulders, and kissed her, using a little restraint at first, then showing her how fervent and serious he was as he tried to get his tongue in there.

Barbara turned her head to slide her mouth away from his and Ross moved his hands around to her back, keeping her, holding her tightly to him.

Close to his ear she said, 'Ross—'

'Barb, don't say anything. Let it happen.'

The strange thing was that she could, easily, close her eyes and let it happen. She felt warm and comfortable; slightly tight. She was in a hotel room with a man. Ross smelled good. He was fairly attractive. If he would keep quiet and not say anything, she could rationalize being here and go to bed with him and maybe, as he said, it would be better than she had ever had it before.

But Ross said, 'God, you turn me on,' and breathed through his nose and it was like a movie. A not very good movie. She realized she was not part of what was going on. She was an observer, perched up somewhere watching the two of them on the couch.

As Ross's left hand came around to close on her breast, she said, 'I was just thinking.'

'What?' Ross breathed.

'What Mitch would do if he saw us like this.'

Ross pulled away to look at her, his expression grimly serious. 'That doesn't do a lot for the mood.'

'What do you think he'd do, though?' Barbara asked.

'I don't think he's in a position to do anything. You mean something physical?'

'Whatever,' Barbara said. 'The thing is, he's unpredictable. You wouldn't think that, would you?'

'I would say he's fairly steady,' Ross said. 'If he tells you he's going to deliver, he delivers.'

Barbara leaned back against the cushion. 'He can also be – I was going to say cold-blooded and I can't think of any other word for it. Not vicious or mean, but—'

'Barb, why don't we talk about Mitch later on. Here, have some more.' Ross reached for the champagne, filled her glass and raised it to her mouth, helping her with the first sip. 'Let's not ruin a nice glow,' Ross said.

She took another sip of the champagne as he quickly refilled his own glass. Ross took a gulp, turned to get back to Barbara, but not in time.

'Did you know Mitch was in the Air Force during the war?'

'Barbara, come on.'

'I said he was unpredictable, you said he was steady. And we're both right in a way.'

Ross took a cigarette out of a pack on the table and lighted it, for the moment resigned.

'Did you know he was in the Air Force?'

'No, I didn't. What was he, a mechanic?'

'See?' Barbara said. 'No, he was a fighter pilot. Everyone assumes he was a grease monkey. But at twenty years old he was a first lieutenant. He flew a P-Forty-seven.'

'That's interesting,' Ross said.

'You know what's more interesting?' Barbara waited a moment. 'He shot down seven German planes in less than three months.'

'No kidding?' Ross seemed interested now. 'He's never mentioned it.'

'He also shot down two Spitfires.'

'Spitfires?' Ross frowned. 'Those are British planes.'

'I know they are,' Barbara said. 'Mitch was returning to his base, I think he was over France. The two planes dove at him firing cannons, thinking for some reason he was German. To protect himself, Mitch turned into them. He fired and with two bursts – he says it was pure luck – he shot down both of the planes.'

Ross was intent now. 'My God, really?'

'There was a hearing,' Barbara went on, 'an official investigation. Mitchell explained the situation as he saw it and, because of his experience and record, he was exonerated, as they said, of any malicious intent or accidental blame. The general, or whoever it was, closed the hearing. Mitch stood up and said, "Sir, I have a question." The general said, "What is it?" And Mitch said, "Do I get credit for the Spitfires?" He was held in contempt of court and sent home the next week, assigned to an air base in Texas.'

'I can picture him,' Ross said, nodding. 'Young and wild.'

Barbara shook her head. 'Quiet and calculating. He hasn't changed that much since. Always mild-mannered, the nice guy – until someone steps over the line and challenges him.'

'Or fools around with his wife.'

'He's never had to worry about that.'

'It began,' Ross said, 'with you wondering what he would do if he walked in here.'

'Right,' Barbara said. 'What do you think?'

'Barb—' Ross paused. 'I don't think you're quite ready for this sort of thing. Or my timing is bad or something.'

'I thought we were going to talk.'

'Let's talk some other time,' Ross said. 'It is getting a little late.'

11

Mitchell was in the kitchen when he heard the front door open. He hadn't eaten. He had been here more than two hours, sitting in the den most of the time, waiting for her, wherever she was. He was in the kitchen deciding if he should make a sandwich, wondering if it would be all right. It was his house, but now he didn't live here. It gave him a strange feeling. With the sound he moved away from the refrigerator. Looking at an angle through the doorway, past a corner of the dining room to the foyer, he saw Barbara, her hand on the partly open door. He heard a man's voice, outside, say, 'We'll make it again real soon, okay?' But he didn't place the voice until Barbara closed the door and turned and saw him. Mitchell said to himself, Ross. God Almighty, Ross. Already. He saw the look on her face. Surprise? Caught? Caught in the act. Or momentarily startled. When she came into the kitchen her expression was calm, composed.

'How long have you been here?'

'A little while. Not long.'

'I went out for dinner.'

'I thought you might've. Where'd you go?'

'The Inn,' Barbara said. 'I think it's going downhill. Getting noisy.'

Mitchell nodded. 'Very popular I hear with unescorted ladies.'

'I wasn't alone.'

'I know you weren't.'

There was a silence. They were standing only a few feet apart, looking at each other, waiting. It was in Mitchell's mind that he was going to stand there and not say anything as long as it took to outwait her. But the stubborn feeling passed. She looked good. In black, with pearls. She looked better than ever. She had been out to dinner with Ross. He knew it. But if she didn't want to tell him about it, if she wanted to keep him hanging – she had every right to turn and walk away if she wanted to. He felt dumb. A big dumb jealous husband putting his wife on the spot.

He said, 'I was thinking about making a sandwich. Is that all right?'

She waited a moment, her eyes still holding his. 'I don't know. I'll have to ask my lawyer.'

'Have you hired one?'

'For God sake, we haven't even *talked*.' She put her purse on the counter and moved past him to the refrigerator. 'I have no idea what's going on in your head and you ask me if I've hired a lawyer.' Opening the refrigerator she looked at him again. 'What kind of a sandwich do you want?'

'I don't care. Anything.'

'Hot dog?'

'That's fine.'

'Just tell me one thing, all right? Are we talking about a divorce?'

'Barbara – I don't know. I don't know what you're thinking either. The little bit we've talked, I probably haven't made much sense.'

'Not a hell of a lot. Do you want a beer?'

'All right.'

He watched her go into the refrigerator and move a pitcher of orange juice to reach the beer. As she handed him the can Barbara said, 'Are you going with the girl or not?'

'No.'

'What does that mean? No, not at the moment, or no, you're not seeing her anymore?'

'Barbara, she's dead.'

She waited, her hand holding the refrigerator door open. 'You mean she died? Something happened to her and she died?'

Mitchell wasn't sure why he told her. It came out of him. She was dead and he had to say she was dead. He couldn't pretend she was a girl from another time who had moved away or dropped out of sight. She was dead.

He put the beer can on the counter and took the photograph out of his coat pocket and showed it to Barbara. He didn't say anything. He held it up to her and watched her face.

Barbara turned from the refrigerator, letting the door swing all the way open.

'Is that the girl?'

'No, a friend of hers. It's the man I'm interested in. Have you ever seen him before?'

Barbara took the picture from him to study it and he felt his hope die. There was no hint of recognition on her face. She said, 'No, I don't think so.'

'It's not the man who was here, with the accounting service?'

'Definitely not. He was skinny and his hair was longer.'

'I was hoping,' Mitchell said. 'Well . . .' He took the picture from her and dropped it on the counter.

'Mitch, who are they?'

'They work at a model studio. I was there today. I had a feeling, I don't know why, and I took their picture.'

'They're friends of yours,' Barbara said, 'or what? Why were you there? – a model studio.' There were so many questions she wanted to ask him, that she wanted to know, *now*, and he stood quietly looking down at the photograph, staring at it with his calm closed-mouth expression. 'Mitch, will you please, for God sake, tell me what's going on!'

Behind her, the bright inside light of the refrigerator showed milk cartons and the pitcher of orange juice, cans of beer, jars, packages wrapped in butcher's paper, dishes covered with silver foil.

'I want to tell you,' Mitchell said. 'But it doesn't have anything to do with you. It's happening to me; I don't want to see you involved in it.'

'Mitch – whatever it is – it's happening to *us*. I'm already involved. As long as I'm your wife I'm involved.'

He looked at her, not saying anything. He walked over to her and slowly, carefully, put his hand on her shoulder. As she looked up at him he reached around her to push the refrigerator door closed.

'All right,' Mitchell said. 'Let's sit down.'

*

There were four cigarette stubs in the ashtray. A drink, half-finished, was forgotten, the ice melted. Barbara sat across the coffee table from him, sitting forward in the low chair. During the past half hour she had not taken her eyes off him.

'But what if she isn't dead?'

'I know she is.'

'You see people shot in the movies. It can look real—'

'I thought of that,' Mitchell said. 'She's dead. I saw her face. Her eyes were open, with a look I've never seen before. She wasn't breathing. She wasn't faking it, she was dead.'

'What would they do with her? Where do you keep a dead body?'

'I don't know. Maybe they buried her somewhere.'

'With your gun and your coat.'

'My fingerprints on the gun. My permit—'

'*If* they kept her body,' Barbara said. 'If they still have it, or know they can get it.'

'That's their whole point,' Mitchell said. 'I pay, or they tell the police where to find her.'

'All right, what if you go to the police and tell them first?'

'Tell them what?'

'The whole thing,' Barbara said. 'I mean you wouldn't be going to them if you actually did it. They'd realize that.'

'I don't know where the girl is. I can't prove anything.'

'At least you could tell them exactly what you saw. Then it's up to them to investigate and find out who did it.'

'How?'

'I don't know. It's what they do.'

Mitchell thought for a moment and came at it from another angle. 'Let's say there are suspects, they're arrested. Let's say they actually did it. Do you think they're going to implicate themselves, tell the police where to find the girl's body?'

'Then look at it this way,' Barbara said. 'If they saw the possibility, that it might happen – the whole thing blow up in their faces – then they wouldn't have kept the girl's body.'

'They haven't necessarily kept it. It's probably hidden somewhere.'

Barbara shook her head. 'If there's the least possibility they could be tied in with the murder, they don't want a body around that could be found by someone, accidentally discovered, and used to implicate them. Mitch, why would they take the chance?'

'You're saying they got rid of her. Put her somewhere she can't be found.'

'I think so,' Barbara said. 'They say if you refuse to pay, they tell the police. That could have been a bluff. They frighten you enough and you pay. If you don't they have nothing to lose. So if they didn't get rid of her body before, they would the moment they see police beginning to close in.'

'Then nothing can be proved.'

'Go to the police and tell them. Let them worry about it.'

'Barbara, once it's told – you don't edge into something like this. I tell them a girl's been murdered, it's out, everybody knows about it. It's in the papers, the whole story. I'm fooling around with a young girl and she ends up dead.'

'Can't it be approached, you know, confidentially? Keep it quiet?'

'I don't see how. Not when someone's been killed.'

She stared at him a moment. You're afraid of the publicity? Is that what's bothering you?'

'Barbara, the girl died because of me, because I knew her. That bothers me more than anything. The publicity—' He paused. 'I don't see this, if it got in the papers, as what you'd call bad publicity. I see it as something that could destroy our lives, affect our kids, ruin, wipe out everything I've worked for, built up. Listen, I feel this more than I can explain it to you. I mean I want to do what's right, I want to see them caught. But I'm also realistic, practical about it.'

'I told Ross,' Barbara said, 'I thought you were sometimes cold-blooded. But that isn't really the word.'

'Use it if you want,' Mitchell said. 'I'm saying I don't feel, my conscience doesn't tell me I have to go to the police. Like that's the only way.'

'But what other way is there?'

Mitchell paused. 'What if – I don't know how – I handled it myself?'

'Mitch, please. Don't say that. They've already killed some-one.'

'So have I. With six machine guns.'

'Mitch, that was different. My God, I don't have to tell you that.'

'I'm not saying I'm going to. I'm saying what if.'

Barbara stood up. 'Mitch, look, if there isn't a body, you can refuse to pay them. If there's nothing they can hold over you – the threat of telling the police – then you're out of it. There isn't a thing they can do.'

'But they'd still be loose,' Mitchell said. 'They killed that girl as coldly as you can do it, and they'd still be loose.' He looked up at his wife. 'I'm in this, Barbara. I'm not going to run, I'm not going to try and forget about it and hope it goes away. I'm going to do something.'

That was exactly what she was afraid of.

*

Barbara made him an omelet with cheese and onion and green pepper. He stood at the counter to eat it, with French bread and an avocado, and the beer she had handed him earlier. He was tired, but he didn't feel like sitting down. He was thinking about Leo Frank and picked up the photograph again. He was think-ing about getting in the car and driving down to Detroit. It would take him about twenty-five minutes, that's all. Start with

Leo, because he still had a feeling about Leo. Walk into the model studio and this time talk to him. Lead him with questions and watch his reaction.

Barbara said, 'Did you tell them you'd pay?'

Mitchell shook his head. 'No.'

'Do they think you will?'

'I don't know.'

'Mitch, even if you wanted to pay them' – she paused as he looked up at her – 'where would you get the money? Over a hundred thousand dollars?'

'I've never considered paying, so I haven't thought about it.'

'We don't have that kind of money. Do they think you just keep it in the bank?'

'Barbara, I don't know what they think. I guess they figure I can get it if I have to, at least ten thousand bucks at a time. The first payment's due tomorrow.'

'And another one a week from tomorrow,' Barbara said, 'and another a week later. Can you put your hands on thirty thousand dollars that fast?'

'I could if I had to.'

'You'd have to sell some stock, wouldn't you?'

'Or borrow it from the bank.'

'But without borrowing – you can't touch the trust funds, can you?'

'No. Or the depreciation investments. In fact, I just sold most of our fooling-around stock last month and put the money into five-year municipal notes. We can't touch that either.'

'So if you wanted to pay them off,' Barbara said, 'how much do you think you could raise?'

'If I had to.' Mitchell paused. 'I don't know, maybe forty or fifty thousand without too much trouble.'

'Do you think they'd settle for that?'

'Are we just thinking out loud or what?'

'You said the one sounded as though he knew as much about you as your accountant.'

'He knows about the royalty. That's enough.'

'What if you showed him exactly how much you can pay?' Barbara said. 'Whatever the amount is, but that's it and no more. Do you think he'd settle for it?'

Mitchell put his fork down. He looked at his wife, at her

drawn fixed expression, and knew she was serious. 'You think I'd make a deal with them?'

'Mitch, they *killed* that girl. If you won't go to the police then you have to pay them. Don't you see that? Or they'll kill *you*.'

'You think if I pay them, that's all there is to it? They go away, we never hear from them again?'

'Talk to them when they call,' Barbara said. 'Tell them you'll show them facts and figures, what you can afford to pay. If you can convince them that's it, why wouldn't they take it?'

'You make it sound easy,' Mitchell said. 'Expensive, but easy.'

'How much is your life worth?' Her voice was calm; the concern, the fear, was in her eyes.

'I don't know, if I got close enough to talk to one of them,' Mitchell said, 'I'm liable to break his jaw.'

Barbara closed her eyes and opened them. 'Mitch, go to the police. Will you please?'

He finished the beer in his glass and placed it on the counter. 'Talk to one of them,' Mitchell said then. 'Not all of them. Just one.'

'What do you mean?'

'That could have possibilities,' Mitchell said. He nodded, thinking about it. Yes, it sure could. Get one of them alone and talk to him. If he could first find out who they were.

'What are you talking about?'

'Nothing really. Maybe an idea; I don't know.'

'Would you like some coffee?'

'No thanks. I want a bed more than anything else.' He looked at her for a moment, saw no response in her eyes and started to turn away.

'Mitch—'

There it was, a good sound. Soft, familiar. He turned to look at her again.

'What?'

'God, I miss you.'

'I miss you too.'

'Then don't go,' Barbara said. 'Stay here.'

'I'm sorry.' He wasn't sure how to say it, but he knew he was going to try. 'I'm really sorry I hurt you. I don't know why – it was a dumb thing I got into.'

'I know.' Barbara nodded slowly. 'Let's not talk about it anymore, all right? Let's go to bed.'

12

Janet came into his office and placed two accounting ledgers on his desk. She went out and came in again with his stock portfolios, insurance policies, bank books and trust fund agreements in plastic folders.

'Martin wants to know,' Janet said, 'if you're blowing town.'

Mitchell looked up at her. 'That's what he said, uh? Blowing town?'

'He said, 'What's he going to do, take the money and blow town?''

'Tell him I'm going to Hazel Park,' Mitchell said. 'I'm going to quit gambling on machine parts and put it on the horses.'

'I don't think he'd believe you.'

'Martin doesn't believe anything unless it's on a balance sheet.'

Janet held a long piece of calculator tape curling in her hand. She reached across the desk to give it to Mitchell. 'That's the total. Martin says you couldn't possibly raise any more than that before April of next year.'

Mitchell looked at the total, at the bottom of the tape. 'That's all, uh?'

'I can ask him to come in if you want to talk to him.'

'No, that's fine. Did he put it all on one sheet?'

'It's there on top. Itemized.'

'Very good.'

Janet waited. 'You're not really going to the track, are you?'

'No,' Mitchell said, 'I'm going to run away with a seventeen-year-old go-go dancer. Listen, I want you to go to the bank after lunch.' He picked out a personal checkbook from the stack of folders and portfolios. 'Here, and get me ten thousand dollars.'

'Ten thousand?'

'In hundreds. That'll fit in a number ten envelope, won't it?'

'I don't know,' Janet said. 'I've never put ten thousand dollars in an envelope.'

'When you get back, try it,' Mitchell said. 'Number ten manila.' As she was going out he said, 'And get me my home.' He waited for the sound of the buzzer and picked up the phone.

'Barbara . . . yeah, it comes to fifty-two thousand. That's it till next spring. . . . Yes, I'm going to talk to him, if I can find him. He's the one to talk to. But I'll have to go to the other guy first, Leo . . . No, I won't. I'm going to give it some more thought and probably later on, if I can get away, see if I can find him.' He paused. 'Barbara, I still miss you. . . . God. Barbara, it's going to take more than one night, you know, to get back where we were, but I can't think of a better way to do it. . . . I know, it's like starting over. It's a good feeling. Listen, I'll call you later, let you know if I'm going to do anything. . . . Okay, I'll see you.'

He missed her again, or still missed her, right now. That was the good feeling, wanting to be with her, wanting to touch her. He had said to her it was like starting over. Or like coming home after a long business trip. Last night, undressing together in the bedroom had reminded him of that, of coming home and going up to the bedroom, no matter what time of the day it was, and making love, not doing much fooling around but getting right in there and doing it, feeling the sweat breaking out on their bodies. There were other times for fooling around and being naked together and making it last. Though she didn't have to be naked to arouse him. She could sit down in a chair, holding her skirt to her thigh as she crossed her legs, and he would want to make love to her. She could be sewing a button on his coat and look up at him, over the top of her reading glasses, and he would want to make love to her: undress her in the stillness of a Sunday afternoon with sunlight framed in the bedroom windows and the phone pulled out of the jack and make slow love to her, feeling her make her gradual change from lady to woman. Dressed, she was a lady. In bed she was a woman. Cini had been a girl, dressed or naked. Cini seemed a long time ago. And if she were alive she could be forgotten. But because she was dead he had to remember her.

He had to see Leo again and talk to him. Speak to him

quietly, sincerely, and watch for reactions when he offered a bait. He had read books on customer and employee relations; how to win friends, close deals, improve your personality and make a million dollars. He hadn't finished most of them. He was not a salesman or a joiner or a joke-teller. He was himself. He relied on common sense but was not afraid to gamble. He gave his word, and delivered. So he would take it a step at a time and maybe Leo – if he was one of them – would reveal himself and maybe he wouldn't.

It would be simple if he knew who they were and he had a gun. Walk in and shoot them and walk out again. There, that's done; now back to work. He could see himself doing it: pointing the gun at three men in a cramped office full of nude photographs and pulling the trigger. It was funny he pictured Leo's office. But he could also picture himself with a cannonball tennis serve and a flawless backhand, or the forty-five-year-old rookie hitting a fastball into the upper deck at Tiger Stadium. Picturing had nothing to do with doing it. Nor was killing a man in an FW-190 or a Messerschmitt at three hundred yards the same as looking in a man's face and pulling the trigger. He told himself he would never be able to kill like that, coldly, impersonally. Still, he wished he had a gun. Just in case he was wrong.

•

He walked out of the office that afternoon wishing he had on his old loose sagging sport coat too. He was wearing a gray knit suit that was tailored to fit snugly and he was conscious of the thick envelope against his chest in the inside coat pocket. He put his cigarettes in a side pocket, checked the other one to make sure he had his car keys, and told Janet he'd see her tomorrow.

She said good night and watched him go down the hall: three-thirty in the afternoon and ten thousand dollars in his coat pocket.

Out in the plant the shifts were changing. Mitchell nodded to employees, calling some by name, looking around, being the friendly approachable boss as he walked toward the rear door and the parking lot outside. He noticed, over in the snack-bar area, a number of employees from both shifts, by the vending machines and the big Silex coffeemaker. Second-shift men standing and sitting around the pair of long cafeteria tables drinking coffee. That was all right; they had some free time yet.

But there were first-shift men hanging around who ordinarily couldn't get out fast enough to go home or stop at a bar.

There was a guy in a raincoat at one of the tables sitting with his back to Mitchell. When he turned to say something to John Koliba and a couple of others at the end of the table, Mitchell recognized him.

Christ. That's all he needed right now.

Mitchell walked over.

Ed Jazik, the Local 199 business agent, was saying, 'What does he give a shit? Closes the plant, lives like a fucking king on what he's got in the bank, what he's been stuffing in the bank while all the hourly assholes are busting their balls to make car payments, washing machine payments, trying to save something for a pair of shoes for the kids, maybe a new dress for the wife once in a while.'

Mitchell stood there listening a moment. He was thinking, Where has this guy been? And why do I have to get him? He hadn't heard union management people talk like that in fifteen years.

Mitchell said, 'Excuse me.' And when Jazik turned and looked up and John Koliba and the others saw him, showing some surprise, he said to Jazik, 'I don't want to interrupt anything important, but you happen to be talking to my employees on *my* time, that I'm paying for. If you want to make a speech then go rent a hall somewhere and let's see how good you do.'

Ed Jazik said, 'You hear that? *My* time. His time, his plant, his profit. You think he gives a shit about the rank and file?'

Mitchell said, 'Rank and file? What're you doing, reading it out of the union book? Rank and file. These guys work for me, I know them. I can't get along without them, all right? And they can't get along without me bringing in the business. So why don't you get out of here and let us get some work done.'

'He's saying he don't give you any time to listen to your rights or think for yourself,' Jazik said. 'It's *his* plant. *His.* He owns it. You don't want to play his way, he's going to take his fucking baseball and bat and go home.'

'You see that much,' Mitchell said. 'I own it. Good. Then you see I have the right to ask you to leave.' That was better. A little calmer.

'We got a few minutes,' Jazik said. 'Let's talk. You listen for a change, I'll tell you how I see conditions here.' He raised up enough to turn his chair sideways to the table and sat down again, crossing his legs.

Mitchell was aware of the men watching him. The boss standing there. On the spot. The union guy trying to push him around a little and get him mad. He had to ignore what the guy said and handle it smoothly – handle it somehow – but, above all, not argue with the guy in front of his employees.

Tell him you don't have time to talk. No, that wasn't handling it.

The guy was waiting, posing, sitting low in the folding chair, legs crossed and an elbow on the table. Sure of himself. Or with nothing to lose. No, Mitchell decided, he was confident. He liked people watching him.

Mitchell said, 'What did I say to you the last time you were here you wanted to talk?'

Jazik shrugged. 'Some bullshit. I don't remember.'

Mitchell kept his eyes on him. 'I said, you want to talk, let's wait till contract time. That's what it's for and we can talk all you want. You said maybe some people don't want to wait. Well, I talked to a few people.' As he spoke, Mitchell's gaze began to move over the solemn faces of the men standing around the table, stopped briefly on John Koliba and moved back again. 'I asked them, how's everything going? No complaints. I said to them well, anytime you got a problem come in and tell me about it. We'll work it out.' He stared at Jazik again. 'That's how we do it here, which I tried to explain to you.'

Jazik listened to every word without moving. He shook his head then, slowly. 'That's not what you said.'

'No?' Mitchell seemed surprised. 'What'd I say?'

'You refused to talk to me, first.'

'Until contract time. That's right.'

'Then you said, we get in an argument, you threatened me, you said, we get in an argument you're liable to try and knock me on my ass.'

Mitchell shook his head. 'No, I said if we got in an argument I was liable to forget who you are and I *would* knock you on your ass. There's a difference.'

Looking at Jazik he knew he was not going to stop now to be polite or waste any more time on him, dumb hotshot son of a bitch sitting there in his raincoat with the collar up and the blank cool look on his face – seeing the guy and, for some reason, seeing the one named Leo sitting in the chair in the nude-model office, a brief glimpse of him in his mind that was there and gone.

Mitchell said, 'Now I'm going to tell you again. Walk out of here right now, or I'll knock you on your ass and throw you out. Either way.'

Jazik, staring at Mitchell, took his time getting up. He was bigger than Mitchell, a little taller and heavier through the shoulders.

He said, 'They heard you threaten me.'

'You heard it,' Mitchell said. 'That's the main thing.'

'I could take you to court, you know that? Threatening bodily abuse and harm.'

'Hey,' Mitchell said, 'let's knock off all the bullshit. Are you going to leave or not?'

'What I want to see,' Jazik said, 'is you try and throw me out.'

Mitchell hit him on the word 'out,' his mouth still slightly open. He hit him with a hard right hand. As Jazik came up off the table, Mitchell hit him with another right, not as solid as the first one. Jazik took it and came at him again. Mitchell feinted with the right this time, threw a left as hard as he had ever thrown one, and saw the men near Jazik jumping out of the way as Jazik hit the cafeteria table and carried it back with him five or six feet before the table turned over and he went down with it to sit on the floor.

Mitchell waited, to see if Jazik was going to get up or if anyone had anything to say. The first- and second-shift men there looked at Jazik and then at him, but nobody said a word.

'Somebody show him out,' Mitchell said finally. He turned and walked away. They watched him head back through the plant toward his office.

Janet was straightening his desk. She looked up, surprised, as he came in. 'I thought you'd left.'

'Get me – what's his name?' Mitchell said. 'The guy that's president of one-ninety-nine.'

'Isn't it Donnelly?'

'Yeah, Charlie Donnelly. Get him for me, will you?'

Janet dialed the number, asked for Mr. Donnelly, said who

was calling and handed the phone to Mitchell. He didn't sit down. He stood by his desk waiting, watching Janet go out of the office and close the door.

'Charlie? Harry Mitchell over at Ranco . . . Fine . . . Yeah, I know, in about a week, ten days. I'm looking forward to seeing you, Charlie, and I mean *you*, because I'll tell you right now I'm not going to negotiate with that stiff you assigned to us – Jazik. The son of a bitch walks in my plant – a sign says authorized personnel only – he walks in starts talking to my employees. A week ago he grabs me in the hall, threatens me with a slowdown. . . . I didn't think you did. . . . Right, so why should I have to take that kind of shit? Charlie, the guy's living back in the Thirties. Where'd you get him anyway?' Mitchell paused for about a minute, listening. He said then, 'If you got a maverick, *you* teach him. I'm not going to break the son of a bitch in for you, I'll break his goddamn neck first. I'm too old for that kind of bullshit. I've been there, Charlie, so have you. We don't need it. We can sit down and talk, right? Twelve years neither of us has ever raised our voice. You give me the contract, we change a few lines and sign it. What'd you send me this clown for? We could do it over a diet lunch.' He waited again, listening, beginning to calm down. 'Yes, that's fine. Listen, I'm sorry if I blew up. I got a few things on my mind, I don't need any—' He paused again, patient, letting the union president explain again how they liked the guy's enthusiasm but he was new and maybe they'd have to sit on him for a while or send him to charm school. Everything was going to be all right. Mitchell would never see the guy again, or at least not for a year or so, if the guy learned anything and was still around. That was good enough. They took another minute getting to good-bye, see you soon, and Mitchell hung up the phone.

Going through the outer office he said to Janet, 'I'll try it again. See if I can get out of this place.'

13

Peggy was the only one in the lobby when Mitchell walked in. She had her coat on, ready to leave.

'You quitting already? It's only five-thirty.'

'I've taken my clothes off eleven times,' the girl said, 'and put them back on again. That's enough for one day.'

'Where is everybody?'

'You mean Doreen?'

'Well, now that you mention it.'

'I don't know. I haven't seen her.'

'How about the other girls?'

'Sickies. Leo lets you call in sick once a month.'

'Is he here?'

'In back.' She moved past him to the door. 'If you see him, tell him I've left.'

'Yeah, maybe I'll stick my head in, say hello.'

She took a moment to look at him again as she opened the door. 'You don't have anything better to do?'

'Tell you the truth,' Mitchell said, 'not that I can think of.' He felt dumb standing there waiting for her to leave.

'Well—' The girl gave a little shrug and finally walked out. The door swung closed behind her.

Leo Frank sat at his desk studying a list of job applicants, trying to remember faces and match them to the names. They were mostly dogs: for some reason a lot of fat broads lately. He couldn't figure out where all the fat broads were coming from, or why they thought anybody would pay to look at them naked. Most of them would have trouble showing themselves for nothing.

He heard the front door close. Peggy leaving. Independent broad. Hire them, pay them good dough, they call in sick or leave anytime they felt like it.

He heard the footsteps in the hall, coming this way, and thought of Peggy again. But as he looked toward the doorway he knew it wasn't Peggy. It was a man. It was the guy. For some reason he was sure of it and had a moment to get ready, to prepare a pleasant expression before Mitchell walked in to stand in front of his desk.

'Well,' Leo said, 'our favorite customer. I hope what you're here for is to give me that picture you took. That wasn't very nice of you.'

'No,' Mitchell said, 'I came to deliver the money.' As he spoke, his hand came out of his inside pocket with the envelope.

'What money you talking about?'

'That I was supposed to leave out at the airport,' Mitchell said. 'I wondered if I could drop it off here.'

Leo frowned and shook his head, wishing to God he wasn't alone. 'Man, I don't know what you're talking about.'

'Ten thousand,' Mitchell said. 'The down payment.'

'You want to give me ten thousand?'

'It's all here.' Mitchell took out the packet of hundred-dollar bills and laid it on the edge of the desk.

'Wait a minute,' Leo Frank said. 'You want to give me ten thousand bucks? What for? I mean, man, I'll take it, but what for?'

'I guess I was wrong,' Mitchell said. 'I thought you were in on it.'

Leo was staring at the money. He had to take it a step further. 'In on what?'

'Well, if you're not involved, there's not much sense talking about it, is there?'

'You see ten grand laid out,' Leo said, 'you can't help but be a little curious.'

'I owe it to these three guys, but I don't know where to find them.'

'That's a strange situation,' Leo said. 'I never heard of anything like that before.'

'One's a skinny guy with long hair, one's a colored guy. I thought maybe the third guy was you.'

Leo laughed, made a sound that resembled a laugh. 'Why'd you think that? I mean why'd you think I was one of them?'

'I don't know, I guess it's just a feeling. The fact you run this place. You see all types of guys come in and out.'

'What's that got to do with it?'

'Well, there was a girl involved in this. She used to work here.'

'Man, there're fifty girls used to work here. Turnover, man, I guess you have it in your business – guys quitting, absenteeism, that kind of situation – but, man, nothing like I got to put up with.'

'You're right there,' Mitchell said. 'I guess every business's got its problems like that.'

Leo couldn't take his eyes off the stack of hundred-dollar bills. 'That's ten thousand bucks, uh? Doesn't look like what I'd picture ten thousand.'

'All hundreds,' Mitchell said.

'I'm trying to think of a way I might be able to help you,' Leo said, 'but I'm stuck. Three guys, man, they could be anybody.'

'No, they're somebody,' Mitchell said. 'The trouble is I got to find them to pay them the dough.'

'You want to pay them personally, is that it?'

'See, I was supposed to leave it in a locker out at the airport, but I forgot which one.'

'That's a problem.' Leo shook his head. 'What I mean to say, I wouldn't want to see anybody not get that money if they got it coming.'

'They got it coming all right,' Mitchell said, 'but it's up to them to collect it.'

'I sure wish I could help you,' Leo said.

'I wish you could too.' Mitchell paused. 'Well, I might as well be going.'

As he started for the door, Leo stood up. 'Say, you wouldn't happen to have that picture on you, would you? The one you took?'

Mitchell paused to look at him. 'Why?'

'I was just curious how it came out.'

'You're in it,' Mitchell said. He turned again and walked out.

Leo waited, listening to the footsteps in the hall. There was a silence before he heard the front door close, and again silence. He was still tense and anxious, but he was also proud of himself at the way he'd handled Mitchell, and he wasn't sweating too much. He picked up the phone and dialed Alan's home number. No answer. He tried the theater and was told Alan was out. The son of a bitch, he was never around when you wanted him. Leo decided to go across the street. Christ, have a couple of drinks.

*

Leo lived in a duplex on an old tree-shaded street of two- and four-family flats. Mitchell stood on the porch by the pair of front doors and rang the bell for the lower flat. He waited. The door opened partway and Mitchell saw the stunned, wide-eyed look on Leo's face before he noticed his silky wrinkled black-and-red pajamas and bare feet.

'How you doing?' Mitchell said.

Leo backed up as Mitchell came in. His stringy hair was uncombed, matted flat against his head; his eyes had a glazed watery look. He said, 'How'd you know where I live?'

'I looked it up in the book,' Mitchell said. 'Mrs. Leo Frank, Jr. That your wife?'

'My mother. She used to live here. I mean we did, we lived here together before she died.'

Mitchell looked around, at the dark woodwork and pale-green rough-plaster walls, heavy, velvety-looking draperies, closed, heavy stuffed chairs with doilies on the arms and headrests. Everything was dark and old and reminded him of other living rooms, some in places where he had lived, some in the homes of friends; dark, solemn, never changing.

'I was just putting the water on for coffee,' Leo said. 'You want some? Or a beer, or a drink?'

'No thanks, but go ahead,' Mitchell said. He followed Leo through the dark dining room to the kitchen. There was an old smell to the place. The wallpaper was stained. The linoleum in the kitchen was worn, coming apart at the seams. He watched Leo, at the stove, place the kettle on a burner and turn up the gas.

'You probably wonder what I'm doing here.'

'It crossed my mind.' Leo opened a cupboard and looked in.

'It was something you said last night.'

Leo closed the cupboard and turned to the sink that was full of dishes. He said, 'What was that?' and began rinsing a coffee mug.

Mitchell didn't say anything until Leo looked over at him. 'We were talking about employee relations.'

'We were?'

'In your office last night. You said, "I guess you have the same problems in your business, absenteeism and so on." '

'Yeah?'

'How did you know what business I'm in?'

There was a pause, a silence, and Mitchell felt it, his gaze holding on Leo who was scratching or touching or fooling with the crotch of his red-and-black silky pajamas.

'I don't know what business you're in. I just assumed you're in business. The way you dress and all.'

'I could be working for somebody,' Mitchell said. 'I could be a salesman or an engineer, anything. How'd you know I had my own company?'

'Hey, listen, I'm not even sure now what I said. I was just making a point about it's hard to keep people nowadays, that's all. Am I right? Isn't that what I said?'

'I don't know,' Mitchell said. 'I had the feeling – I thought about it after, in the car – you knew exactly what I did, the company, everything.'

'Man, I don't even know your name.'

'It's Mitchell. My company's Ranco Manufacturing.'

'It's nice to know you,' Leo said, 'but listen, man, I think you heard it wrong. I never said I knew what business you're in. We never even talked before. How could I know?'

Mitchell stared at him for a moment, then shrugged. 'Yeah, maybe so. I guess I heard you wrong.'

'Well – you sure you don't want some coffee?'

'Thanks, but I got to make a call. I was down this way, that's why I stopped in. I'm sorry if I troubled you.'

'No, it's no trouble at all. I've probably made the same mistake myself.' Leo was behind Mitchell, following him to the front door. As they reached the door, and Leo opened it, the phone rang in the front hall and the kettle began to whistle in the kitchen. 'Everything at once,' Leo said.

Mitchell wanted to wait. He tried to think of a reason, but Leo was letting it ring, pushing the door closed. 'I'll see you around,' Leo said. He got Mitchell out and closed the door on him, hurried to the phone in the hall, but it stopped ringing as he reached it. The kettle was still giving off a shrill whistle. Leo got to it, steam pouring out, and took the kettle off the stove. He didn't make a cup of coffee though. He poured a vodka and Seven-Up instead. In fact he had three of them while he was getting dressed.

*

Mitchell sat in his car, four houses down from the duplex. He was watching Leo's house and the white T-bird parked at the curb. He remembered Barbara saying the man who had been in their house, the skinny guy with long hair, had gotten into a white car. Looking at the car – that he hadn't noticed before, when he arrived – the gut feeling was stronger than ever. Thirty minutes later, when Leo Frank came out of the house and got into the white car, Mitchell's gut feeling moved up into his mind where he could look at it and reason and believe – not *know*, as O'Boyle would say, but believe – that Leo was one of them. Mitchell said to himself, Stay with him.

•

'Leo, what'd I say? At my office, right? Jesus, you come here.'

'I went to your office,' Leo said. 'Man, you're out to lunch. I got to talk to you.'

'You tell me he's following you, so you come here. Jesus.'

'No, today I haven't seen the guy at all. Maybe he's quit, I don't know. Yesterday he comes in the studio again. Says hello, that's all. How you doing? Later on I go out have something to eat. I look over, the guy's sitting there having a cup of coffee. I go home last night, I see his car drive by twice, maybe three times.'

Alan was having a corned beef sandwich and a bottle of red pop. He wasn't paying any attention to Doreen dancing topless on the stage, grinding out a slow rock number for the last of the lunch trade. He was tense because Leo was half in the bag and it wasn't three o'clock yet. But he had to appear calm and convince Leo that everything was all right, that the guy didn't know anything, the guy was groping, taking a shot in the dark.

'Let's say he really did forget the locker number,' Alan said. 'Okay, I call him again and tell him. I *been* calling him, the son of a bitch is out following you around.'

Leo was hunched over the table with his drink, his back to Doreen as the rock number ended and Doreen started down from the stage. 'But why me?' Leo said. 'Why's he picking on me?'

'Leo, stop and think, will you? Because you knew his girl friend. She used to work for you.' Alan looked up as Doreen, still topless, approached their table.

She touched Leo on the shoulder as she went by and said,

'Hey, baby, I want to see you before I leave. You still owe me for last week.'

Alan waited until she was past them, going toward the bar. 'Look, he pulls this cute stunt because he's got no place else to go – hey, you listening to me?'

'Yeah, I'm listening.'

'He's got no place else to start. But what's he prove? Nothing. The only thing is, we don't want to take any chances, right? You're going to finish that drink before I finish this corned beef. So why don't you do it and get out of here?'

Leo drank down the rest of his vodka and Seven-Up. He wanted another one, but Alan would say something and get nasty about it. He'd stop off someplace else, down the street, before going back to the studio.

'Okay, I see him again I'll let you know.'

'On the phone,' Alan said. 'Don't ever come to the theater or my place unless I tell you it's all right. Now get out of here.'

Leo paid his check at the bar, walked down past the stools into the dark front part of the place. He had his hand on the door to push it open, then moved forward quickly, off balance, as the door seemed to open by itself. He stopped to avoid bumping into the guy coming in – the *guy* – feeling the shock of suddenly seeing him, appearing out of nowhere.

Mitchell stepped back, holding the door open. He said, 'How you doing?'

'Man, I don't know,' Leo said, trying hard to smile. 'We keep running into each other, don't we?'

'I was just over at the studio. I thought I'd stop have a beer.'

'You get your money's worth?'

'It was pretty good. Mary Lou.'

'Yeah, well, I'll see you around,' Leo said.

Mitchell nodded, with a pleasant expression. 'You probably will.'

He stopped inside the door, at the pay phone, and called his office. When Janet came on he said, 'Any calls?' He listened to her say, slightly agitated, 'Any calls? That's all you've been getting are calls. All day yesterday and today.' Mitchell said, 'Give me the important ones, any customers,' and made a list of them in a pocket notebook as Janet dictated the names. 'Anybody else?' Nothing important, she told him. A man had called three times yesterday and twice this morning. She recognized his voice after the first time, but he wouldn't leave a name. Mitchell thanked her, said he'd see her later and hung up.

He walked from the dim front area, down the bar through pink spotlights, to a stool next to the service section with its rows of glasses and trays of olives and cherries and lemon twists. When the elderly bartender he had spoken to once before took his order, a draft beer, Mitchell half turned on the stool to watch a good-looking dark-haired girl finish her dance and come down among the tables, slipping a blouse on over her bare breasts. Most of the tables were empty. Lunchtime was past and only a few beer drinkers were left, scattered around, one guy eating a sandwich. The place was quiet. He turned to see Doreen come out of a door at the end of the bar, wearing slacks and knotting a white shirt to show off her dark slender midriff. Doreen didn't see him. He watched her go toward the tables and heard her say, 'Hey Alan, what happened to Leo?' Her words momentarily clear in the silence before the rock music started again, filling the place with sound, and now a thin blond girl was dancing.

There was the name – Leo – like a signal. And another name – Alan. The guy at the table eating the sandwich, the guy with thin shoulders and long hair – looking at his back, seeing Doreen standing by him, talking, then walking away, toward the front door.

He was aware of the feeling again, the tightening in his stomach that was a real feeling, unmistakable, telling him something, giving him something to think about. He waited perhaps a minute – until he realized he might miss his chance if he waited any longer. Mitchell picked up his beer and walked over to the table where the skinny guy with long hair was sitting.

'I understand you been trying to get hold of me.'

Alan was taking a bite of the corned beef sandwich. Chewing, his eyes raised and he said, 'What?'

Mitchell pulled out a chair and sat down, putting his beer on the table. 'I understand you called me three times yesterday and a couple of times this morning.'

'I did? What'd I call you?'

'You probably been wondering about the money – why I didn't deliver it.'

110

Alan took another bite of the sandwich. 'Man, this is weird. I'm having lunch, a guy I never saw before sits down says I called him.'

'You've seen me before,' Mitchell said.

'You sure of that?'

'Not a hundred percent,' Mitchell said, 'but I've got a strong reason to believe it. Put it that way.'

Alan's tongue sucked at his teeth. 'Okay, I give up. What's the game? Some kind of con?'

'The other way around,' Mitchell said. 'Only it isn't a con. You said it yourself one time on the phone. You said, "This is no con."'

'I got an idea,' Alan said. 'Why don't you get the fuck out of here? You don't, I'm going to call the management, tell them you're bothering me.'

'You don't want the money?'

'What money?'

'The ten grand. If I don't know the locker number how'm I supposed to deliver it?'

'Weird,' Alan said. 'No shit, you on something or what?'

'How about your accounting service,' Mitchell said. 'You still got that?'

Alan's expression was bland, but he was silent, hesitant, before he said, 'You mind if I leave you? Man, you're talking to yourself anyway.'

Mitchell watched him get up, reach into a tight pocket for a wad of crumpled bills and drop two of them on the table.

'You going home? Back to work?'

'I'm getting the fuck away from you, man, is where I'm going.' Alan walked off, toward the front door.

Mitchell said, 'Hey, where do you live? Case I want to talk to you again.'

Alan didn't answer or turn around. He walked down the length of the bar and out the door.

Mitchell sat at the table for a couple of minutes, finished the glass of beer and went over to the bar, where the bartender he had talked to once before was drying glasses.

'That guy just left,' Mitchell said. 'Alan something? You know his last name, what he does?'

'You know his first name you know more about him than I do,' the bartender said.

'How about Doreen? She coming back?'

The bartender, who had learned in forty years to do his job and mind his own business, said, 'Which one's Doreen?'

*

The printed card on the mailbox of 204 said D. MARTIN. Mitchell looked at the other names once more – passing the box that had been Cini's, where a man's name appeared now – and came back again to 204. D. Martin had to be Doreen. He pressed the button and waited in the narrow tiled foyer. Close to him, the voice from the wall speaker said, 'Hey, love. Get up here.' With the loud buzzing sound he pressed the thumb latch and the door opened. She was careful about her name on the mailbox, but she let him in without asking who it was.

He found out why as she opened the apartment door and he saw the look of surprise on her face.

'Hey, I thought you were somebody else. Four o'clock this dude's supposed to be here.'

'Well,' Mitchell said, 'that gives us ten minutes anyway.'

'You serious?' She moved aside to let him into the atmosphere of dim lights, Aretha Franklin in the background, incense burning on the coffee table and Doreen in billowy orange pants and a tight white blouse open to the waist.

'He's always late anyway,' Doreen said. 'You probably got twenty-five minutes, and if you're anxious, love, you won't need that much. You want a drink?'

'I guess so. Bourbon?'

'Anything you want. Rocks?'

'And a splash of water.'

She went through a door into the kitchen. Mitchell sat down on the couch and lighted a cigarette. He heard her say, 'How come we didn't make it the other day? You act like you're all ready, you leave.'

He didn't answer, but waited until she was in the room again, handing him the drink.

'Leo was a little mad I took that picture.'

'Man's got hemorrhoids or something. He always acts uncomfortable.' She sat down on the couch, moving slightly with the blues beat of the music.

112

Mitchell took a sip of the drink. 'Who was that guy he was with in the bar today, the skinny guy?'

'You were there? I didn't see you.'

'At the bar. Leo left, you asked him where Leo was.'

'You mean Alan?'

'Yeah, Alan. I met him before. What's his name?'

'Alan Raimy.'

'That's it. Raimy. What's he, a good friend of Leo's?'

'I guess he's a friend.'

'You know where I can get hold of him?'

'Now we're getting to it,' Doreen said. 'Aren't we? You're not making conversation, you want to know something.'

'Where I can find him, that's all.'

She was thoughtful, off somewhere in her mind or listening to the music, then looked abruptly at Mitchell again. 'You weren't taking that picture of me, were you? You were shooting Leo.'

'He happened to be there, that's all.'

'Come on – I don't think you're a cop,' Doreen said. 'Cini would've found out and told me. But, man, you're up to *some-thing*.'

'Where's he live? I won't tell him how I found out.'

'Ask Leo, you so anxious.'

'I did. He said he didn't know.'

'If he's got no reason to tell you,' Doreen said, 'that's reason enough for me. I may like you, so far. But that doesn't mean I know you, or want to know you or what you're doing.'

'Does he live around here?'

'I don't know.'

'Where does he work?'

'For some reason,' Doreen said, 'I don't seem to be getting through to you.'

'No, it's my fault,' Mitchell said. 'I forgot you're a business-woman.' He took the number 10 manila envelope out of his coat pocket, opened it and laid a one-hundred-dollar bill on the coffee table.

Doreen looked at it, unimpressed. 'I make that in five minutes, sport, with the shoe clerks.'

'All right, you said something about twenty-five minutes.' Mitchell pulled out four more one-hundred-dollar bills and laid them on the table. 'Twenty-five minutes' worth and you don't even have to move your tail. Where do I find him?'

'How much more you got in there, love?'

'That's it. All we got time for.'

She looked at the five one-hundred-dollar bills and was thoughtful again. 'I'll ask you a question,' she said finally. 'Nobody can say I told you anything about him. I'm only asking you a question, you dig?'

He watched her, deciding to let her do it her own way, and nodded. 'Go ahead.'

Doreen's nice brown eyes raised to Mitchell again as she said, 'Do you like dirty movies, love?'

*

Mitchell decided one hard-core porno would last him a long time. Barbara said she couldn't believe it. She would say, 'My God!' in a startled whisper and nudge Mitchell's arm with her elbow. She nudged him all the way through *Going Down on the Farm* until, at the end, the ratty-looking guy and the girl with stringy hair kissed. After all they had done to each other on the screen for the past sixty minutes, in positions Mitchell had never heard of or ever imagined, they kissed in the Duck Head bib overalls, wearing nothing underneath, and walked out of the barn toward a pickup truck. The main feature was over and the house lights came on. Mitchell reached over for his wife's hand.

'We'll wait a few minutes.'

Barbara sat unmoving now. 'I don't believe it.'

'You said that.'

'My God, we've led a sheltered life.'

'As they say, whatever turns you on.' He let his gaze move to the sides, turning his head slightly to see the rows emptying, but didn't look all the way around.

'Did you see anything,' Barbara said, 'that – interested you?'

'Well, I don't know. There're a couple numbers we could look into.'

'You know, they didn't kiss at all, until the very end.'

'I guess their mouths weren't ever close enough.'

'Where do they get the actors?'

A light, somewhere behind them, went off. Then it came on again and Mitchell heard the familiar voice.

'Okay, mom and dad, the show's over. Time to go home.'

A silence followed. He was waiting or had walked away. Mitchell didn't look around. He said to his wife, 'Not yet.'

'Mitch, now I'm scared.'

'He can't hurt us,' Mitchell said.

In that moment he hoped he was wrong about Alan. Because Barbara was here and it would be easier if he was wrong. But he still had the gut feeling and he knew – no, he wasn't certain yet, though he would bet on it – that Alan was one of them. And if he was, then face the next fact. Alan was capable of killing. He could have a gun. Under his coat, in his office, somewhere. So if Alan was one of them he would have to first get Barbara out of the way, then approach him carefully. Hold back and be nice. Don't do anything dumb. He wished Barbara didn't have to be here. But he had to *know* about Alan – not simply feel it – and there wasn't any other way to do it. Barbara was the only one who could identify him.

He said to her, 'All right, let's go.'

They took their time walking up the aisle, Mitchell with his hand on her arm. The theater was empty now. As they came out of the aisle he saw Alan in the lobby, watching the last few patrons straggling out.

'I can't see his face,' Barbara said.

They saw him reach over to flick a wall switch and the lights on the marquee, outside the theater, went off. On the wall next to him was a poster in a glass cabinet advertising a coming attraction. *The Gay Blades*. A color drawing of several young men who appeared to be wearing only jockstraps and were holding swords in the air. Mitchell hadn't noticed the poster coming up. Guys with jockstraps and swords. He saw Alan turn, take a few steps his way, look up and instantly stop.

Barbara stared at him. Quietly, she said, 'He's the one.'

'Go to the car,' Mitchell said. 'Wait for me there.' When she hesitated, he said, 'Barbara, please get out of here.'

He walked with her, stopping when he was even with Alan, a few feet away. Barbara kept going and Alan's gaze followed her as she went out through the glass door. When he turned back to look at Mitchell, he said, 'I've seen you someplace. Hey yeah, you're the weird guy in the bar this afternoon.'

'That was the third time,' Mitchell said.

'Third time what?'

115

'Do you want to play let's pretend,' Mitchell said then, 'and go through a lot of bullshit or do you want me to give you the money?'

Alan hesitated. 'What money?'

'You asked for ten thousand dollars, delivered today.'

'I did?'

Mitchell, starting past him, got about four steps.

'Now wait up,' Alan said. 'Tell me this again about the ten grand.'

Mitchell shook his head. 'I must have the wrong guy.'

'Why do you think I'm the one?' Alan saw Mitchell turn again to walk off. 'Now wait a minute!' Quietly then, he said, 'Who told you where to find me? Leo?'

'I spoke to him,' Mitchell said. 'He wouldn't take the money. So I came here. Now do you want it or not?'

'You want to give it to me, that's fine.'

'Have I got the right guy?'

'You seem pretty sure.'

'I want to hear it from you,' Mitchell said.

Alan nodded past Mitchell. 'There's a guy in the office right there. Another guy up in the projection room – if you think you're going to pull something. I'll tell you something else. I've got a gun on me.'

Mitchell took the envelope out of his pocket and held it out in his left hand. 'Is this for you or isn't it?'

'I said if you want to, give it to me, if you're sure.'

'And I want to hear you say it.'

'All right, for Christ sake, yeah! I'm the guy, now gimme it!'

Mitchell gave him his right balled into a fist, went in after him and hit him again, hard, with the same right hand. Alan shattered the glass showcase as his back slammed against it, tried to roll away, screaming, and stumbled to his hands and knees. Mitchell stood over him, waiting.

'You touch me again, honest to God—' Alan spit blood, his head hunched between his shoulders. 'I'll scream loud enough to bring somebody quick, I swear it!'

'You already have,' Mitchell said. 'I think everybody's gone home.'

'There's a cop always outside when we close. You touch me, honest to Christ, I'll yell loud enough to get him.'

Mitchell stooped slowly to a squatting position next to Alan. He said, 'We don't need cops. What do you want to call the cops for?'

'You touch me—' Alan's hair hung in his face. He reminded Mitchell of an animal that had been beaten and was terrified.

'I'm not going to touch you. I want to talk to you.'

'You cut my mouth up. Christ.'

'I got carried away,' Mitchell said. 'There's something about you makes me want to kick your fucking face in, but I'm all right now. All I want to do is talk to you. Show you something. That's all.'

'What?'

'Am I talking to the right guy? I mean are you in charge? I don't want to waste my time otherwise.'

He waited, then heard Alan say, 'You're pulling some kind of shit. You go to the cops you're the one gets nailed.'

Mitchell shook his head. 'What do you keep talking about cops for? Do I look stupid? I don't want any cops in this. But I don't like dealing with more than one person either. I can talk to one person and reach an understanding. But you get a crowd involved – and three's a crowd, buddy – then I'm never sure if they all agree with each other. You follow me?'

'You want to talk,' Alan said, 'so say something.'

'I want to talk to you, but I have to show you something too. I have to show you facts and figures.'

'What facts and figures?'

'Can you read a balance sheet?'

'Come on, say it.'

'Look,' Mitchell said, 'I know I have to make a deal with you. I don't want to blow everything I've got, go to prison for life. But I can't give you what you're asking, because I can't give you something I haven't got. You come to my office at the plant tomorrow night, eleven-thirty, after the second shift, I'll show you my books, my investments, trust funds. I'll show you where my dough is and exactly how much I can pay you. You're the one's been doing the talking – I mean if you're the one – you know about capital-gains tax, things like that, then I think you'll understand it and, hopefully, take a more realistic approach. You understand? But you got to come alone or there's no deal. Maybe you decide no, you'd rather call the cops on me.

I'll have to take that chance. But I promise you this, there's no deal unless you and I sit down together and talk it over. If we don't then you get nothing for your trouble.'

Alan looked up at him. 'I could be walking into something.'

'Buddy, you could also be dying right now. Tomorrow night, eleven-thirty.' Mitchell rose, putting the envelope back in his pocket.

'The ten grand,' Alan said. He got up on his knees and held out his hand.

'No,' Mitchell said, 'you're pretty convincing, but I'm still not sure I've got the right guy.'

Alan watched him walk out. Son of a bitch, pulling something; he was sure of it. He saw the car at the curb – the bronze Grand Prix, and – yes, you bet your ass it was – his wife standing by the car. Old Slim. Slim legs and reasonably large knockers. A very nice combination. Alan walked outside – shit, the guy wasn't going to do anything to him now – and got a good look at her as she got in the car, not noticing him, but showing him some thigh. Jesus, her legs were something. Little muscle line down the outside of the calf. Thin strong legs. Good squeezing legs, get the scissors around you.

As the Grand Prix pulled away, taillights growing smaller in the darkness, he was thinking, That could be looked into again. There could be a part for Slim in this somewhere.

14

Alan said, 'Are you listening to me? If you're busy I can wait, man, if you're busy. I don't want to interrupt you or anything.'

Bobby Shy was listening. He could blow coke and not miss a word; there wasn't any trick to that. He was dipping into the Baggy again with his Little Orphan Annie spoon – little chick with no eyes or tits but she was good to hold onto and bring up to your nose, yeeeeeees, one then another, ten dollars worth of fine blow while Alan was talking out of his cut mouth, telling about the man coming to see him.

They were in Doreen's apartment because when Alan called he said he wanted to meet there. Alan, Bobby and Leo. It was one-thirty in the afternoon. Doreen was in the bedroom asleep.

Bobby had to grin at Alan's cut-up puffed-up mouth. Man had hit him good. That shit, are you listening to me? Talking but trying not to move his mouth. Like the mouth wasn't there. Like the man hadn't hit him. The man had looked easy, but the man didn't fuck around, did he? Bobby sat at one end of the couch, his feet in black socks on the coffee table. Leo sat at the other end of the long flowery couch, but Bobby could still smell that cheap shit he wore. Alan was standing, moving around some, shoulders hunched up, fingers in his tight little front pockets, looking at him.

Bobby tossed the Baggy over to the coffee table. He better save a blow for Doreen when she woke up, else she'd kill him. He said, 'I hear you. I'm sitting right here, ain't I?'

'It's important we clear this up first,' Alan said. 'The guy didn't happen to be there. Somebody told him where to find me.'

Leo was sitting forward on the deep cushion, ready. 'I didn't tell him *anything*. I didn't even tell him your name, for Christ sake, anything.'

Alan kept his eyes on Bobby Shy. 'Leo says he didn't tell him.'

'Man, I heard him ten times now. I believe him just so he quit saying it.'

'All right,' Alan said. 'If Leo didn't tell him that leaves only one person.'

'Hey, me? I talked to the back of the man's head a couple times, that's all.'

'I'm not talking about you,' Alan said.

'Well, they only three of us.'

Alan shook his head. 'Doreen. If it's not Leo told him then it's Doreen. She was in the bar right before he came up to me.'

Bobby thought about it. 'Unh-unh. She wouldn't tell him.'

'How do you know?'

'Because we friends,' Bobby said. 'She know I found out I'd throw her off the roof.'

'Let's talk to her.'

'No need to.'

'I want to be sure,' Alan said.

'Hey, look. I'll talk to her after a while,' Bobby Shy said. 'You understand what I'm saying? I'll ask her about it and I'll let you know.'

'Long as you do it,' Alan said. Get the last word in and let it go. Black sleepy-eyed son of a bitch had to be handled with gloves. Don't disturb whatever was going on inside that fuzzy coked-up head. Leo was just as bad in his own way. Hold his hand or he'd fuck up. Jesus, what he had were a couple of beauties. A fat-ass juice head who was liable to melt with a little heat and a bad-ass spade gunslinger who blew fifty bucks a day on his highs. Jesus, the way the guy was turning out, these two were no help at all. The guy was coming on strong all of a sudden, different than the kind of straight-A stiff he had looked like at first.

'So, as I mentioned,' Alan said, 'the guy tells me he wants to talk about his financial situation. That's all he says. Except I got to come alone. Why?'

'That's the question,' Bobby Shy said. 'Now what's the answer?'

'Right away, I think he's pulling some kind of shit. Like the cops are there, waiting in the bushes. I walk in, he makes a payoff and they hit me. But then I think, why just me? If the cops are on it they'd want all of us. Right?'

'Or,' Bobby said, 'they take you, figure you'll tell them about the rest.'

'Come on,' Alan said. 'It's easier to hit all three. It's done. We're standing there holding the fucking money.'

'Doesn't answer the question, does it?' Bobby Shy said. 'Why he wants you to come alone.'

'I think we only got one way to find out,' Alan said. 'I go see the guy.'

Bobby Shy's gaze stayed on him. 'You and him don't happen to have something going, do you?'

'You want to go instead of me?' Alan stared back at him. 'I don't care, man. You go, find out what he wants. Then it's your ass if he's pulling shit, man, not mine.' Alan waited. That ought to be enough. He didn't want to overdo it.

Bobby Shy grinned out of the deep flowery cushion of the couch. It was a lovely high he could feel all over him with everything clear and cool and not to be wasted hassling this skinny puff-mouth little dude with the hair. He said, 'Hey, be nice. You go see the man, tell me what he says. I believe you. Why shouldn't I believe you? We all in this.'

Leo Frank said, 'Ask him who told you. Ask him if it was me. You'll find out.'

Alan gave them each a little more time. No hurry. No need to talk anymore. Okay, wrap it up. 'All right,' he said. 'Meet at my place tomorrow. Same time.' He started for the door, then turned and looked at Bobby again.

'That tour bus stick-up. I finally figured who the cat was.'

Bobby Shy's eyes were half closed. 'Is that right?'

'Paper said you got over four thousand.'

'Shit.'

'You're a regular fucking cowboy, aren't you?'

'I thought you'd like it.'

'I don't know,' Alan said. 'Kind of dumb, but stylish.'

'You trying to tell me something?'

Alan winked at him. 'I'm saying I know you did it, man, that's all.'

*

Bobby Shy sat on the edge of the double bed looking down at Doreen: soft brown face a little puffy with sleep, the long black eyelashes she stuck on one at a time closed over her eyes. Sweet girl breathing quietly, her face raised, her naked body forming a half twist beneath the sheet, giving him the firm curve of her hip against the thigh.

He said quietly, 'Doreen?'

He said her name again and this time gently squeezed her bare shoulder. 'Hey, baby, come on. Time to get up, cook me something.' His hand moved from her shoulder to the pillow next to her, pulled it across her body and laid it on his lap. The movement opened her eyes. They stared at him calmly, moved to look at the square of daylight on the window shade and came back to his face again.

'What time is it?'

'About three.'

'Seven o'clock this morning, man wants to start all over. I say hey, get your ass out, baby, go to work. He say, real surprised, "I'll pay you." '

'What man was that?'

'Seven in the morning. I tell him, baby, I don't even do it for fun seven in the morning.'

'His name Mitchell? Was a friend of Cini's?'

Doreen didn't move; she kept her eyes on Bobby Shy's face and after a moment, said, 'No, it wasn't him. Somebody else.'

'Was he here yesterday?'

'Who?'

'Man name Mitchell.'

'Yesterday. Yeah – about four. I told him I was expecting somebody.'

'What else you tell him?'

'I told him to come back sometime.'

'What else?'

'What do I know I can tell him? I don't *know* anything.'

Bobby Shy raised the pillow. He saw her eyes briefly before he dropped the pillow over her face and pressed down on it with his hands spread open, his arms rigid. He turned his head to the side as she clawed at him and kicked and her body thrashed beneath the sheet.

When he lifted the pillow he saw her eyes again, like they'd been open all the time. She gasped and said almost immediately, 'I don't *know* anything to tell him!'

'You know me,' Bobby Shy said. 'You know people I know.'

She was rigid, afraid to move; afraid to say the wrong thing.

'He ask you any questions?'

'He was only here five minutes. I ask him he want a drink, he say yes, I give him one.'

'He come to buy or talk?'

'I told him I was busy, he finish the drink and left.'

'You don't answer none of my questions,' Bobby Shy said. He raised the pillow again and had to force it down over her face, fight through her hands trying to push it away. He saw her eyes again and could put himself in her place and know what she was seeing. Then he was looking down at the pillow, feeling her body twisting against him, her legs coming up and straightening and coming up again. He saw, close to him, her underarm and a trace of powder and fine little black dots in the deep hollow. She was thin and wiry, tough little hundred-pound chick would fight as long as she could stay alive and probably keep moving after she was past it. Her legs straightened again and stiffened. Her arm, raised, close to his face, seemed to go limp and come down slowly, outstretched.

Bobby Shy lifted the pillow to see her eyes still open. They looked dreamy. She breathed in air and let it out and began to take short little quick breaths like she'd been running. Her eyes stared at him with the dull dreamy look, something gone out of them. Sweet girl going to sleep, too tired to speak.

Bobby Shy said, 'One more time. You tell him where I or anybody I know works or lives?'

Doreen's head moved on the pillow, just a little, from side to side. 'I didn't. Please—'

'Hey, you feel all right?'

'Believe me? Please, I didn't tell him nothing.'

'I believe you,' Bobby Shy said. 'I believe everybody.'

'I told him I was busy. That's all I said to him.'

Bobby Shy leaned down and kissed her on the cheek. 'Baby, why don't you sleep some more? You going to sleep, hey, keep telling yourself, I ain't ever going to talk to that man again. I ain't ever going to look at him. He come here, shit, I slam the door in his face. Hey, Doreen?' Bobby Shy said, 'Do that, everything will be lovely.'

*

Alan drove Leo's white T-bird out to Ranco Manufacturing. His own car, a yellow Datsun 240Z, had been gone almost two months. Stolen. Parked in front of the movie theater not ten minutes in the no-parking zone while he ran in to check receipts on his day off and the car was gone when he came out. He called the police every day for three or four weeks, reminding them it was a yellow Datsun 240Z, for Christ sake, with an eight-track Panasonic outfit, wire wheels and Michelin X radials – asking them how many yellow Datsun 240Z's did they think there were in Detroit or northern Ohio or Indiana or wherever cars went to get sold or dumped. They told him, each time, don't worry, it would turn up. Of course it would probably be stripped of the eight-track Panasonic outfit, the wire wheels and the Michelin X radials, and would probably need some bodywork, but it would turn up. The pricks. Alan stopped calling the police right after he found out about Harry Mitchell of Ranco Manufacturing and looked him up, checked him out, got his D and B and everything but a urine specimen and knew he was the guy to hit. The one he and Leo had been waiting for.

Alan parked the T-bird across the street from the plant, a half block away, and watched as the line of headlights, the second-shift employees, came out the drive from the parking lot behind the place and turned into the street. Some of the cars came out and made a little jog over to the Pine Top Bar. Alan could see the green neon sign in his rearview mirror, a couple hundred feet behind him. He waited until the driveway cleared, then waited another fifteen minutes to be sure. He didn't like it at all.

He would have to watch what he said, in case Mitchell's office was bugged. He would accept no money tonight, even if he was offered the whole load, in case the cops were waiting in the next room or in the goddamn closet. What could they get him for?

Murder? What murder? What girl?

Answer: Yeah, I know a few girls worked there. Big turn-over; they leave, you never see them again.

He had been out to Mitchell's house, hadn't he?

Answer: Yeah, I was there once. I explained it to his wife. I'm starting up a personalized accounting service for households, people who spend a few thousand a month and don't like to bother with bills and bank statements. That's my background, accounting.

Quick thinking wins again. He almost told Mitchell's wife he was a real estate salesman. This was much better. He could point to his background, and hope they didn't look into it too closely.

All right. Mitchell had asked him to come out and look at his books. Almost his exact words. That's all he knew and that's why he was here.

What else?

He couldn't think of anything else, of any way they could nail him and make it stick. But he still didn't like it.

*

The Thunderbird made a lazy circle through the empty parking lot, crept toward the plant and came to a stop not far from Mitchell's Grand Prix. There was a silence before the car door slammed.

Mitchell stood in the light that came from above the rear

door. When he saw the figure coming toward him, he pulled the door open and held it.

'Mr. Mitchell?'

Mitchell didn't say anything.

'Mr. Mitchell?' Alan walked up to him, taking his time. 'I understand you'd like me to look at your books.'

'There's nobody here,' Mitchell said. He went in first, letting Alan catch the door and follow.

'My, you got some machinery, haven't you? What is it exactly you make, Mr. Mitchell?'

Alan grinned, beginning to relax, looking around as he followed Mitchell through the plant and along the hallway to the front offices, past clean metal desks and filing cabinets in bright fluorescent light into Mitchell's office. Mitchell closed the door and nodded toward his desk.

'There. That represents everything I owe or own, my net worth as of right now. Help yourself.'

Alan walked around the desk, looking down at the forms, ledgers and bankbooks. 'What is it you want me to do, see if everything's in order?'

'I told you there's nobody here,' Mitchell said. 'There's no hidden recording device of any kind. You can look if you want.'

Alan sat down at the seven-foot glass-top desk. It was easier not to say anything than to nose around looking for a bug. He began studying the titles on the forms and statements.

Mitchell stood across from him. 'If you know what you're doing, it'll take you three or four hours to go through all this. If you don't know what you're doing it could take you forever and you still wouldn't know.'

Alan grinned up at him, 'Don't worry about me, Mr. Mitchell. I bet I can read this quicker than your own accountant.'

'I had a feeling you could,' Mitchell said. 'You took Biz Ad in college and what happened?'

'I found there's more to be made in the film business,' Alan said pleasantly. 'But I like to keep my hand in accounting, so to speak.'

'In other people's accounting.'

'Yes sir, pick up a little extra here and there.'

'You going to go through everything?'

'I'll look enough to get the feel of it anyway.'

'The government takes sixty-five percent of my salary.'

'I see that.'

'We live on the rest. The balance of my royalty each year has been going into municipals and other long-term investments. Past royalty income is in trust funds and neither can be touched. You understand?'

'Yes sir. Like so many people who make a lot of money, you don't seem to have any.'

'That sheet in front of you, it itemizes everything, adds, subtracts and comes up with a figure. You see it?'

Alan nodded. 'Fifty-two thousand.'

'That's what I can put my hands on right now,' Mitchell said. 'Not a dime more than that before next April.'

'That's when your fiscal year ends?'

'When we pledge our allegiance to the I.R.S.'

'What about next year?' Alan said. 'Same amount, uh? Unless you can convert some of these other stocks.'

'I'm not worried about next year,' Mitchell said. 'There's something about your life-style tells me you probably won't be around. I'm thinking only of the present, and I'm thinking of my family. I've worked hard to leave them something and I intend to do it without selling my company or house or changing my way of life. So I'll deal with you right now, at a figure you'll see is the going rate. Fifty-two thousand dollars. If you insist on more, then I won't pay you anything. If you go through with your threat to inform the police, then I'll tell them everything I know and you'll be up to your neck in it. I think I'd have a fairly good chance of beating the charge. Even better than you'd have. But I don't want to take that chance. Mainly because of what it would do to my family.' Mitchell paused. 'So do you want fifty-two thousand dollars or a lot of trouble and a reasonably good chance of going to jail?'

Alan looked at Mitchell but didn't say anything.

Mitchell waited. He said then, 'How you split it is up to you. A hundred and five cut three ways is thirty-five thousand each. Fifty-two split is seventeen-three . . . if you split it in thirds, but that's up to you.' He waited again.

'Look at it this way. Whatever you get is better than nothing. I might have shown you a debit balance with all kinds of liens against me, including the I.R.S. You see what I mean? You threaten me with a murder conviction and jail, and all the while the government could have had first crack at me.'

'You never know,' Alan said, 'do you? Life is full of surprises.' He was thoughtful again. 'How long would it take you to get your hands on the fifty-two?'

'Five days. Something like that.'

'Well, let's take a look at it.'

'You want to come here?'

'Maybe. I'll let you know.'

'One other thing,' Mitchell said. 'Keep your buddies out of it. Pay them what you want, but I'm only dealing with you. Otherwise it's off.'

'It's all right with me.' Alan thought a moment and then got up from the desk. 'Answer me something. Who was it told you where to find me?'

Mitchell gave him a surprised look. 'Your friend Leo. Who'd you think?'

He watched the car drive out of the parking lot, then walked back through the plant to his office, sat down at the desk and wrote himself a note.

Call O'Boyle in the morning. See what his friend can find out about Alan Raimy and Leo Frank.

And went straight home.

15

'I don't know,' Leo Frank said, 'deal looks clean and simple, then all of a sudden it gets complicated. There must be something. I mean the guy's got *some* dough, hasn't he?'

Bobby Shy looked over at Alan. Those two were talking. Bobby sat on a pillow with his back leaning against the wall. He was uncomfortable but he was listening, getting it clear in his mind. There was a funny sound in the talk: somebody jiving somebody.

Alan was over by the window that had a tree painted on the shade, a brown heavy line for the trunk and a green circle for the leaves. Alan was home. He was smoking a joint, exhaling with barely a trace of anything coming out of his mouth.

He said, 'The man has money. I told you he had money. He can get his hands on more money when he cashes in his stocks and bonds and shit. But the government has got him by the balls. He owes them over a hundred and fifty grand on his income tax the last two years and he's got to pay up. If he doesn't, they make him sell his house, his business, everything.'

Leo said, 'Then why did he have money the other day, in the envelope?'

'Because he had to hold us off,' Alan said. 'He was afraid we might jump and call the cops on him. So he let us smell the dough figuring we wouldn't do anything right away. That gives him time to set up the meeting.'

'I don't know,' Leo Frank said.

'I know you don't,' Alan said. 'Jesus, I'm glad he talked to me and not to you. He might be a fuck-up in business, but he had that much sense.'

No, Bobby Shy was thinking, something is not right. He didn't like the sound of the talk. He didn't like being here in Alan's apartment. The place looked bare, like he'd just moved in and hadn't put anything where it belonged; and yet it was full of all kinds of weird shit on the walls, on the floor, even hanging from the ceiling. There were psycho designs and names and words in bright aerosol paint sprayed all over the white walls and on the shades – like the men's room of a jive joint or a New York subway station. Man had gooseneck lamps you could twist around in every direction, blacklights and colored mood lights in white globes, Indian bells and shit, birds and mobile shapes hanging down, balls on aluminum sticks that hit against each other, rugs that looked like they were made out of animal hair, pillows from India laying around, a couple of straw chairs and all these big red and green and purple and yellow pillows. Like they'd turn the men's room in the jive joint into a turkish whorehouse.

'I mean,' Leo said, 'if a guy makes that kind of dough, how come he doesn't have any left to pay the government?'

'He invested it. Look,' Alan said, 'he's supposed to pay the government quarterly, every three months. If he doesn't he has to pay a penalty at the end of the year, like six percent. But he figures he can put the dough to work and make more than six percent on it. So he invests. Only the stock he invests in goes down. A business he puts dough in folds. So he's not only lost the money he invested, he still owes the fucking government the income tax he didn't pay.'

Leo was nodding, trying to understand it. 'Don't they give him time to pay?'

'They call him in,' Alan explained, ready for that one. 'He talks to a clerk in the Internal Revenue office. He says look, I'll pay. Give me some time. The clerk looks over the guy's tax return. Shit, he sees the guy spends more on booze than he makes in a year and he throws the fucking book at the guy. Pay up, right now.'

Leo said, 'You know this for sure?'

'No, I'm making it up,' Alan said. 'Leo, I saw the correspondence with the Internal Revenue office, their stationery, Department of Internal Revenue across the top. I saw his books, I saw his bank balance. The guy gives us five bucks and they want to know where it went.'

Alan squeezed the joint between his fingernails and got a last suck out of it before he dropped the burned brown stub in an ashtray. He said, 'If you want to know something, I'll tell you. I had a gut feeling the guy was too perfect. We wait for somebody like him like a guy waiting for the most beautiful chick in the world. She comes along, man, there she is. But it turns out her fucking breath smells or something.'

'Jesus, all the time we put in it,' Leo said. 'And the girl—'

'That brings us to something else,' Alan said. 'The girl. This part I don't like, what we have to do.' He looked directly at Leo Frank. 'You know why?'

Leo had a puzzled look. 'I don't even know what you're talking about.'

'Leo, I asked him. He said it was you told him where to find me.'

'I didn't! I never even gave him your last name!'

'Leo, I ask him. I said hey, who told you where I work? He says who do you think? Your friend Leo. His exact words.'

'Honest to Christ, I *didn't*.'

'Leo,' Alan said, 'the show's over, or almost over. I don't give a shit really, it's done. You let me down. Okay, live and learn.'

Bobby was still watching Alan, wondering why Alan hadn't mentioned this before, first thing when they came in. He was wondering also why Alan was so cool about it. Alan should be stomping Leo with words, cutting him up; but he was passing it over like it didn't matter. Live and learn – shit.

'But,' Alan was saying, 'we do have a problem. Somebody got killed. He saw it. At the time he didn't know about us, but now he does.'

Bobby Shy spoke for the first time. He said, 'He knows about you two. He don't know about me.'

Alan looked at him. 'That's right. That's why you're going to have to do it. You can walk up to him, shake hands and blow him away. Man won't even know what hit him.'

'For what?' Bobby Shy said. 'What do I get out of it?'

'Peace of mind,' Alan said.

'I look nervous to you?'

'All right,' Alan said. 'You want to take a chance? He knows she's dead, right? He knows three of us did it. Not just me and Leo, also a spade wears a stocking over his face and packs a thirty-eight Special. Bobby, you been to Jackson. I believe you lived there ten years, robbery armed? You really want to take a chance? His conscience gets to him, he goes to the police and they start ripping the fucking walls out looking for us. Hey Bobby, you want that to happen?'

Bobby Shy grinned. 'Listen to the man. Wants me to clean up his mess.'

'I thought you were the pro,' Alan said. 'One likes to pull the trigger.'

'Giving me some sweet jive now.'

'Shit, you walk up, ring his bell, he opens the door, it's done.'

'That's how you do it, huh?'

'Why not?'

Bobby Shy nodded. 'Maybe. Do it in the man's house. Make it look like a B and E.'

Alan was grinning now. 'Hey, possibilities, right? You like it?'

'I'll think on it,' Bobby Shy said.

Alan had him; he could feel it. He said, 'While you're thinking I'll do a time-and-motion study on the man and I'll let you know when. In fact, you want, I'll go with you.'

'Hold my hand?' Bobby Shy said. 'I appreciate it.'

'We just have to stick together,' Alan said, and looked over at Leo to include him. 'I mean we start something, we have to finish it. Then – we got time, we got nothing else to do – we look for another guy. Why not?'

He got them out of there and sat down on a pillow to smoke another joint and relax. Jesus, all that footwork took it out of you. Slipping and sliding around, juking the spade and fat Leo right out of their socks. Shit, right out of their shares. But the guy could still be pulling something and Alan decided he'd better think on that a while.

The funny thing was he started thinking about the guy's wife again. At home, in the living room standing there mad with her legs a little apart. Getting in the car in front of the show, giving him the show, her legs apart again, nice glimpse of some inside thigh. He said to himself, Now come on, there's a role in this piece for Slim. How about it? He sucked on the joint and pictured her at home, alone again, and started to put something together.

*

They went out the door of the apartment building and walked around the corner toward Leo's car. Leo expected Bobby Shy to say something, say it and then maybe hit him. He never knew what Bobby Shy was going to do. He always felt uneasy when he was with him – quiet, easy-moving black dude could have a gun on him right now.

Leo said, 'You going home or where? I'll drop you.'

'I think over Doreen's,' Bobby Shy said. 'I got half my clothes there now. I don't know *where* I live.'

He sounded calm. He didn't sound on the muscle at all. Leo said, 'Listen, I'm telling you the truth. I didn't tell the guy where to find Alan.'

'What difference does it make?' Bobby Shy didn't bother to look at him.

'It makes a difference. Alan's trying to blame me,' Leo said, getting a little excited about it now. 'If the guy told Alan it was me, then the guy's lying.'

'Yeah, okay.' Bobby Shy didn't see the point yet.

'And if the guy lied about me – for some reason, I don't know why he would – then he could be lying about not having any dough.'

'Alan believe him. He see the books.'

'Let's say Alan also believes I told on him.'

Bobby Shy still didn't look at Leo, but he began to put it together in his head. 'You saying Alan is dumb to believe the man?'

'I'm not saying that. We know Alan isn't dumb. He's got a weird fucking mind, but he isn't dumb.'

'We finding out maybe the man ain't so dumb either,' Bobby Shy said. 'So what you trying to say?'

'I'm saying either Alan's lying or the man is.'

Bobby Shy walked on a few paces, thinking about it, before he said, 'Or both of them.'

'Or both,' Leo said. 'I thought of that.'

'It's a shame, ain't it?' Bobby said. 'Everybody trying to mess up everybody.'

'We picked the wrong guy,' Leo Frank said. 'That's the whole thing. We picked the wrong fucking guy.'

*

It took Bobby Shy the rest of the day to locate a whole lid of Colombian reefer. It was Doreen's favorite. He brought it to her and said he was sorry he doubted her word. No, he hadn't doubted her really, it was only he had to be sure. It turns out, he told Doreen, it was Leo told the man. Because that's what the man told Alan, and why would the man lie about it?

Doreen looked up at him with the eyes, sitting on the edge of the flowery couch, rolling two professional joints, and said, 'You never know who you can trust, do you?'

'Deal we been working fell through,' Bobby Shy told her.

And Doreen said, handing him a lighted joint, 'I admire you, love, but please don't tell me about it. They some things I don't want to know.'

'Man was going to pay us a hundred and five grand so we don't tell stories on him,' Bobby went on. 'But Alan talk to the man, he say he find out the man don't have any money. Owe it all to Uncle Sam.'

'Alan told you that, huh?'

'He's the only one talk to him.'

'You believe it?'

'That's where we're at,' Bobby Shy said.

'Well, you could talk to Alan again, put a pillow over his face.

'Yeah, I could do that.'

'Or,' Doreen said, 'you could go see the man.'

'I could do that too.'

'Ask him, how come if he's broke he's carrying all that money around in an envelope.'

Bobby Shy held the reefer, about to take a drag. 'You see that envelope of his?'

'He took it out of his pocket and put it back,' Doreen said. 'It was thick.'

'Leo say they ten grand in it.'

Doreen nodded. 'I believe it.'

'What I want to know,' Bobby Shy said, 'why he showed it to you.'

Doreen drew in on the joint. It calmed her and gave her confidence. She said, 'He mentioned something about he wanted to give it to Alan. I forgot to tell you that the time you ask me.'

'You forgot to tell me.'

'He just mentioned wanting to see Alan. It didn't seem like any big thing.'

'He showed you the money?'

'Little bit of it.'

'And he gave you some?'

'He took it out, peeled off a hundred. That's when I told him I was busy.'

'That's all, huh? You didn't tell him anything about Alan. Where he lives or works—'

'Hey, Bobby,' Doreen said. 'What're you worried about Alan for? He tell you the deal's off – he's not worried about you, is he?'

'That's a point,' Bobby said.

'Alan saw the man's money? In the envelope?'

'I believe he did.'

'And he's just going to forget about it?'

'That's another point.'

'Something's going on, baby, Alan hasn't told you about.'

'As I said a minute ago, that's where we're at.'

'And as I mentioned,' Doreen said, 'you could go see the man. Find out if he's still got his envelope laying around someplace? You understand what I'm saying?'

Bobby Shy nodded. 'Could do that.'

'Like at night. Late.'

'After everybody's asleep.'

'Man, that little envelope,' Doreen said. 'It holds more than a whole bus full of people, don't it?'

*

They were back where they had been for twenty-two years, and it was even better than it had been for a long time. He wanted to be with her. He felt good with her. There was nothing to hide now, no excuses that had to be made.

It was Sunday, sixty degrees and a clear sky, and they decided not to think of anything or anybody but themselves today. They played three sets of tennis outside, at a high school court near their house. It was a little windy, but it didn't matter. It was good to be out, together. They played hard and perspired, Mitchell more than Barbara, going all out and beating her 6–3, 6–3, then letting up a little and having to put the pressure on again and come from behind to beat her 7–5 in the third set. He shouldn't have let up. If you go out to play you go out to win, even if you're playing your wife. Barbara was glad he felt that way. When she did beat him, once in a while, she knew she had won on her own and had not been given anything.

Several times, working to beat Barbara, he had thought of Cini. Cini alive. He wasn't sure why. He couldn't picture Cini playing tennis. She would laugh at the idea. She was a girl made to be held and played with in other ways. She was soft and vulnerable, a little girl. Barbara was also a little girl – running hard, swinging, chopping, stroking the ball, saying to herself, 'You dummy!' when her shot went out or hit the net – but she was a little girl in a way that was different. She could turn off being a little girl. She could be a lady or a woman or even a grandmother, and she would be natural, at ease, on all these levels. Though at home as they showered together and made slow love in the afternoon, alone in the silence of the house, it was hard to imagine her as a grandmother.

Lying on the bed, looking at each other, Barbara said, 'It's better than that dumb movie, isn't it?'

And Mitchell said, 'Way better. You have to be in love to find out.'

'Do you feel that?'

134

'Of course I do.'

'Tell me.'

'I love you.'

'There isn't any other way to say it, is there?'

'I don't know of any.'

'It's good to hear. That's something,' she said. 'It's always good to hear. I get a feeling inside when you say it.'

'Even after—?' He paused.

'Don't.'

'I was going to say, even after all these years?'

'It gets better.'

'I guess if you want it to it does.'

'Do you remember when you used to come home from trips? Even if you were gone only a day or two, we couldn't wait.'

'I was thinking about that the other day.'

'Were you really?'

'Why would I lie? I'd rather make love to you than – I don't know, name a good-looking movie star.'

'Paul Newman.'

'Than Paul Newman.'

Barbara smiled. 'You really do love me, don't you?'

'What do you think I've been trying to tell you?'

'It's different now, isn't it? Do you feel it?'

'Like starting over.'

'Being *in* love rather than just loving.'

'I guess there's a difference.'

'You were letting me win in the third set, weren't you?'

'I got tired about in the middle.'

'Mitch, I love you.'

And he said, 'Then we've got nothing to worry about.'

They stood at the counter in the kitchen to eat hot homemade chili with French bread and hard butter – Barbara wiping her eyes, Mitch blowing his nose – and drank ice-cold Canadian beer from stem glasses. Late Sunday lunch was chili or hot dogs. Saturday Mitch fried hamburgers and onions. Today was the first time they had observed either of the rituals in almost three months. It was good to be back.

It was good to sit on the couch in the den and watch an old Gary Cooper movie, *Good Sam*, and remember they had seen it together before they were married. It wasn't so good – not at first – when the friends dropped in, three couples who were close friends, coming from a cocktail party. But it did get better with good talk and drinks and the chicken they sent out for, and by ten o'clock the house was quiet again. At eleven-thirty, after the late news, they went to bed and for a little while longer it was the way it had been for so many years, holding each other as they went to sleep.

*

She said very quietly, 'Mitch?'

'What?'

'There's somebody downstairs.'

'I know there is.'

Mitchell was lying on his back, his eyes open now for several minutes in the darkness of the bedroom. He was fully awake – tense, listening – with the knowledge that someone was in his house. Raising his head he could see the outline of the windows, a bleak wash of moonlight on the wall facing the bed and the dark shapes of the open doorway and the dressers on either side. He felt the covers tighten as Barbara moved, rolling slowly away from him. The telephone was on her night table.

'Wait,' Mitchell said.

'I'll dial the operator, tell her to call the police.'

'No, not yet. Wait.'

Barbara lay motionless, listening. 'He's coming upstairs.'

'I think so. Is the flashlight still in my closet?'

'On the top shelf.'

'Close your eyes. Don't move.'

'Mitch—'

'Shhhh.'

More than a minute passed before he was aware of the figure in the doorway. Mitchell closed his eyes and let his head sink into the pillow. He breathed with his mouth slightly open. There was no sound in the room, but he could feel the presence of someone and, after a moment, a slight bump against the foot of the bed. Mitchell waited, breathing in and out slowly. When he heard the clink of metal, a faint sound across the room, he opened his eyes again and saw the figure standing by his wife's dresser. A pinpoint of light passed over the surface and went off. The figure moved across the doorway to the other dresser. Mitchell heard a clinking sound again, his loose change. He saw

136

the envelope, briefly, in the pinpoint of light. He saw it lifted from the dresser as the light went off and the figure turned. Mitchell closed his eyes. He opened them again after only a moment, saw the room empty and raised the covers to get out of bed. Barbara whispered his name, an urgent sound, but he didn't look at her now. Mitchell went to his closet and got the flashlight from the shelf above his suits. He was careful not to make noise, but didn't waste time stepping out into the hallway.

The figure was almost to the stairway that turned once as it descended to the front hall. Mitchell started toward him. He took a few cautious steps, and then he was moving quickly, reaching the man and seeing him come around, at the same time bringing the flashlight up turned on, the beam momentarily in the black man's face before Mitchell slammed his left in straight and hard, chopped with the flashlight and felt it come apart as the light went out and the black man grunted, made a noise, and fell backward down the stairway. Mitchell reached for the light switch. The hall lights came on in time for him to see the man hit the wall at the landing and fall down the remaining stairs to the foyer. Mitchell was moving then, his hand sliding down the railing. He got to the man and planted a foot on the wrist of his outstretched arm. He reached down to take a .38 Special out of the man's belt and the envelope out of his inside coat pocket. With the envelope came a woman's nylon stocking.

Above him his wife called his name.

As she appeared on the landing he said, 'Get the camera. And a flash.'

*

They were in the den now. Bobby sat holding a handkerchief to the side of his face. He would dab at his cheekbone and then look at the fresh blood spot that appeared on the cloth.

Mitchell was unloading the .38. He put the cartridges in his pajama pocket and the empty revolver on the coffee table. As he sat down across from Bobby Shy he looked over at his wife.

'Why don't you see if you can find a band-aid?'

Barbara stood in the doorway, behind Bobby Shy, in her nightgown. She seemed to want to say something, but Mitchell's calm gaze held her off. He was in control. As she turned away Mitchell looked at Bobby Shy again.

'You got pictures of me,' he said, 'and now I've got pictures of you and Leo. All but Alan. You want some coffee or a drink or anything?'

Bobby Shy's eyes raised, his hand holding the handkerchief against his face. 'Man bust in your house, you always serve him drinks?'

'On special occasions.'

'Maybe you thinking I'm somebody I'm not.'

'We can waste a lot of time,' Mitchell said, 'or we can get to the point. I know your voice, I can identify you.'

'How come you ain't call the cops?'

'Now you sound like your friend Alan,' Mitchell said. 'You think I want the police involved? The only thing I want to know, why you bother to steal ten grand when I'm going to give you more than fifty thousand. Hand it to you.'

'You going to give me fifty thousand?'

'Fifty-two,' Mitchell said. 'That's the figure. Alan told you, didn't he?'

'About what?'

'Maybe you haven't seen him. You see him today?'

'What fifty-two thousand?' Bobby Shy said.

'Or he meant to tell you and he forgot.'

'Hey, I'm asking you, what fifty-two thousand?'

'The figure we agreed on. What I can afford to pay. He didn't tell you about it?'

'He say something about you owing the government.'

'Oh.' Mitchell nodded and was silent, giving the man time to think about it.

'You don't owe them anything?'

'Everybody owes the government. What's that got to do with it?'

Bobby Shy took the handkerchief away from his cheek, but didn't look at it. 'You made a deal with Alan?'

'It was Alan I spoke to,' Mitchell said. 'The payment's supposed to be for three of you, however you split it up.'

'Or however he don't split it,' Bobby Shy said.

Mitchell shrugged. 'Well, that's not my problem, is it? Who gets what.'

'When you make this payment?'

'In a few days. When I get it together.'

'Where?'

'Look,' Mitchell said, 'why don't you talk to Alan about it? I told him I'd pay. You want to know anything else, talk to him.'

'I'm going to do that,' Bobby Shy said. 'Yeah, have a talk.'

Mitchell nodded. 'I would.' He watched Bobby Shy get up, look at the handkerchief and put it in his pocket. 'Don't you want a band-aid?'

'Thanks, I don't think I need it.'

'You can sit, rest your head some more if you want.'

'No, I'm fine.'

As Bobby Shy turned and started to walk out Mitchell said, 'Hey, you forgot something.'

Bobby Shy looked back at him. 'What?'

'Your gun,' Mitchell said.

*

Alan didn't usually go to the movie theater until late in the afternoon or early evening, unless he needed some extra spending money. Then he'd make a day of it at the theater. Take tickets for a while in the afternoon, pocket a handful of them, then resell them later and keep the money, when he worked the ticket booth in the evening while the girl was on her relief. Twenty tickets were usually enough. Twenty times five was a hundred dollars and the guy down in Deerfield Beach, Florida, who owned the theater, never knew the difference. The money went for sugar candy and cigarettes – very often for the two teen-aged sisters who lived in the building. Laurie, fourteen, and Linda, fifteen. He would let them come to his apartment after school and take their clothes off and listen to music and smoke dope and sometimes drop a little acid. Little teenyboppers with skinny white bodies. Groovy little girls who squealed and giggled when they got turned on and loved to jump on Alan, on the Indian pillows, and undress him and do everything they could to turn him on too. Alan called it playing with his kids.

Laurie and Linda and the rock music were turned way up when Bobby Shy knocked at the door.

Alan, still dressed, went over and opened the door a crack with the chain on. He said, 'Hey, Bobby,' grinning but not liking it one bit, closed the door, took the chain off and let him in.

Bobby Shy looked at the little naked girls on the pillows.

They looked back at him, not turning away or trying to cover themselves. They stared at him with knowing little smiles and gleams in their eyes.

Bobby Shy said, 'Get rid of the fuzzies. We got something to talk about.'

Alan got the warning in the man's quiet, cut-dry tone. Bobby was in a mood, so don't mess with him or ask questions. But stay loose; don't ever look scared. Alan clapped his hands once and said, 'That's it for a while, kids,' like a stage manager. 'Let's take a break.'

The girls pouted and said awwww and oh shit, but Alan got them into their clothes and out of there in a couple of minutes. He closed the door and looked over to see Bobby taking a chair away from the table in the dining-L. He placed it in the middle of the floor and sat down. Alan sat against the wall on a pillow, yoga-fashion, and began building a joint. When he finished it and looked up again, reaching toward the low coffee table for a match, Bobby, seated about fifteen feet away, facing him, was screwing a silencer attachment into the barrel of his .38 Special.

'Hey now, come on,' Alan said, 'don't fool with guns in here, okay? The goddamn piece's liable to go off.'

'It's due to go off,' Bobby Shy said, 'unless you give me the straight shit when I ask you a question.'

'Come on, what *is* this?' The extension on the barrel was pointing at Alan now; he could see the little round black hole. 'Are you kidding, or what?'

'This number don't kid,' Bobby Shy said. 'You ready for the question?'

'Man, what're you on?'

Bobby Shy crossed his legs and rested the butt of the revolver on his raised knee. 'The question,' he said, 'is how much did the man say he give you?'

'Give *me*?'

'Give you, give us – say it.'

Alan was silent. He stole a little time by lighting the joint and tossing the matches back on the coffee table.

'You went out to see him, didn't you?'

'What's the answer?' Bobby said.

'Before I can talk to you, you go out on your own and see the guy. Is that it?'

Bobby turned the revolver on his knee slightly, a couple of inches, and shot a pig off the coffee table – a blue ceramic jar shaped like a pig that seemed to explode from within because there was no sound relating the exploding fragments to the gun.

Alan sat up straight, his back against the wall, his eyes open. He said, 'Bobby, listen to me for a minute, all right?'

'Man pull shit on me,' Bobby said, 'he got to be very brave or stoned out of his head.' His gaze lowered, he pulled the trigger and shot a fairy-looking figurine he never did like off the coffee table. It flew apart, was gone, with bits of it landing in Alan's lap. 'Which are you,' Bobby said, 'brave or stoned?'

'My mind is clear, man,' Alan said. 'Think about it a minute. How am I going to tell you with Leo sitting there? I called you later, you were gone. I called Doreen's, nobody answered.'

'She was home.' Bending his wrist, Bobby raised the trajectory of the revolver and shot two birds off a mobile hanging to Alan's left.

'All right, maybe she was home. I'm saying nobody *answered*, for Christ sake.'

The barrel shifted past Alan to ten o'clock. Bobby squeezed the trigger and shattered the globe of a mood lamp hanging from the wall.

'You could be shooting into the next room, for Christ sake!' Alan said. 'What if you hit somebody!'

Bobby sprung open the cylinder of the .38 and began reloading it, taking the cartridges from his coat pocket. 'I'm going to hit somebody, you don't say what the man offer us. Last call,' he said, snapping the revolver closed and putting it squarely on Alan. 'How much?'

'You know as well as I do,' Alan said. 'Fifty-two thousand.'

Bobby Shy smiled. 'Don't you feel better now?'

'Look,' Alan said, 'how was I going to tell you if I can't find you?'

'Tell me now, I'm listening.'

'All right, the man made us an offer. Fifty-two thousand, all he can afford to pay.'

'You believe it?'

'I looked at his books,' Alan said. 'Yes, I believe him. The way he's got his dough tied up he can't touch most of it. He offers fifty-two. All right, let's take it while he still believes it'll save his ass. But – here's what we're talking about – what do we need Leo for?'

'I don't see we ever needed him.'

'Leo spotted the guy. He did that much. But now he's nervous, Christ, you don't know what he's going to do next.'

'So me and you,' Bobby said, 'we split the fifty-two.'

Alan nodded. 'Twenty-six grand apiece.'

'And we go together to pick it up.'

'And we go together to hit the guy, whether we do it then or later.'

'All this time,' Bobby Shy said, 'what's Leo doing, watching?'

'Leo's dead. I don't see any other way.'

Bobby Shy thought about it. 'Yeah, he could find out, couldn't he?'

'We can't take a chance.'

'Man's too shaky, ain't he?'

'Do it with the guy's gun,' Alan said. 'How does that grab you?'

'Tell Leo we want to use it on the man.'

'Right. He hands it to you.'

'I guess,' Bobby Shy said, 'seeing he's a friend of yours, you want me to do it.'

'Not so much he's a friend,' Alan said, 'as you're the pro.' He grinned at Bobby Shy. 'Don't tell me how you're going to do it. Let me read it in the paper and be surprised.'

16

It was the next day that Alan panicked.

He came out of the men's room and there they were, a patrolman and a plainclothesman he knew right away was a cop, standing by the door to his office. So he walked down the aisle and took a seat and watched the last fifteen minutes of *Going Down on the Farm,* now in its Second Smash Week. Saved by his bladder.

Maybe the plainclothesman was on the vice squad and they

were cracking down on dirty movies again. That was a possibility. Or maybe they were selling Police Field Day tickets to local merchants. Yeah, or they were here to give him a good citizenship award. Bull*shit*, Mitchell had changed his mind, hit by his straight-A conscience, and blown the whistle. That had to be it. After only a couple minutes of thinking about it, Alan was convinced Mitchell had gone to the cops. As the picture ended and some of the audience began to leave, Alan moved down the aisle to the fire exit and went out that way, into the alley.

He got away from there in a Michigan Bell telephone repair truck, a Chevy van, that was parked near the end of the alley with the key in the ignition. He drove out North Woodward for no reason other than it was the quickest way to get some distance.

But within a few miles he began to calm down and think about it again. Maybe the cops weren't after him. Maybe they really were from the vice squad. Every other year or so there was a crackdown on porno movies. No explicit sex within five feet of them actually doing it. No front shots of guys, though beavers were all right. Alan hated censorship. He hated himself a little now for running. He should have somehow found out what they wanted. Call and see if they talked to anybody. But was he really running? Or was he going this way for a reason? His instinct telling him what to do before his head even realized it. Like everything was clear and simple and he knew all the time what he was going to do. Why not? Put the plan to work that he'd been thinking about. A little luck wouldn't hurt; but if his timing was off he could always improvise, or try it tomorrow or the next day. The plan in general would work, one way or another.

He turned off Woodward into downtown Royal Oak, took the telephone company truck up to the top of a municipal parking structure and left it there. He'd pick up something else on the way out, something a little sportier.

At the pay phone by the entrance he dialed Mitchell's home number. He listened to Barbara say hello three times, then hung up. He dialed a local number next.

'Hey Richard, how you making it? Alan. Listen, I'm out your way, Bobby asked me to pick him up some scag. ... Man, I

143

don't know. That's what he said, scag. Maybe he's changing his habits or it's for a friend, I don't know. ... Yeah ... No, he'll pay you next time. Bet on it, you know Bobby. ... At the parking thing in town ... Man, the big fucking five-story parking lot whatever the fuck you call it building ... Yeah, I'll be up on top.'

Alan went down the street to a drug store and paid a buck forty-seven for a package of ten Plastipak disposable U-80 Insulin syringe/needle units.

By the time he got back to the roof of the parking structure, Richard the dealer was there. Alan didn't see him – skinny young black guy with a big grin and a newspaper folded under one arm – until he stepped out of the red panel truck that had SUPER-RITE DRUGS painted on the side in white letters along with an RX prescription symbol.

'Jesus,' Alan said, 'nobody will ever say you don't have some kind of a fucking sense of humor.'

'It's a touch,' the dealer said, grinning. 'I seen the truck in the used-car lot. I said, man, I got to have it.'

'In your name?'

'Shit, my cousin's name. He still in the slam.'

'Bobby's got to see it,' Alan said. 'Too fucking much.'

'Yeah, Bobby have something to say. Speaking of Bobby.' He handed Alan the folded newspaper. 'Shit never been his pleasure, but as you say, maybe it's for some chickie friend. You need anything for yourself?'

Alan took the envelope out of the newspaper and folded it into his pocket. 'You have it in the truck?'

'No man, but I can get it right now.'

'I got to be somewhere,' Alan said. 'In fact, I'm late.' He paused a moment. 'Hey, you wouldn't let me use your truck, would you?'

'Use my truck – how'd you get here?'

'Guy dropped me off. Listen, it's a long story. What I got to do is see a man wants to buy some smoker movies. Take me about a half hour at the most.'

The dealer wasn't sure and wasn't grinning now. He said, 'The man live around here?'

'Over in Southfield. He wants to buy some movies, you know, for his club; but he's got some old equipment and he doesn't know if it's any good. I got to look at it. Half hour's all, Richard. You don't have any stuff in the truck, do you?'

'It's clean.'

'Then what're you worried about? It isn't even in your name.'

'I got a piece in there.'

'So keep it there,' Alan said. 'You want to stand on the roof of the fucking parking lot with a piece in your hand?'

'You want to get stopped with it?'

'Stopped for what? I'm a very careful driver, obey all the traffic regulations. I'm not worried about the piece. I don't even know where it is, I don't want to know. All I want to do is see a guy.'

'Something I don't like,' the dealer said.

'What don't you like? Richard, hey, go have a cup of coffee or something, I'll be back in half an hour. No shit, scout's honor.'

That's how Alan got the panel truck with SUPER-RITE DRUGS written on the side. That was also how he got the piece, another Lucky Jackpot of the Year Award for clean living. It wasn't in the glove compartment – which he had to bust open, snapping the lock with a screwdriver – it was up under the instrument panel, hanging there in a wool sock: a kind of automatic he had never seen before, a cheap little Saturday night gun without a name or number, but it had nine live ones in the clip and that's what counted.

It was turning out to be a good day.

*

It was, in fact, the first warm sunny day in almost a month: a clear sky finally, now that it was the middle of May, temperature in the high sixties. The touch of wind was cool, but the stockade fence held off the gusts that came across the yard and it was almost hot on the patio.

Barbara reclined in a lounge chair with the backrest set low, her eyes closed, her face raised to the sun. The first good hot feel of sunshine in three months, since Mexico. She wore a yellow bikini that once had been her daughter's. With her flat-sunken stomach, firm thighs and trace of the winter-vacation tan, her body seemed made for the bikini. But she had a feeling about wearing one and she put it on only for backyard sunning or if she was off somewhere with Mitch, alone.

Lying there she thought of Mitch. She thought of the girl and wondered what she had looked like. No, she couldn't do that. She thought of Mitch again and hoped he was at the plant and if she called him he would answer. But she didn't get up to call. Mitch handled matters his own way. She would have to be patient and wait, not nagging or pleading or telling him to be careful. If you want him, she thought, that's the way he is. And she wanted him.

She thought about the house and having the storms taken off and the windows washed and the lawn cut and fertilized and the swimming pool cleaned out. She tried to think of the name of the pool maintenance company they had called last year. Aqua something. Aqua-Queen—

'You got a nice navel.'

Her eyes opened abruptly. The sun was on a line over his shoulder, a halo behind him, and for a moment until she shielded her eyes, she could not see his face clearly.

'I like a nice deep navel in a little round tum-tum,' Alan said. 'Please don't move, lady, till I tell you to.'

She had started to push up out of the chair, swinging her legs to the side away from him. She stopped as he took the newspaper from under his arm, opened one fold and showed her the gun inside.

'You see it?' He folded the newspaper, putting it under his arm again. 'Now you don't. But you know where it is.'

Barbara stared at him. 'What do you want?'

'You remember me? Silver Lining Accounting Service.' Alan smiled. 'What was the line? We make a mistake we eat it. Something like that.'

'I know who you are,' Barbara said. 'I know what you are.'

'So I don't have to introduce myself and give you references,' Alan said. 'Now what I want you to do is get up, put your little sandals on and go in the house. I'll be right behind you.'

When Barbara swung her legs to his side of the lounge and bent over to straighten her sandals, to slip them on, Alan got a good clear shot of her breasts. He said, 'Jesus, I don't know what he was fooling around with that skinny chick for.'

Then, inside the house, after he had checked to make sure the doors were locked, following close behind her, his eyes holding on the movement of her hips, he said. 'Jesus, I bet you start that thing going it takes all night to shut it off. My, having that right at home.'

He took her into the kitchen and told her to get up on the table and fold her legs under her like an Indian. She sat there watching him, not sure what he was doing until he took the package of disposable syringes and the envelope out of his pocket.

Alan used an egg poacher. He got the water boiling, set the aluminum tray over it and cooked the heroin, diluted with a spoonful of water, in one of the concave sections of the tray, where the egg would go. Alan grinned and said, 'Shit, man, gourmet cooking; Bobby'd take one look at this setup and have to get one.' Bobby mostly blew coke, though, he told Barbara. Bobby said shit messed him up and made him sick.

She watched him bend over the egg poacher and carefully draw the white-powder-turned-to-liquid into a syringe, pushing the plunger in to release the air bubbles then drawing it out again slowly, getting almost every drop of the liquid.

When he turned to her, holding the syringe so that the needle pointed up, he said, 'It won't feel hot. Maybe a little warm going in.'

'I don't want it,' Barbara said.

'Lady, it's just scag. Give you a nice slow ride uptown, see the lights.'

'I don't *want* it.'

'Jesus, I'm not hooking you. I just want to make you quiet and easy to handle. Put your leg out, either one.' His free hand reached toward her.

When she pulled away from him, holding onto the edge of the table, he slapped her hard across the face. She made a sound, more of surprise than pain, and he hit her again.

'Now put your leg out!'

He grabbed her by the ankle and pulled. Barbara fell back against the curtain covering the lower part of the window, off balance now, on her elbows. Alan turned, taking her leg under one arm, squeezing the ankle and pushing the syringe into the vein that popped out beneath his thumb. He felt her tighten and try to draw her other leg free, but not in time to kick him or push him away. His thumb raised over the syringe, stroked it down slowly and the lady was on her way.

•

She remembered the feeling from a time before, lying in a hospital bed after the nurse had given her the shot. Like that, but a deeper, more complete feeling: her mind and body wrapped in comfortable comforting softness, floating without moving in warm water that had no wetness, floating without moving to keep afloat, suspended in the good feeling. She was aware but not sure if she was awake. It was not something to think about because there was nothing, no reason to think. Being, without touching, lying on a bed, her bed, their bed, that had always been firm but now had no feeling, as though she were lying not on the bed but in the bed and the bed was warm motionless water. Someone else was in the room. The skinny man. Skinny legs and shoulders and long hair, his hair hanging, his skinny face looking down at her. Now he was closer to her and she felt him touch her, his hand on her thigh, on her stomach. She said, 'I'm so tired.' His voice, someone's voice, said, 'Then why don't you go sleepy-bye? Close your eyes—'

*

'How was it?'

Her eyes were open. She was looking at the white ceiling. She thought of the hospital room again. No, she was at home, lying on her bed. In bed. Someone had spoken to her, a sound of words, or a dream. There was light in the room, maybe time to get up, but she felt more asleep than awake: the nice drowsy early-morning feeling of peace and quiet and a warm bed. Roll over and look at the alarm clock on the bed table. Next to the telephone. The telephone had been moved and was in the way. She raised her head from the pillow. It was only six o'clock. It seemed later. She let her face sink into the pillow and closed her eyes. A few more minutes. Lying on her side she drew her legs up. Her body was warm, but she felt a chill, a draft, on her back and she reached down for the sheet and blanket. Her hand felt only her bare thigh and hip. She turned, opening her eyes and pushing up on one arm, still with the drowsy feeling, but with awareness and memory clicking in her mind. She was naked except for the yellow bikini bra covering her breasts.

'I asked you how was it?'

'What time is it?'

'Six.'

'You were here all night?'

148

'It's six in the evening, Slim, not the morning.'

She sat up, too quickly, almost falling back down again, seeing Alan at the foot of the bed, and had to put her hands behind her to support herself, closing and opening her eyes with the warm light feeling in her head, but also aware of herself reclining naked in front of him, like a painting, a model in a painting. The Nude Maja. By— She rolled to the edge of the bed, trying to push her legs over the side and get up.

Alan came around from the foot of the bed holding the syringe upright in one hand. As her feet touched the floor he pushed her down again, effortlessly.

Alan smiled at her. 'Feel pretty good, huh? You been up and away almost three hours. Tomorrow you may be a little constipated, but you'll get over it.'

She had nothing to cover herself with so she lay without moving her hands flat on the bed at her sides. A patient watching her doctor.

'What did you do to me?'

'Guess.'

Barbara stared at him but said nothing.

Alan grinned. 'You squirmed around a lot. You don't remember? You moaned, said a few things. Nothing dirty.'

'What did you do to me?'

'Give you a hint,' Alan said. 'You can't ever knock anybody up doing it.' He grinned at her and winked. 'Now I got to shoot you up again. We're about ready to get out of here.'

As Barbara started to push up, to lunge at him or get past him, Alan hit her with a fist, chopping it quick and hard into her upturned face. 'Be nice,' Alan said. He got her leg under his arm and squeezed the ankle to pop the vein.

The telephone rang.

*

Leo began that day with a vodka and Seven-Up. It didn't help any. He had two more, not wasting much time. Usually the vodka picked him up and a couple of them would give him a nice glow; but he still couldn't feel anything. He ordered another one and said to the owner of the Kit Kat, who was behind the bar, 'You haven't seen them today by any chance, have you?'

'Not since last night,' the bar owner said.

'They were together though, last night?'

'I don't know if they came in together. What I told you before, they left together.'

'What time was that?'

'I don't know what time. They're sitting at the bar, they got up and left.'

'I'll have another one,' Leo said.

The bar owner looked at him because Leo had only taken an inch off the top of his fourth drink; but when he came back with a fresh vodka and Seven-Up Leo was ready for it. The bar owner moved away and Leo sat there alone. One other guy was sitting up toward the front end of the bar with a Strohs.

Leo hadn't been able to locate either of them yesterday, to find out what the hell was going on. Alan hadn't been home or at work. Doreen said she hadn't seen Bobby or Alan all day. Bobby disappeared sometimes, but not Alan. He always knew where Alan was, or Alan knew where he was. Since getting into this deal they'd seen each other every day. Now, all of a sudden, Alan wasn't anywhere around.

Drinking the vodka Leo thought it over carefully, seeing Alan in his apartment the last time and remembering what he'd said. It was over. The guy couldn't pay. But the guy knew who they were. They couldn't take a chance on the guy not going to the police. Then sounding friendly toward the end, saying they had to stick together and maybe, after a while, look for another guy to hit. Why had he sounded so friendly? The whole deal blows up. They kill the girl for nothing. They have to kill the guy now. And Alan sounds friendly, not the least bothered about it or nervous. If they were supposed to stick together then where the hell was Alan? Like they were ditching him.

There were guys he hung around with a long time ago used to do that, ditch him. Sometimes they'd just take off running and leave him behind when he couldn't catch up. Or he was supposed to meet them somewhere and they wouldn't be there. Or he'd find out they'd all gone to a show and nobody had bothered to call him or come by his house. Once he was sixteen his mother let him use the car a lot, a blue six-cylinder Plymouth coupe, and for a while they let him drive them around and hardly ever ditched him. He hadn't seen any of them in a long time now. Not since he worked at his first motel as a night clerk, a six-buck place out on Telegraph. They found out he could fix them up with young fifteen-dollar broads out of high school and sometimes they'd come by two-thirty in the morning half loaded on beer.

Something was going on.

He wondered if maybe Alan had seen Mitchell again. Or if Bobby had seen him and put the guy away. There was nothing in the morning *Free Press* or the early edition of the *News*. It could be too soon. They could have taken the guy somewhere and dumped him and his body hadn't been found yet. He said to himself, What's the matter with you?

Leo went to the pay phone near the entrance. He had to get the number of Ranco Manufacturing from the operator because it was out of the city, in Fraser. When he dialed the number and asked for Mr. Mitchell the girl's voice asked who was calling please. He said, 'Tell him Alan Raimy.' He waited. When he heard Mitchell's voice, recognizing it immediately, he hung up the receiver and held it down hard in the cradle until he was sure Mitchell was off the line. He lifted it to his face again and dialed Alan's apartment. Still no answer. He dialed the movie theater. Alan wasn't in yet. Was he expected? Nobody seemed to know. He dialed Doreen's number again. No answer.

Leo had two more vodkas and Seven-Up at the bar. He was sure something was going on. He was beginning to be sure they didn't want to be seen with him. Because something was going to happen to him and if they were seen with him anytime before it happened they could be taken in and questioned. This way, if they were questioned for any reason, they'd say no, they hadn't seen him in a couple of days. And nobody could prove otherwise.

What the hell was he doing sitting here? Making it easy for them. The whole thing had looked easy. Foolproof, Alan had said. They'd have to be fucking idiots to blow this one. It was their chance to make it for life. Christ, his life was going by so fast all of a sudden. Christ, what had he done, accomplished? Worked at some motels. Handled some broads. Got them their business but had to pay when he wanted a little. Even the dumb-looking ones nobody wanted and didn't last, he had to pay. Three arrests for pandering. Two suspended, one conviction. Ninety days in DeHoco, fucking Detroit House of Correction. Famous milestones in the life of Leo Frank. When his mother died he was the beneficiary of a $25,000 life insurance policy and a year-old T-bird. Hot shit, his troubles were over. He'd invest it in some kind of business. He rented a storefront and set up the model studio; that took five. He met Alan, loaned him almost ten and pissed away the rest of it in less than a year. Alan had bought a sports car and fixed up his apartment with a lot of weird shit and hadn't paid him back as much as a dime of the ten he borrowed. All Alan ever did, pushed him around, ditched him, insulted him—

Leo walked back to the phone and dialed Ranco Manufacturing again. This time, when Mitchell came on, Leo didn't hang up.

He said, 'Mr. Mitchell, this is Leo Frank. From the model studio? ... Yeah, how are you? ... Listen, I'd like to talk to you sometime soon, I mean today, you get a chance. ...'

*

Mitchell could have walked – the Pine Top was across the road and only a block down – but it might have looked funny. Where was the boss going, walking off at two o'clock in the afternoon? It was an industrial area of small plants, warehouses and vacant lots for sale. There wasn't anyplace he could be walking to except the bar. So Mitchell drove over and parked the Grand Prix in the lot on the side of the green-painted cinder-block building, among the pickup trucks and sedans with hardhats on the rear window ledges.

Mitchell had been inside only a few times before. He remembered nothing in particular about the place: a bar that looked like hundreds of other bars, a country ballad on the jukebox and about a dozen workingmen sitting around drinking Strohs, most of them at the bar. The first person Mitchell recognized was Ed Jazik, the 199 business agent. He was alone at the bar. Mitchell walked past him and Jazik didn't turn around or seem to notice him. He saw Leo Frank at a table against the wall, fooling with a plastic swizzle stick. A drink and another stick were on the table.

Standing up extending his hand, Leo gave him a big smile. Mitchell took the hand firmly, giving the limp thick flesh a little pressure, and heard Leo's voice catch as he said, 'I'm glad you could make it. I didn't meeeeean ... to take you away from

152

your work.' There was a hint of relief in his expression as the waitress came over and Mitchell sat down. 'What would you like?'

'Nothing,' Mitchell said.

'Well, I might as well have another one,' Leo said to the waitress, 'long as you're here.' As the waitress left he took a moderate sip of his vodka drink and looked over at the bar and toward the front, avoiding Mitchell's gaze.

'Place does pretty well for the afternoon,' Leo said. 'I bet they got some go-go in here they could do even better.'

'Three-thirty and eleven-thirty they do their business,' Mitchell said, 'when the shifts let out.'

'I imagine it's strictly shot and a beer, huh?'

'I imagine,' Mitchell said. He waited, in no hurry, watching Leo sipping at the drink, then lighting a cigarette, working up his nerve.

'I understand,' Leo said, 'you finally got in touch with Alan, the guy you were looking for?'

'I saw him,' Mitchell said. 'Then he came out to see me. He tell you about it?'

'He mentioned it. Ah, fine,' Leo said to the waitress, taking the fresh drink and handing her his empty. He stirred the drink for a moment. 'What I been wondering, why you told him it was me said where to find him.'

'I didn't tell him it was you.'

'He said you did. He said' – Leo grinned – 'your exact words, your friend told me, Leo Frank.'

'Somebody's mistaken,' Mitchell said. 'I didn't tell him anything.'

'Well, why would he tell me that?'

'You know him better than I do,' Mitchell said. 'Why would he?'

Leo thought about it. He took about a third of his drink and thought about it some more.

'I don't know. It was like he was blaming it all on me.'

'Blaming what all on you?'

'I mean, well, you know. What he talked to you about, the deal? It fell through, didn't it?'

'He told you that?'

'Well, see, I really don't know much about it, you know? I

153

was just trying to get you two guys together. As a favour is all. And he says you said it was me told you where to find him.'

'Leo,' Mitchell said, 'I know you, I know Alan and I know the colored guy. I got his name, Robert Shy, and the number off his driver's license. I know where all of you live or work. I know it's you three that killed a girl named Cynthia Fisher and I know it's you three I have to pay to get out of this. Leo, why don't you have another drink?'

He could smell Leo's after-shave. The man seemed afraid to move, sitting there holding onto his glass and looking directly at Mitchell now. He tried a little drink, shaking his head.

'You got it wrong if you think I'm in on it. Alan told you that?' Like he couldn't believe it.

'Leo,' Mitchell said, 'why don't we quit beating around? I made a deal with Alan. Evidently he hasn't told you about it yet. Or the colored guy. He came to see me, he didn't know about it either.'

'Alan said you couldn't pay, you owe the government.'

Mitchell nodded. 'That's what the colored guy said.'

'Bobby came to see you?'

'Leo, let's talk about Alan. I made him an offer. I said I'd give you guys fifty-two thousand bucks, because that's all I can afford to pay. He looked at my books, he said all right, he'd settle for that. I said, you're going to split with your partners? I don't want them on my back, I want it done. He says, of course.'

'He told us you didn't have any money. You owed the government.'

'Leo, I know that. You want to talk about that, talk to Alan.'

'Son of a bitch. I knew something was going on.'

'You want another drink?' Mitchell looked over toward the bar. He didn't see Jazik now. 'I'll have one with you.'

'The son of a bitch. Yeah, vodka and Seven.'

Mitchell raised an arm to the waitress and held up two fingers.

'I knew it,' Leo was saying, 'by the way he acted, the way he talked, he was pulling something.'

'If you expect me to feel sorry for you,' Mitchell said, 'that's quite a bit to ask, isn't it? Under the circumstances.' He was surprised at his own tone and the fact he could be calm and talk to Leo and not punch him through the wall. When the waitress brought their drinks, Mitchell raised his glass.

'I'm sorry I can't wish you luck, buddy. But I'm sure you can understand I don't give a shit what happens to you. Or to Alan, or the colored guy, Bobby.'

Leo took a drink. 'I'm telling you I'm not as involved in this as you might think.'

'Well, you're sort of mixed up in it then.'

'It was Alan's idea.'

'I believe it,' Mitchell said.

'What they did to the girl? Honest to God, I told them I wouldn't have any part of it.'

'You were there though, weren't you?'

'You can't prove that.'

'I'm not trying to prove anything,' Mitchell said. 'I'm trying to get this settled, over with. Even if I have to pay fifty-two thousand. I've made that clear.'

'You pay and it's over with all right,' Leo said. 'He's already set it up. Once you pay him he puts Bobby on you. Or he does it himself. Jesus, for all I know they're both in it. They were together yesterday. Bobby knows Alan was pulling something, but they're still hanging around together.'

'Like they're taking you out of the picture,' Mitchell said, 'splitting two ways.'

'I don't know. Christ, you never know what he's thinking, Alan, he's got a weird fucking mind.'

'I don't know either,' Mitchell said. 'But I have to take his word and pay, or else I face a murder charge with a good case against me.'

Leo was staring at him, thinking. After a moment he leaned in close to the table. 'What if you went to the cops on your own? Told them the whole story.'

'I think the odds are I'd go to jail.'

'No. I back you up. We make a deal with the cops. I testify against Alan and Bobby. I go on the stand, say they killed the girl – if the cops'll let me plead, I don't know, say just to the blackmail part. And that's the truth, I was never for killing the girl.'

'I don't know,' Mitchell said. 'It'd be only your word. They'd still have a case against me.'

'What case?'

'The girl's body. My gun, the film—'

'You want to know something?' Leo said. 'There is no girl's body.'

'What do you mean?'

'It's at the bottom of Lake Erie, in all the pollution and shit.'

'Since when?'

'Since they did it. You believe she's on ice somewhere because you can't take a chance she isn't. Right? Alan figured that. You see her killed and that's what you remember. It sticks in your mind. It scares the shit out of you and you agree to pay. Only now you know Alan and Bobby did it. They can't take a chance. You pay or you don't, either way they kill you.'

'Or us,' Mitchell said. He was silent a moment. 'What about the films?'

'In the lake with the girl.'

'And my gun?'

Leo hesitated. 'It's somewhere else. Case they need it again.'

'If nothing can be proved against me,' Mitchell said, 'then I'm out of it, huh?'

'You can think so,' Leo said, 'but they're still going to kill you, whether you pay or not. Listen, they do it easy.'

Mitchell watched Leo finish his drink. He picked up his own glass, untouched, and placed it in front of Leo.

'For the road.'

'You going?'

'Why, we have anything else to talk about?'

'I'm telling you they're going to kill you.' Leo was tense, staring at him again. 'You haven't said anything about what you're going to do.'

'I don't know yet,' Mitchell said. 'Think about it, I guess. Or wait and see what happens to you. Then I'll know if they're serious or not.'

*

The way Ed Jazik's car was facing, away from the bar, into a vacant lot, he could watch Mitchell's Grand Prix through his rearview mirror. Coming out a few minutes ago he had looked at Mitchell's car and had come very close to smashing a window and doing the job right then. But Mitchell probably had seen him inside. Or he might come out too soon. When Mitchell did come out, and Jazik watched him drive the short distance up the road and turn into his plant, he was glad he waited. It would've been easier to smash the window and do it here, but doing it over in the plant parking lot would be better, because his employees would come running out the back door and see it. The shift changed in a half hour. Then give it another half hour or so, wait till after the office employees all went home, then go over there. Pull in the drive, turn around to be facing out and keep the engine running. Take about half a minute.

Jazik went back inside the Pine Top and ordered a Strohs at the bar. His fourth one this afternoon. He looked over at the guy Mitchell had been talking to: fat clown in a striped suitcoat tight across his shoulders, hunched over the table with two drinks at once. Slob was probably a customer of Mitchell's, owned some manufacturing plant. Fat son of a bitch sitting there, nothing to do, nothing to worry about. The guys that had it all looked alike.

*

The package for Mr. Harry Mitchell arrived by United Parcel while Janet was clearing her desk, ready to leave for the day. The label imprint bore the name of a Detroit luggage shop, and by the compact size of the carton Janet was fairly sure it was a case of some kind. She opened the carton to find the case, or whatever it was, gift-wrapped in silver-and-white-striped paper with a ribbon and bow. There was no card on the outside.

Mitchell looked up as Janet came into his office and placed it on his desk.

'What's that?'

'I don't know. It's not your birthday, is it?'

'Who's it from?'

'The card must be inside. Do you want to open it or should I?'

'You do it.'

He watched Janet slit the taped ends with a letter opener and slide the case out without tearing the paper: a black attaché case with chrome clasps and lock. It was shiny, inexpensive-looking, like plastic passing for patent leather. Janet turned the case to face Mitchell, picked up the ribbon and began winding it around her hand, watching as he snapped open the clasps and raised the top half. She couldn't see inside.

'Isn't there a card?'

Mitchell picked up a small folded piece of product literature. 'It's a Porta-Sec,' he read. 'Your portable executive secretary from Travel-Rama . . . made of genuine Hi-Sheen Tuffy-Hyde.'

Janet wasn't sure what to say. She tried, 'Do you like it?'

'What I've always wanted,' Mitchell said.

She hesitated another moment. 'There isn't a card?'

'I don't see any.'

'Do you know who it's from?'

'Not offhand. Maybe they forgot to put it in.'

'I'll call the store if you want.'

'No, that's all right.'

'Well, if you don't have anything else for me . . .'

'Not that I can think of,' Mitchell said and looked up at her pleasantly. 'I'll see you tomorrow.'

He waited until Janet was out of the office and the door closed before he picked up the little envelope from the empty case and took out the card. Printed in pencil it said, HAPPY 52 SPORT! HOPE TO SEE THOUSANDS MORE!

*

John Koliba, second-shift leader, came out of the Quality Control room and walked down the aisle toward the last Warner-Swasey in the row of turning machines. It was a quarter of six, he would recall later. He was going over to tell the operator to shut the machine down and change the turret adjustment for a run of bushing plate stops. He wasn't sure if he happened to look over at the rear door first or if he heard the explosion outside and then looked over, because it all happened like at the same time. He heard it and, through the glass part of the door, saw the flames shoot up inside the car that was parked about thirty feet away. It wasn't a very loud explosion, a dull, sort of muffled sound, but heavy. Most of the other employees working toward this end of the shop heard it too and were right behind Koliba by the time he was outside and saw that it was Mr. Mitchell's car on fire. Koliba yelled at a couple of guys to get fire extinguishers. Then he ran back inside and through the plant to get Mitchell. But when he got to Mitchell's office the door was closed and for a moment he didn't know what to do, if he'd be interrupting him or what. He said to himself, For Christ sake, and banged on the door. The voice inside said, 'Come in.'

Koliba pushed the door open, stood there looking at Mitchell behind his desk and said, 'I don't mean to bother you, but somebody just fire-bombed your car.'

By the time Mitchell and Koliba got there all the second-shift men who could shut down and get away from their machines were outside in the parking lot. The two men with the fire extinguishers were covering the car with blasts of white foam, but not doing much good. The flames filled the interior of the car and smoke billowed out of a partly open window. Finally one of them edged in close enough to get a door open and shove the megaphone nozzle of the extinguisher inside and let go. The car filled with foam and the flames seemed to be smothered. Cars were being moved out of the near vicinity of the fire. A man would be watching with concentrated interest, then realize his own car was parked close to the Grand Prix and wake up and run to get it the hell out of there. Beyond the fire and thick smoke, for several minutes cars were pulling out and making turns all over the parking lot.

Mitchell stood watching, his hand on the rim of a metal waste bin of scrapped parts. He said to Koliba, next to him, 'Why'd you say it was a fire bomb?'

Koliba's little eyes, squinting, held on the car. 'I seen it before.' Mitchell didn't say anything and Koliba looked at him. 'What else could it be? You leave a cigarette on the carpeting?'

Mitchell still didn't say anything.

'You ever seen wiring catch fire inside a car? Under the hood, yeah, but not inside.'

'Maybe it was the gas tank.'

'The tank didn't go. Not yet it didn't,' Koliba said. 'It started inside, gasoline or something. But it wasn't poured in, you know, sloshed around the upholstery and the guy throws a match in. No, because I heard it. I was going over to Number Six and I seen it blow up, like the guy lit a wick or a rope soaked in gas or something and got the hell out before it went. Otherwise, he'd a thrown a match, I'd have seen him.'

Mitchell was staring at the car, at the interior filled with foam that was like soapsuds.

'No chance of it being an accident?'

Koliba looked at him again. He said, 'Shit, you know as well as I do who done it.'

A machinist, coming out from the plant, spotted Mitchell and hurried over. 'I called the fire department. They're on their way.'

'Fire department, the fire's out,' Koliba said.

'You think it's out,' the machinist said. 'They make sure.'

'Tear the car apart doing it,' Koliba said.

'Yeah, well you think it's out,' the machinist said, 'all of a sudden the son of a bitch blows up on you.'

Mitchell wasn't listening to them. He had thought of Alan Raimy first – coming out and seeing the car burning – the hip creepy guy Alan, wondering why he would do something like this. He didn't think of Ed Jazik or remember Jazik at the bar across the street until Koliba said you know as well as I who did it. Koliba knew; there wasn't any question in his mind. It was as though everything lately had to do with Alan Raimy and the fat guy and the colored guy and dealing with them had become his primary business. But he was still operating a plant and had a maverick union management guy on his back. Jazik seemed a long time ago. Except that he was here and now, as real as the burned-out car. Something else to be handled. All right, call the local and yell at the president again. Or let it go. Maybe Jazik felt better now. He couldn't concentrate on both Jazik and Alan Raimy. One of them had to be set aside. Jazik. Though he should keep his eyes open. Maybe for another slowdown. Jazik shows off and maybe wins a couple of new friends in the shop. So maybe there would be more breakdowns to watch for. Christ.

He looked at the metal bin he was leaning against, at the hundreds of machined parts that had been scrapped during the past two weeks. He reached in and picked out of the bin a switch actuator housing and held it in the palm of his hand. It looked fine, except the inside diameter was off tolerance maybe a thousandth of an inch. Mitchell held the part in his hand as he walked over to the wet, smoking car and looked inside at the gutted scorched interior that was steaming glistening charred black and smelled of burned vinyl and rubber.

Somebody said, 'Mr. Mitchell, you better get back. That gas tank's liable to go.'

Next to him, John Koliba said, 'It'd a gone by now. Look, see the pieces of glass on the seat? Down in the springs. I bet you anything it was a bottle of gasoline exploded,' Koliba grinned, his little eyes squinting. 'I hope it was lead-free gas, uh? Don't want to pollute the air.'

Right away he thought maybe he shouldn't have said it. Mitchell didn't smile or seem to think it was funny. He was looking at something he was holding in his hand.

'What's 'at?' Koliba said. 'Something you found?'

Mitchell opened his hand to show him the metal part, the switch actuator housing. 'Nothing. Piece of scrap.'

'I thought maybe it was something you found in the car.' Koliba watched Mitchell turn to walk away. 'You gonna call the cops?'

'I don't know, I'll think about it,' Mitchell said.

He walked back toward the plant. Koliba watched him toss the scrapped part in the air about a foot or so and catch it in one hand, then toss it up again and catch it, playing with it. His car was burned up and he didn't seem to think anything about it. Christ, I'd have the cops here, Koliba was thinking. Not the local cops, the goddamn F.B. fucking I., they'd take the broken glass or prints or something and pin the son of a bitch. Koliba heard the sirens then, out on the road coming this way. He looked over toward the drive with renewed interest to watch the fire engines arrive.

*

At six o'clock, sitting in his office with the Hi-Sheen Tuffy-Hyde attaché case on the desk in front of him, Mitchell called his home.

The phone rang seven, eight, nine times. He was about to hang up when he heard his wife's voice say hello.

'Hi. You sound like you've been sleeping.'

There was a long pause before she said yes, she'd taken a nap and just woke up.

'No tennis today – how come?'

There was a pause again. 'I didn't feel like it,' her voice said. 'I guess I was tired.'

'From what?'

'I don't know. Working around the house. I guess.'

He said, 'Are you all right?'

'I'm fine.'

Maybe she was, but she sounded funny. He said, 'The reason

I called – I won't be home tonight. For two reasons. First I've got to work on something, a design, and I don't know how long it's going to take me. Maybe all night, or longer. And, I don't have a car. It's out of commission and I won't be able to get another one from the leasing place until tomorrow. I'll tell you about that later. The main thing, I'll be in my office or in Engineering – you've got that extension in your book – so if you need me for anything, be sure and call.'

There was a silence on the other end of the line.

'Barbara?'

'Yes. I'm here.'

'What's the matter? Don't you feel good?'

'I'm fine really. Just a second.'

He waited several moments before she came on again.

'What time will you be home tomorrow?'

'I guess the usual. If the car isn't delivered, I'll get a ride with somebody. So I'll see you then.' He paused before saying, 'Barbara, I miss you.'

The lifeless voice said, 'I miss you too. God, I miss you.' And hung up.

Mitchell replaced the receiver and sat with his hand still holding it, hearing her words and the voice he barely recognized. She hadn't said good-bye or given him a chance to say it. He thought about her, picturing her by the telephone in the kitchen, though she was probably in the bedroom if she had been taking a nap. He couldn't imagine her sleeping this late in the afternoon.

Well, he'd see her tomorrow. Or he could call later. Right now he'd better put his design hat on and get to it. He took the new attaché case and the switch actuator he'd fished out of the trash bin, went into the drafting room of the Engineering Department and turned on the fluorescent lights that always seemed brighter and colder at night, with no one else in the room.

*

Leo got stopped by the Royal Oak Police coming across Ten Mile Road. He was sure the cop was going to make him get out and walk a line and stand on one foot and try and pick up a quarter – that's it, in for a breath test; he'd blow a twenty, the shape he was in, and spend the night in the tank. But the cop

162

didn't make him get out. Maybe his luck was turning. The cop asked him for his operator's license and registration and asked him where he was going. Leo said he was going home. He said he had to go to the bathroom something awful and maybe that's why he was hurrying a little. He probably looked like he was in pain. He had used the bathroom excuse he'd learned from somebody a few times and sometimes it worked. Even cops had to go to the bathroom and unless the cop was sadistic he'd understand. This cop didn't waste a lot of time giving him the speech on safety and how they were just trying to keep people alive or any of that shit. He gave Leo a ticket for thirteen miles over the limit and told him to stop at the next gas station.

The plan: he was going to go home and pack a few things, his new double-knit houndstooth check, stop by the studio, get whatever dough was in the box, lock the place up and move to a motel, maybe out around Pontiac somewhere, contact Mitchell in a day or two and talk to him again about going to the cops. Maybe cops never smiled but they could be understanding and they were known to make deals. Give one guy a year, something like that, for blackmail, to get two guys for airtight first-degree murder. That was the plan.

But when he got home to the flat in Highland Park, he started worrying again what he should do with his mother's things, all her clothes and crappy jewelry. He should have sold the place and her stuff a year ago, right after she died. Now he'd have to leave it for God knows how long. He was sure somebody would break in and steal everything and wreck the place. The goddamn neighborhood was going to hell, becoming overpopulated with heads and freaks and hustlers, people supporting their habits. So he worried about that for a while. Until he decided he'd better take a couple of downers and sleep off some of the vodkas and Seven. He didn't have a glow now; he had a headache and a tired, heavy feeling.

When he woke up it was dark. By the time he got to the model studio it was after ten.

He emptied the metal box in his office, thirty bucks, got some pills, hair spray and after-shave out of the drawers, stuffed them in his coat pockets, went out to the desk in the lobby and checked the box there, empty, which he knew it would be but checked anyway. He was sitting there thinking. Okay, don't waste any more time, go downtown or out to Pontiac but do it now.

He looked over and saw Bobby Shy watching him, over by the hallway and near the furniture, standing there with his hands in his pockets, watching him.

Leo said, 'How'd you get in? Man, I didn't hear a sound.'

'I walked in the back,' Bobby Shy said.

'The door was locked. How could you walk in?'

'I don't know,' Bobby said, 'but here I am.'

'Where you been? I been looking all over for you, for two days.'

Bobby said, 'Where have I been? I was where I was. What you mean where have I been?'

'Two days I haven't seen either of you. Man, I was starting to wonder.'

'We're fixing up something to take care of the man,' Bobby said. 'I need his piece.'

'You're gonna use his gun on him?'

'That's the idea.'

'Tonight?'

'You want to know all that?' Bobby said. 'Why don't you get me the piece, not worry about it?'

They went back to the office. Leo opened the top drawer of the file cabinet, felt around and came out with the .38 Smith & Wesson.

'I almost forgot I had it. I don't have the bullets,' Leo said. 'Alan kept them.'

'I'll see Alan about that,' Bobby said. He took the revolver and put it in the right-side pocket of his jacket.

Going back to the lobby Leo said, 'I'll tell you the truth, I was starting to get nervous. I don't know what happened to you guys, where you could be. Then, you know, you start imagining things, like something's going on and they're leaving me out of it.'

'We wouldn't leave you out,' Bobby said. 'You part of the group.'

'You know how you start thinking when you don't know what's going on.'

'Man,' Bobby said, 'sit down at the desk and take it easy. Think about nice things.'

'I'm not worried now,' Leo said. 'I was a little nervous, but I'm okay now.'

Bobby steered Leo over to the desk and gently, with his hands on his shoulders, sat him down.

'What're you doing?' Leo said. 'Hey, what's going on?'

'Nothing going on,' Bobby said. 'I want you to sit down and rest, man, take it easy.'

'Yeah, but I don't get it.'

'What's to get? Sit there, man, don't move for a while. Let your body relax, feel at peace. There now.'

Bobby walked away from the desk to the front door counting one, two, three, four and a half steps. He opened the door, gave Leo a nod and a little smile and walked outside.

The place next to the nude-model studio, also closed but with a light burning inside, was a dirty-book store. Bobby stepped into the alcove of the doorway, stood with his back to the street and the headlights of the cars passing, took the Smith & Wesson and five .38 cartridges out of his jacket and loaded the revolver. Glancing at the street, at the few cars going by but not studying them or worrying about them, he walked back to the front door of the model studio, counted one, two, three, four and a half steps past it, stopped, faced the black-painted plate glass in front of the 'D' in NUDE MODELS, raised the revolver belt-high and fired it at the glass, getting the heavy report and a hundred and twenty square feet of shattering glass and the 'D' disappearing in front of him, gone, all at the same time. There was Leo still sitting behind the desk like he hadn't moved. Bobby didn't know if Leo had been hit. He extended the .38 in front of him and shot Leo four times, hitting him dead center in the chest, getting that last one in before Leo slid down behind the desk. Bobby didn't need to go in and check. He knew Leo was dead about the time he reached the floor.

17

Mitchell said, 'Tell him I'll call him back,' and hung up the phone.

He was in the Engineering office, sitting on a high stool under the bright fluorescent lights. He leaned over the drafting table again to study the cutaway drawings he had made of a clasp lock assembly. They were crude drawings, rendered freehand, without using the T-square. Lying open on the table was the black attaché case he had received the day before. Next to the case was the switch actuator he had taken out of the scrap bin, also the day before.

He drew a rectangle, representing the open case, looking down into it; then drew a top-view indication of one of the two clasp locks that were on the facing of the case.

Vic, his superintendent, came into the Engineering office and stood looking down at the board.

Mitchell said, 'Yeah?'

'That five hundred feet of number eight rod was due yester-day, it's not here yet.'

'Call them up.'

'I did call them. They said they'd see what they can do.'

'Call them again,' Mitchell said. 'Tell them the rods aren't here by noon they can bend them around their ass and make Hula Hoops, we'll go someplace else.'

'They'll say okay, and the rods'll get here about four, five o'clock.'

'But you'll have them,' Mitchell said.

Vic was staring at the drawing. 'What're we in, the luggage business now?'

'I'm trying to figure out,' Mitchell said, 'how to snap this open – see, it's one of the clasps – and make an electrical connection inside.'

'For what?'

'For example, if you wanted a light to go on when you opened the case.'

'Like a refrigerator.'

'Only the case isn't plugged in.'

'You got to have a battery inside.'

'I know that,' Mitchell said. 'I'm trying to figure out how to connect with the battery without messing up the case, changing the way it looks.'

'It's a pretty nice case.'

'You see the problem?'

166

'I think that switch actuator's too big. All you need's a little spring of some kind.'

'Maybe you're right.'

'Well, I guess you'll think of a way,' Vic said, 'if that's what you want to do, light up a briefcase.'

'It's kind of what I want to do,' Mitchell said.

*

He had the attaché case with him when he went back to his office and stopped at Janet's desk.

'You remember the name of the place this came from?'

'I wrote it down, in case you wanted me to check on the card.'

'I found the card,' Mitchell said. 'It was in there all the time.'

Janet said, 'Oh?' and waited.

'What I'd like you to do, go there sometime today and get me another case, just like it.'

'You want another case,' Janet said, 'just like that one.'

'I was fooling with the lock and I sprung it.'

'Maybe it can be fixed.'

'I'd just as soon have another case, a new one, if it's okay with you.'

'Certainly it's okay.'

'Thank you.'

'Mr. O'Boyle called again. I told him I gave you the message the first time.'

'Get him for me, will you?'

'Yes sir, Mr. Mitchell.'

He looked at her. 'Janet, I have a reason for wanting another case. Will you accept that, take my word for it?' He went into his office.

*

'I've got another one for you to look up,' Mitchell said into the phone. 'Robert Shy. I'll give you his address, his driver's license number if it'll help.'

'Is he a friend of Leo Frank?' O'Boyle's voice asked.

Mitchell hesitated. 'Why?'

'You haven't seen the paper this morning?'

'I spent the night here. Something I had to do.'

'Get a paper,' O'Boyle said. 'Page three, a picture of the model studio with the window blown out.'

167

'He have an accident? What happened?'

'He was shot four times. You give me the name of a guy to check on and three days later he's dead. Now do you want to tell me what's going on?'

'Was it a robbery, what?'

'He had forty-three dollars on him, a comb, a can of hair spray and a bottle of Beach Boy after-shave lotion. No, it wasn't a robbery and you're not answering my question. Mitch, what's going on?'

'Wait a minute, Jim. What about Alan Raimy?'

'What about him?'

'What'd you learn?'

'The only one I've found out about so far is Leo Frank. You remember Joe Paonessa, the assistant prosecutor you were so nice to? I checked with him. He called me yesterday afternoon to tell me what they had on Leo.'

'What?'

'Mitch—' O'Boyle sounded impatient, let his breath out, probably shaking his head.

Mitchell said, 'Come on, tell me.'

'Leo Frank was arrested once,' O'Boyle said, 'for indecent exposure, three times for pandering, one conviction, served ninety days. What I want you to understand,' O'Boyle said then, 'the prosecutor's office checks him out as a favor, and the next day the man's dead. Now what do I tell Joe Paonessa when he calls?'

'Wait and see if he does.'

'Mitch, the man was murdered.'

Mitchell said, 'I don't know what to tell you, Jim. I mean right now I don't have anything to tell you. Maybe in a couple of days.'

'I'm going to come over and talk to you,' O'Boyle said.

'I won't be here.'

'Mitch, I give the prosecutor's office two names. One of them is found murdered. Now what are they going to do? They're going to call me and say how do you know this guy, what was his problem? And they're going to look for the other name, Alan Raimy. Now I know Leo and Alan are involved in the blackmail, obviously. Joe Paonessa doesn't know that, naturally I didn't mention your name. But he could think about it and put it together and you could look up to see the police at your door. Before we get to that, I want you to tell me the whole thing. All right?'

'I don't see you have to tell them anything,' Mitchell said. 'Tell him they're clients of yours. They come in, you want to check them out first. Jim, guys who commit crimes go to lawyers, don't they? Or guys who've committed a crime and see they might get caught? Tell Joe what's-his-name they came to you, but haven't told you the whole story yet. They owe on a gambling debt, something like that, and have been threatened. Jim, you're the lawyer, you can think of something.'

'I want to talk to you today, Mitch.'

'All right. But later on, okay? I've got things to do and I'm running out of time.'

'Mitch, promise me – you won't do anything until you've talked to me.'

'We'll see,' Mitchell said. 'But I may not have a choice.'

*

Alan pulled the bedroom phone out of the jack and took it with him when he went downstairs. He got the *Free Press* off the front steps and read about Leo while the water was boiling. That Bobby. Goddamn gunslinger had to blow the place up. Style but wild. Man loved to pull the trigger. Yeah, Alan said, and smiled.

It was working, he told himself, pouring the coffee. Everything was working. He went down a checklist in his mind.

Leo out of the way.

Guy's wife upstairs, under control.

Panel truck in the garage. Stolen but as good as clean, because Richard the dealer sure wasn't going to any police.

Guy busy at his plant, not knowing what shit was going on.

That was the luckiest jackpot great-timing break of all, the guy not coming home last night. Jesus, so he didn't have to sneak Slim out and hide her in some motel and leave a phony note saying she was out for the evening or visiting her mother or some goddamn thing – which the guy might buy or might not. That had been the riskiest part of the whole idea and it turned out to be nothing to worry about.

He placed the coffeepot and cups, the paper and the telephone on a tray and carried it upstairs to the bedroom. She was lying in the big king-size bed with the sheet covering her and seemed to be still asleep. But her eyes opened as he set the tray on the night table. She watched him put the gun in his pocket and plug in the phone.

'Where did you sleep?' she asked him.

'Hey, Slim, come on. That wasn't a dream you were having. That was for real.'

'Did you give me another injection during the night?'

Alan grinned at her.

'I mean the heroin, or whatever it is.'

'Just the one, before we went to bed. Some other time I'm going to keep you awake for the show.'

'May I get dressed now?'

'You're fine the way you are. Sit up, we'll have some coffee. First though—' He sat on the edge of the bed, picked up the phone and dialed a number.

'Mr. Mitchell, please. Mr. Raimy calling.' Alan looked over at Barbara and winked.

*

'What happened to your friend?' Mitchell said, as soon as he heard Alan's voice.

'Who's that?'

'Leo.'

'Never heard of him. Listen,' Alan said. 'I've been thinking about you and getting very bad vibes, like you're trying to pull some kind of shit on me. You ever get that feeling?'

'If you're nervous, see a doctor,' Mitchell said. 'If you want to get this done, then let's do it.'

'You got the fifty-two?'

'I can have it today.'

'Okay. We'll do it tonight.'

'Where?'

'Get the money, go back to your office and stay there. I'll call you.'

'I assume,' Mitchell said, 'you want it in the briefcase you sent.'

'You assume correct. Now, one other thing.'

'What's that?'

'No police. Okay?'

'No police.'

'Not that I don't trust you but, man, I don't like taking a chance. You understand? So I'm going to have somebody with me.'

'Who, Bobby?'

'Hey, you've been busy. No, somebody else. Hang on a second.'

Mitchell waited.

Barbara said, 'Mitch?'

His chair came upright as he straightened and the arms banged against the desk. 'Barbara! Where are you? ... Barbara!'

There was a silence before Alan came on the line again.

'You see it now, sport? If I find out you got the police in this – man, if I even feel it – no wife. I'm taking a chance. You may not even give a shit about her and I'm left holding Slim, but I don't see any other way to do it. You give me the fifty-two, I give you your wife. Shake hands and go home.'

'Where are you?' Mitchell said.

'What difference does it make? I'll call you later.'

'Let me talk to my wife again.'

'Don't worry, I'll take good care of her.'

The line went dead.

Mitchell pressed the phone button down, raised it and dialed his home. He listened to the phone ring ten times before he hung up.

He waited, picked up the phone again and this time put in a call for Ross.

*

Alan didn't say anything until the phone stopped ringing. 'That's hubby checking up.'

'It could be somebody else,' Barbara said.

'It doesn't matter. We're not answering the phone today.'

'I have a tennis match this afternoon. If I don't show up they're going to wonder. Someone may come over.'

'Let me worry about that,' Alan said. 'Till we leave here we don't answer the phone or the door.'

'Where are we going?'

'Hey, don't talk for a while, okay?' He picked up the phone again and was dialing a number.

After a moment, quietly, he said, 'Bobby, I liked it. . . . Yeah, you're a fucking cowboy. . . . Listen, it's set for tonight. I'm going to call him later, let him know exactly where and all that. But listen, we don't want two cars. Have Doreen drive you out, meet me at Metropolitan Beach, it's just a little bit east of his plant, eight o'clock. . . . I'm nowhere near you and I got things to do. Listen, get Doreen to drive you, drop you off. I'll meet you in the parking area over by . . . you'll see a sign it says TOT LOT . . . where they got all the swings and slides and shit. . . . Yeah, you'll see it over to the right as you come in. Hey, Bobby, and bring the guy's piece. . . . That's right. Take you about forty-five minutes. So, I'll see you at eight. Man, on the button, eight o'clock.'

As he hung up the phone Barbara said, 'What are we going to do until then? That's a long time away.'

Alan turned to look down at her, at the curve of her breasts beneath the sheet and her bare arms at her sides, lying flat, motionless.

'What do you want to do? Play a little tennis? At the club?'

She didn't say anything.

'Or we can shoot scag. Drift off somewhere and, you know, groove around.'

'You do it,' Barbara said. 'I'll watch.'

'Well, you're going to have some before we leave,' Alan said. 'You can bet to that.'

*

Mitchell stood in the small outer lobby looking at the photographic lightbox display of Wright-Way trailers, campers and motor homes. He turned to the glass window with the round opening in it as the receptionist said, 'Mr. Mitchell, he's out of the office right now.'

'Is he in the plant?'

'Esther just said he was out of the office. Did you have an appointment?'

'Not in about three years,' Mitchell said. 'Why don't I wait a while, see if he turns up?'

'I'll try and locate him for you,' the receptionist said.

Mitchell lighted a cigarette and stood looking into the front-office area, at the rows of secretaries and clerks sitting at their pastel green metal desks. After a few minutes the receptionist said, 'He doesn't seem to be in the plant.' Mitchell nodded. He smiled, showing her he was patient and in no hurry.

After a few more minutes he saw the Chief Engineer come out of the hall that led to the plant and go over to one of the secretaries. Mitchell waited. When the Chief Engineer turned from the desk, he saw Mitchell in the lobby, walked over, waving for Mitchell to come in, and pulled open the glass door.

'What're you doing out there? Come on in for Christ sake.'

'I'm waiting to see Ross. I guess they can't find him.'

'I just talked to him five minutes ago,' the Chief Engineer said. 'What do you mean they can't find him? If he's not at his desk he's probably locked in the toilet with some broad.'

Mitchell smiled. 'How's it going? You got any problems?'

'A few things I could talk to you about,' the Chief Engineer said. 'Whyn't you come in my office?'

'How about after I get through with Ross?' Mitchell said. 'He called, it sounded important.'

They were walking down the executive hallway now, approaching Ross Wright's office. The Chief Engineer walked him all the way to the end, to Mr. Wright's secretary's desk. He said, 'Esther, tell him Mr. Mitchell's here. And listen, then send this guy down to my office when he's through, in case he forgets.'

That's how Mitchell got in to see Ross, sitting behind his black desk with a big smile on his face.

When the door closed behind him, Ross said, 'Mitch, how's it going?'

'I called you a couple times this morning,' Mitchell said. 'You never called back.'

'Meetings.' Ross shook his head, poor overworked executive. 'Some of the field people are in this week. I haven't had time to take a leak.'

'Anything I can do for you?'

'I appreciate the offer, but not that I know of. Production's fine, but now it's sales. If you could keep both of them up at the same time, uh? That'd be something.'

'I understand you were out with my wife,' Mitchell said.

'Barbara?'

'That's her name. Barbara.'

Ross had a surprised look for a moment, of innocence, that became serious, sincere.

'I took Barbara to dinner the other night. I thought she might want to talk about it, you know, offer her a shoulder to cry on if she wanted one.'

'Yeah? Did she cry?'

'Of course not. I didn't think she would. I thought maybe if I could find out how she felt about the situation, you know, I could give you the word and maybe help you straighten things out.'

'Where'd you go, the Inn?'

Ross nodded. 'Yeah, had a pretty good dinner. Adequate. It's not as good though as it used to be.'

'Champagne and brandy after?'

Ross nodded again, slowly, as if trying to remember. 'Yeah, I believe we did.'

'Barbara told me about it.'

'Mitch, you're not thinking—' Ross turned on one of his smiles. 'Hey, come on, you're not accusing me of anything, are you? I thought she'd want a quiet place to talk and I still had a suite for a customer'd been there – you know, a sitting room – I thought would be more comfortable.'

'She didn't tell me about the room,' Mitchell said.

'Oh,' Ross said. 'Well, we were only there a few minutes. Had one drink, talked a little bit and I took her home. That's all there was to it. I mean I'd even forgotten we went to the room, the suite. We sat down for a couple of minutes, talked about you most of the time. Hey, about when you were in the Air Force and you shot down the two Spitfires. Jesus, you never told me anything about that before. How many planes you shoot down?'

'Seven,' Mitchell said. 'No, nine.'

'Jesus, goddamn ace, I never knew it.'

'Ross, you still working on your ski slopes? Up north.'

'What?' The abrupt switch stopped him.

'You said, last time we had lunch, you were putting in improvements at your ski resort. Doing some blasting.'

'That's right. They started a few days ago.'

'The guy with the dynamite's there?'

'He should be. Why?'

'I need some.'

Ross stared at him. 'You need some dynamite?'

'About a half dozen sticks,' Mitchell said, 'and a cap, you

know, a detonator. If you called somebody up there, they could be down here with it in about three and a half hours, couldn't they?'

'Yes, but' – Ross was frowning, puzzled – 'what do you want it for?'

'I may have to blow some stumps,' Mitchell said. 'Maybe I won't need it, but I want to be ready just in case.'

'Mitch, I don't know. Dynamite – I mean it's not like handing somebody a dozen eggs.'

'I don't want eggs,' Mitchell said. 'I want dynamite. You can get it for me and I think you want to get it for me, Ross. As a favor. You know what I mean? Because we've always been so close. You and I, and now Barbara. So why don't you pick up the phone and get on it?'

*

O'Boyle was sitting at one end of the couch with his brief case next to him and a file folder open on his lap.

He said, 'Why don't you sit down for a minute? I don't know if you're listening or not.'

'I'm listening,' Mitchell said. He walked from the window back to his desk, but didn't sit down.

'It's a little hard to talk to you.'

'I'm listening,' Mitchell said. 'You talk, I'll listen.'

'You look like you're ready to climb the wall or go through it.' O'Boyle watched him move to the window again, the early-evening light flat and dull against the pane.

'Are you going home for dinner?'

'I don't know yet.'

'You want to get a bite somewhere?'

'Why don't you read me what you've got?'

'I have a feeling you're off somewhere.'

Mitchell looked at his lawyer. 'I'm here. I'll be here. Now tell me about the guy.'

Jim O'Boyle was soft-spoken, intelligent and a successful lawyer. He knew Mitchell pretty well, sometimes; he thought he knew his moods. One thing, he was not going to waste time beating his head against an immovable mind. He looked down at the open file folder.

'Alan Sheldon Raimy,' O'Boyle said, 'Born in Detroit. Was graduated seven years ago from Michigan with a Masters in Biz

Ad, top third of his class, taught accounting on a fellowship, was suspended, fired, for operating an abortion service.'

Mitchell looked over. 'What?'

'He was an abortion broker,' O'Boyle said. 'The little girls called him when they got in trouble, Raimy arranged the operation and took ten percent. Like an agent. He was arrested by the Ann Arbor Police, once, also by the Washtenaw County Sheriff's Department. No convictions until—'

O'Boyle's hand moved down the page in the folder. 'Arrested for embezzlement three years later. Accountant for a chain of women's dress shops in Detroit. He'd send them invoices from phony companies with names that sounded very much like legitimate suppliers, pay the invoices himself and open bank accounts in the phony names. He made over twenty thousand before he was caught, convicted and served a year and a half in Jackson. Since then he's been arrested for, let's see, once for lewd and indecent conduct – he was part of a live smoker act. Alan and two girls.'

'What'd they do?'

'Probably everything. He was arrested again for contributing to the delinquency of a minor. Caught in a motel with a gallon of wine, marijuana and a fourteen-year-old girl. Thirty days in the House of Correction. Another indecency charge, the last one, showing a smoker movie, stag film, dismissed. So that's Alan Sheldon Raimy,' O'Boyle said. 'Now he's gone from dirty movies to blackmail to what else?'

'You want a drink?' Mitchell walked over to the cabinet. He took out a bottle of bourbon and poured two short drinks.

O'Boyle watched him. 'The police are after Raimy. They can't find him.'

'How do you know?'

'Mitch, I'm the first one the prosecutor's office called. Why am I asking about a Leo Frank, deceased, and Alan Raimy? I told them I don't know of any connection between the two. The reason I was inquiring about them is privileged communication. But, I had to tell them if I learned anything I'd get in touch. And that may hold them off and it may not.'

Mitchell handed O'Boyle a drink. He took his own and walked around the desk and sat down.

'I don't know where Raimy is,' Mitchell said.

'But he's threatening you, isn't he?'

'He's doing more than that.' Mitchell took a sip of the bourbon. 'He's got Barbara.'

He described the phone call and hearing her voice briefly on the line. Mitchell spoke quietly, taking his time. He said, 'Yes, he's threatening me. He's going to come here for a pay-off or tell me where to meet him. And if he suspects the police are involved, I never see Barbara again, at least alive. That's what's going on.'

O'Boyle was silent. Questions jumped in his mind, but he tried to ignore them for the moment and concentrate on Mitchell sitting at his desk with a glass of bourbon, in control now after pacing around the room. That part of it was a little frightening. His calm. Almost as though he felt nothing. Or had made up his mind about something and that was it.

'Why didn't you tell me this earlier?' O'Boyle said.

'Earlier than what? He called this afternoon. I'm waiting for him to call back.'

'Before he does—' O'Boyle paused, as if anticipating Mitchell's reaction and wanting to put it off. 'We've got to bring in the police.'

'No,' Mitchell said. A flat statement, that was it. 'I told you what he said on the phone and I believe him. No police. He kills people, Jim. As you said, he doesn't just show dirty movies anymore. What he does, he kills people.'

'That's right, and he can kill you too.'

'Or Barbara, if I don't handle it right.'

'What do you mean, handle it?'

'I have a choice. I can pay him or not pay him. But the first thing I have to do is get Barbara away from him.'

'We agree on something,' O'Boyle said. 'But we still have to call the police.'

'No.' The flat statement again. 'At first, up until a few days ago, I had a vague idea of setting him up. I hand him the money and, somehow flatten him, break his arm if I have to and then hand him over to the police. But I've got another idea now and it may be the only way.'

'Mitch, the police have experience in this kind of situation, a procedure—'

He shook his head. 'Jim, remember when this started you

came here and I told you about it? I put down on tape everything I remembered from the first meeting with them. This afternoon I put some more stuff on tape. Everything that's happened since and what I may have to do. I'm going to give it to you, Jim, and if anything happens to me you'll know who the guys are, what they did, everything. But I'm not going to discuss it with you now and I'm not going to bring the police in, because this son of a bitch, Alan Raimy, I know would walk out of court. How do they get him for murder? How do they prove it? The girl's gone, so is the movie. He says, "What girl?" Arrest him for kidnapping? Maybe. But also maybe he feels he's come too far to give up. Jim, this guy kills people. He could kill again, Barbara or me, and get away with it.' Mitchell paused. 'So I'm going to handle it. One way or the other.'

O'Boyle stared at him, as if trying to read his mind. 'All right, what're you going to do?'

'I'm going to pay him off.'

'I don't believe you.'

'Then don't. I appreciate your help, Jim, your concern, but I'm not going to argue with you.'

'Mitch, I've got an awful feeling you're going to do something – God, I don't know what – that you've got no business even considering.'

'But I do know my business,' Mitchell said. 'Keep that in mind.'

'Now I don't even know what you're talking about.'

And Mitchell said, 'Good.'

*

Bobby Shy was sitting low, looking straight ahead through the windshield at the tree-lined parkway that led into Metropolitan Beach.

'What time is it?'

Doreen turned her hand, holding the top arc of the steering wheel, to look at her watch.

'Just ten after. Staying light longer, isn't it?'

Bobby didn't say anything.

'Now where?'

They were entering the parking area that covered a good forty acres: open empty pavement that reached to a low line of tan-brick structures – the bathhouse, pavilion and maintenance buildings, empty, deserted this time of the year – and a glimpse of Lake St. Clair beyond, flat gray water that extended to the horizon.

'Over to the right,' Bobby said. 'See the truck?'

'That's Alan?'

Bobby didn't answer. Doreen glanced over at him but didn't ask him again. She saw him reach inside his jacket, draw his .38 Special out of the waistband of his trousers and put it on the seat, tucking it in tight against his left thigh. Mitchell's Smith & Wesson was in the right-hand pocket of his jacket.

'Pull up on the left side of the truck,' Bobby said, 'two, three spaces over.'

Doreen was frowning. 'How you know it's him?'

'It's him,' Bobby said. 'Watch me, don't say nothing. I say get out of here, that's when we get. You dig? Not before I say it.'

As they eased to a stop, facing the fenced-off playground area and the sign that said TOT LOT, Alan got out of the panel and came over, relaxed, friendly-looking, with a nice smile.

Bobby smiled back at him. 'You in the drugstore business now?'

'How do you like it?'

'Richard call, he ask if I seen you anywhere. Said you was buying some shit for me.'

'I needed it for something,' Alan said. 'Also I needed wheels and there he was. I figure this is not the day to grab a car and get picked up for joyriding.'

'Richard going to climb up your ass.'

'Let's not worry about Richard right now,' Alan said. 'Did you bring the man's piece?'

'I got it.'

'Let me see it.'

Bobby's hand came out of his side pocket with Mitchell's Smith & Wesson. He looked up at Alan with a mild expression, the trace of a smile, as he took the revolver in his left hand by the barrel and extended it through the open window to Alan.

Alan took it by the grip, his finger curling around the trigger.

'Is it loaded?'

Bobby grinned. 'No, baby, it ain't.'

'This one is,' Alan said.

He pulled Richard's Saturday night gun out of his hip pocket, stepped back with his left foot and shot Bobby Shy three times, in the face, in the neck and in the chest. Doreen was screaming, banging against the door to get it open, then twisting to reach the lock button and pull it up. Alan shot her twice in the back of the head as the door swung open and she went out.

He looked closely at Bobby, slumped in the seat, reached over and got the .38 Special without touching him. He walked around the car to Doreen, his gaze moving over the empty parking lot, then looked down at her lying twisted on the pavement and prodded her in the ribs with the toe of his boot.

Barbara, frowning, looked at him as he got back in the panel. 'I heard an awful noise. Loud noise somewhere.'

'Fireworks,' Alan said. 'Somebody celebrating.'

*

He checked them into a Holiday Inn on the south end of Mt. Clemens. Barbara was a little slow-moving, beginning to drag after her high; but he got her out of the panel without any trouble and into the nice twenty-buck room with a telephone. She said she had a headache. He told her to lie down on the bed, the one away from the door, and he'd take care of her head after a while. First thing, he called room service for hamburgers, fries and a bottle of rosé, mentioning to Barbara as he hung up he always liked wine when he was in a motel with a lady. It was romantic. Alan figured they had at least a half hour before the food came, so he picked up the phone again and dialed Ranco Manufacturing.

He said, 'How you doing, Sport? You got it? ... That's very good. It fits in the case all right? ... Good. Now listen. Eleven o'clock I want you to leave your place and go north on Ninety-four, toward Port Huron. You go past the turnoff to Selfridge Air Force Base, you'll see the sign. Go past about two miles. ... Wait a minute. ... Wait ... wait, hey *wait*, will you! What do you mean you don't have a car?' He listened for a moment. 'Hold on.' Alan put his hand over the mouthpiece and looked at Barbara lying on the bed with her eyes open.

'Yesterday your husband said something about he didn't have a car.'

'What?'

'When he called, saying he wasn't coming home. He said something about his car. What was it?'

Barbara shook her head. 'I don't remember.'

'He just said he's leasing another one. He was supposed to get it today, but it didn't come, it's not ready yet.'

Barbara shook her head again. 'I don't know what you're talking about.'

Alan waited.

Son of a *bitch*. He had to think about it, but he had to tell Mitchell something. He said into the phone then, 'Borrow one. I'll call you back.' And hung up.

*

He let her out of the bathroom after the young kid from room service was gone. The tray, with its metal-covered plates and wine bottle in a plastic bucket, sat on the low sectional dresser in front of the mirror and at first she thought there were two trays.

Barbara could smell the french fries and felt nauseated again. She shook her head when Alan told her to help herself. He didn't seem to care. He was digging into the fries with his fingers, dipping them in catsup and stuffing them into his mouth as he got the wine out and poured two glasses. Barbara took one because she was thirsty and it looked cold. He made her come over to take it. Standing by the dresser she saw herself in the mirror. She looked ill, as though she'd been in bed with the flu. She should have on a robe, not a raincoat. She needed makeup and a hairbrush. But she knew she had no purse with her. The bottom of the raincoat was partly open. She buttoned it with one hand and was aware, then, that she wasn't wearing anything beneath the coat. Alan told her to sit on the bed and be a good girl. The wine was very cold. As she sipped it he let her have a cigarette and she began to feel a little better.

Alan was standing eating his hamburger, getting it done, staying close to the french fries and catsup on the tray. He was hungry. He could worry about Mitchell and wonder if the son of a bitch was pulling something, but he was still hungry and had to eat. The wine was good; it helped him relax. But he wished he'd taken a little longer yesterday afternoon, another twenty minutes, and had Richard get him some reefer. With reefer he could get his head together and see everything clearly.

He said to Barbara, 'He been having trouble with his car?'

'Not that I know of.'

'How was he going to get home?'

'You said he was leasing another one, didn't you?'

'But it didn't come. The day of all days he's got to have a car he says it didn't come.'

'That happens, doesn't it?'

Alan was thoughtful. 'I don't know. He could be pulling something. But I don't have time anymore to fool around.'

Barbara watched him drink his wine and fill the glass again.

'If my husband told you he'll pay you, he will.'

'I take your word for it.'

'This is your idea,' Barbara said, 'not ours. I would assume you have to be optimistic in your business, believe you're going to be paid, or you'd never have gone into it.'

She continued to watch him as he moved to the front of the motel room and pulled the draperies back to look out. It was dark now. She could see the shiny front of a car and neon lights on the street beyond.

'Why does he have to have a car?'

'To go where I tell him.'

'I mean why not meet him at the plant, pick up the money there?'

Alan turned from the window to look at her but said nothing.

'You're afraid of the police,' Barbara said. 'But wherever you tell him to meet you he could bring the police, couldn't he?' Barbara paused. 'But he won't. If he said he'll pay you, he will.'

'Lie down,' Alan said. 'I want to talk to you I'll let you know.'

He went into the bathroom, leaving the door open, came out and poured himself another glass of wine. He sat down now, turning off the lamp next to the chair, sipped the wine and smoked two cigarettes in the semidarkness. Barbara wasn't sure how much time passed, perhaps twenty minutes or a half hour. He came over to the phone, sat on the bed facing her and lighted another cigarette before giving the operator Mitchell's number.

She heard him say, 'You get a car? ... All right, forget it. I'm going to come see you, sometime after your shift lets out. ... Just be there, alone. You know who's going to be with me. I'm going to drive in the parking lot. I don't like it, I drive out and that's all for your wife. I like it, you bring the money out and we do business. ... No, we get there I'll tell you what happens next.' He paused, listening. 'No, she's fine, man. Fact I didn't know an old lady'd be that good. Hey, don't she moan and squirm?' Alan laughed out loud hanging up the phone.

At a quarter past eleven he poured heroin into a Holiday Inn spoon and heated it over a candle he had brought from the Mitchell house. Barbara said to him, as he came over with the syringe, 'Please don't, I'm already sick.' Alan told her this would make her better, popped a vein in her arm this time and shot her high before she had time to kick, scream or say thank you. He didn't use all of the spoon on her; about half of it, good for an hour or so. He took a fresh needle and shot the rest of the scag into his own left arm. Yeeees. Man, that would help over the rough part. Reefer was sweeter, but a touch of scag would do in a pinch.

At ten to twelve Alan brought a couple of blankets and a pillow out of the room and made a nice little bed in the back of the panel, got Barbara into the truck without anyone seeing them that he noticed and took off south down the highway. Barbara was making little moaning humming sounds as though she might be singing. Alan felt pretty good himself. Shit, he ought to. It was payday.

18

Mitchell, carrying a Hi-Sheen Tuffy-Hyde attaché case, let the fire door swing closed behind him. He reached for the wall switches, began killing every other bank of fluorescents and somewhere in the dim empty plant area a voice yelled out, 'Hey! I can't see!'

Somebody was still here.

Mitchell didn't see who it was until he was walking toward the back, toward the sound, and John Koliba stepped out of a dark aisleway between rows of parts bins: Koliba, the white tight T-shirt stretched across his belly, holding a pair of rubber vacuum cups, one in each fist.

'I thought you was gone,' Koliba said. 'I would have swore

you walked by five minutes ago with that case in your hand. I was over in Quality Control.'

Mitchell said, 'I was out here. I went back to my office for something.'

'I guess J didn't see you go back.'

'I didn't see you either,' Mitchell said. 'What're you up to?'

'Well – don't laugh, okay? I got an idea for a kind of handling rig I been fooling with, seeing if I can make it work. On my own time, you understand. Maybe I got something, I don't know yet.'

'Why don't you work on it during your shift?' Mitchell said. And he was thinking, Why don't you get the hell out of here, right now.

'Well, I figured I should do it on my own time. You know, you got designers, engineers. You didn't hire me for that kind of work.'

'No, but if you think you've got something, John, I'm willing to take a chance, I mean pay you for your effort,' Mitchell said. 'Starting tomorrow, work on it during your shift.'

'That's great.' Koliba grinned, his eyes squinting almost closed. 'You got a minute I'll show you what I'm doing, the idea.'

'I'd like to see it,' Mitchell said, 'but let's wait'll tomorrow, okay? Why don't you knock off now, go on home?'

'Yeah, well listen, then I'll show it to you tomorrow.'

'I want to lock up,' Mitchell said. 'The security man's sick or something. He's not around tonight.'

'Right,' Koliba said. 'I'll wash up, be out in a minute.'

'Good, I want to get out of here.'

'Why don't you go ahead? I'll see the door gets locked.'

'No, there's a couple of things I got to check,' Mitchell said. 'Just hurry it up, okay?'

He was thinking, Christ, quit talking, and walked away gripping the attaché case at his side. Behind him Koliba said something about a couple minutes is all. Ahead of him, down the aisle past the turning machines and the rows of stock bins, a spot of light reflected on the glass section of the rear door. He reached the door and looked out.

The reflection was from a light pole. The parking lot was empty. Good.

No, Christ, there was one car parked in a lane over to the far right. Of course. Koliba's. He said to himself, Why did he pick tonight of all the nights? Guy showing initiative, wanting to get ahead. And it's your own fault, you talked to him, inspired him. God. He said, Come on, John, come out right now and get in your car and get the hell out of here, will you? God, get him out of here. But almost as he said it to himself, like a silent prayer, it was too late.

The headlight beams appeared, coming out of the driveway on the side of the plant, the way they had appeared, creeping along the pavement, the time before.

But not a white Thunderbird this time, a panel truck, the square shape of it, red as it reached the light pole, with something lettered on the side, circling slowly through the open parking area. Mitchell watched and he was thinking, it's not him. Somebody else to get rid of. But the truck came around, maintaining its creeping pace, and circled again, headlights sweeping the darkness beyond the cyclone fence.

Mitchell opened the door and walked outside, into the circle of light that came from the spots above the rear door.

As if sensing him, the panel truck, at the far end of the yard, turned and came slowly toward him until he was standing in the beam of its headlights. The truck stopped.

Mitchell raised the attaché case shoulder-high and lowered it again.

There was no response from the truck. The only sound was the low rumble of the engine idling.

'You want it or not?'

There was silence again, lengthening, until finally he heard Alan's voice.

'Whose car's that?'

'Guy working late.'

'Man, you know what I told you.'

'I didn't know he was here till just now.' Mitchell waited. 'Where's my wife?'

There was no answer from the truck.

Mitchell raised the case again. 'Look, this is what you came for. Take it. Let my wife go and get out of here.'

'Come a little closer,' Alan's voice said.

Mitchell walked toward the headlights. When he was about

185

thirty feet away Alan said, 'Okay, right there. Open it up, show me what you got.'

'Where's my wife?'

'You first,' Alan said. 'You show me yours and I'll show you mine.'

'It's all here,' Mitchell said. 'You want to come get it or you want me to bring it over.'

'Man, I told you, I want to *see* it! Now that's the last word I'm going to say.'

Mitchell hesitated. He went down to one knee tnen, placed the case flat on the pavement and flicked open the two clasps with his thumbs.

'Turn it around,' Alan said.

Mitchell turned the case, holding the top open toward him, so Alan could see the packets of ten-and twenty-dollar bills, banded, stacked neatly in rows that filled the inside of the case.

'Pick up some of it,' Alan said. 'Walk up to the front of the truck.'

Mitchell rose with packets of bills in both hands. He approached to stand close to the headlights.

'Hold it up,' Alan said.

Mitchell's head and shoulders were above the light beams now. He could see Alan through the windshield, behind the wheel. He held up the packets of bills.

'Where's my wife?'

He watched Alan turn and say something. After a moment Barbara appeared, part of her rising out of darkness, behind the empty passenger seat.

'Let her out.'

'You bring me the case first,' Alan said.

Mitchell stared at Barbara. 'What's the matter with my wife?'

'She's on something, man. Having a high.'

'Let her out!'

'When you bring the case. Hey,' Alan said then, 'you see this?' He held up Bobby's .38 Special and pointed it at Mitchell. 'No bullshit now, right? You twitch, I'll shoot your fucking eyes out, man. Now bring the case.'

Mitchell walked back to the open attaché case and went down to one knee again. He dropped the packets of bills inside. With his back to the truck he fished a screwdriver out of the front part of the case, beneath the bills, and wedged the tip of it between one side and the top, brought the top down, pressed his weight on it, but it wouldn't snap closed. Mitchell fooled with it for a while.

'What's the matter?'

'I can't get the thing closed. The lock's sprung.'

He rose to his feet with the case, holding the top and bottom together between the palms of his hands, fingers spread wide.

'I'll get something to hold it together.'

'Just bring it here.'

'Take me a minute,' Mitchell said. 'I'll wire it up.'

'Man, bring it over here! I don't give a shit!'

Mitchell stopped to half turn. 'I don't want it blowing away. You'll think I cheated you.' He turned again and started for the rear door of the plant.

'Hold it there!'

Mitchell stopped and turned again. He saw that Alan was out of the truck now, behind the open door, resting the .38 on the window ledge and leveling it at him.

'I'll put a piece of wire or something around it. I come back, you let my wife out I'll give you the dough. Now think about it a minute,' Mitchell said, 'and try not to wet your pants.'

He turned, ignoring Alan and the .38 pointing at him, continued on to the door of the plant and went inside.

John Koliba was coming down the aisle.

Mitchell said, 'John, I think I left the light on in my office. You want to check it for me?'

Koliba waved at him. He said, 'Sure thing,' turned around and headed back up the aisle past the machines.

Mitchell walked over to a section of metal shelving that stood along the back wall near the door. He placed the attaché case on a middle shelf, reached up to the top shelf above his head, and took down an identical Hi-Sheen Tuffy-Hyde black vinyl attaché case with a strand of copper wire wrapped around it once, the ends twisted several times to bind them together.

He said to himself, You don't have a choice. He couldn't walk back out there and pull Alan out of the truck and hit him in the mouth and call the police. That would be good, but how could he do it? Alan had a gun and he was going to kill them. He was certain of it. Maybe he was afraid. He said to himself,

Of course you're afraid. He didn't want to do it this way. And he said to himself, But if you don't you'll be dead, and so will Barbara. So do it.

Mitchell looked at his watch. He waited thirty seconds before he turned to the door.

*

Alan slid behind the wheel again and got Barbara into the seat next to him, within reach. She was awake, groggy but out of her buzz and he didn't want her behind him.

Sitting there, holding the .38 on the window ledge, he told himself to get out, right now. Flip it in gear, floor the gas pedal and get the hell out.

But he had seen the money. Jesus, all those tens and twenties filling up the case. It was there. The guy had it.

But if the guy was pulling something . . .

Get out of here and call him.

No, there wasn't time for any more screwing around. It was right there in the case.

If it's still in the case.

If the guy wasn't out in ten seconds . . .

The door opened. Mitchell, with the attaché case at his side, was walking out into the light.

Alan put the gun on him, after a moment shifting it from the ledge to the windshield as Mitchell walked into the beam of the headlights and came directly toward the front of the truck. He stopped where he had stood before and raised the attaché case to the front of the hood.

'Your money,' Mitchell said. 'Now let my wife go.'

Alan shifted the .38 to his right hand and rested it on the dashboard, the barrel almost touching the windshield.

'Open it.'

Mitchell hesitated. 'You saw the money.'

'I want to see it again.'

'I'm tired,' Mitchell said. 'I don't want to play anymore.'

He took the case off the hood and started around to the passenger side of the truck.

'Hold it there!' Alan turned the gun on him.

But Mitchell kept moving, reached the door and pulled it open. 'I said I'd pay you.' He took Barbara by the arm and helped her out, swung the attaché case up, his eyes holding on

Alan, and dropped it on the seat. 'Here. I'm paying you.'

'Open it!' Alan screamed it at him.

Mitchell slammed the door. 'You open it.'

He walked off, still holding Barbara's arm, keeping her close to him, around the front of the truck and through the beam of the headlights.

'Hold it there! Man, I'll bust you – *both* of you!'

Mitchell stopped, thirty feet from the truck now, and looked around.

'You got it. What do you want me to do, count it for you?' He turned, holding Barbara, and kept going.

Alan had the .38 on him, dead center on his back moving away, halfway to the door of the plant.

But the black attaché case with the wire around it was next to him, right there, two feet away. He glanced at it.

Open it. Do it quick.

His hand reached over and felt the twisted ends of the wire, wrapped around each other two or three times, as stiff as a coat hanger.

They were almost to the building, in the arc of the high spotlights that spread down over the pavement.

'I count to three – you're dead!'

Mitchell stopped. He didn't turn around. He moved Barbara in front of him and pushed her gently, so that if she reached out now she could touch the door.

Alan held the gun on Mitchell's back and kept his eyes on him as his free hand untwisted the wire. He felt it come loose and bent the top strand back, out of the way. He glanced at the case then, turning it so the front of it faced toward him.

He looked toward Mitchell again and began to bring in his hand holding the gun.

'You move, man, you're dead!'

He laid the .38 on his lap and turned to the attaché case with both hands.

*

Mitchell said to his wife, 'Barbara, how're you doing?'

He saw her nod. 'I'm all right. A little sick.'

'When I touch your back, go through the door, fast. Don't hesitate. I'll reach in front of you and open it.'

'Mitch—'

'Right now,' Mitchell said, and moved with her, his hand flat against her back.

*

Alan saw them. He caught a glimpse of them over his shoulder. He wanted to pick up the gun and blast away, catch the guy before he got inside. But even as he saw them he knew it was too late, the way he was twisted around, his thumbs on the metal clasps of the attaché case.

This was what he had come for and he had to open it. Right now.

It was in his mind, for part of a moment, that the case wasn't broken. The lock wasn't sprung. It was closed now. It didn't need the wire to hold it. But again he was too late. His thumbs were already pressing open the clasps.

The panel truck, with SUPER-RITE DRUGS lettered on the body and Alan Sheldon Raimy inside, exploded, blew apart in a burst of fire and scattered pieces of itself all over the Ranco Manufacturing parking lot.

*

Koliba turned from the shattered window in the door to look over at Mitchell standing with his arm around the lady in the raincoat.

'Was he in it?'

'Who?'

'Jazik,' Koliba said. Like, who else?

'I don't know,' Mitchell said. 'Somebody was.'

'I'll call the fire department. Twice in two days. We're keeping them guys busy, eh?' Koliba started to move away. He glanced back to see Mitchell taking his attaché case from the metal shelf against the wall. 'You want me to call the cops, too?'

'If you want to,' Mitchell said. He was taking the lady by the arm again as he looked at Koliba. 'But who're they going to arrest?'

FOR THE BEST IN PAPERBACKS, LOOK FOR THE

In every corner of the world, on every subject under the sun, Penguin represents quality and variety – the very best in publishing today.

For complete information about books available from Penguin – including Pelicans, Puffins, Peregrines and Penguin Classics – and how to order them, write to us at the appropriate address below. Please note that for copyright reasons the selection of books varies from country to country.

In the United Kingdom: For a complete list of books available from Penguin in the U.K., please write to *Dept E.P. Penguin Books Ltd, Harmondsworth, Middlesex, UB7 0DA*

In the United States: For a complete list of books available from Penguin in the U.S., please write to *Dept BA, Penguin, 299 Murray Hill Parkway, East Rutherford, New Jersey 07073*

In Canada: For a complete list of books available from Penguin in Canada, please write to *Penguin Books Canada Ltd, 2801 John Street, Markham, Ontario L3R 1B4*

In Australia: For a complete list of books available from Penguin in Australia, please write to the *Marketing Department, Penguin Books Australia Ltd, P.O. Box 257, Ringwood, Victoria 3134*

In New Zealand: For a complete list of books available from Penguin in New Zealand, please write to the *Marketing Department, Penguin Books (NZ) Ltd, Private Bag, Takapuna, Auckland 9*

In India: For a complete list of books available from Penguin in India, please write to *Penguin Overseas Ltd, 706 Eros Apartments, 56 Nehru Place, New Delhi, 110019*

In Holland: For a complete list of books available from Penguin in Holland, please write to *Penguin Books Nederland B.V. Postbus 195, NL – 1380 AD WEESP Netherlands*

In Germany: For a complete list of books available from Penguin in Germany, please write to *Penguin Books Ltd, Friedrichstrasse, 10 – 12, D 6000, Frankfurt a m, Main 1, Federal Republic of Germany*

In Spain: For a complete list of books available from Penguin in Spain, please write to *Longman Penguin España, Calle San Nicolas 15, E – 28013 Madrid, Spain*